P9-DNJ-957

Praise for the first novel in the Bakeshop Mysteries

Meet Your Baker

"A delectable tale of murder and intrigue . . . This bakeshop mystery is a real page-turner, and we look forward to others in the series, just as tasty."
　　　　　　　　　　　　—*Portland Book Review*

"With plenty of quirky characters, a twisty, turny plot, and recipes to make your stomach growl, *Meet Your Baker* is a great start to an intriguing new series, but what sets this book apart and above other cozy mystery series is the locale. Ashland comes alive under Alexander's skilled hand. The picturesque town is lovingly described in vivid terms, so that it becomes more like a character in the book than just a backdrop to the action."　　　　　　　　　　　—*Reader to Reader*

"This debut culinary mystery is a light soufflé of a book (with recipes) that makes a perfect mix for fans of Jenna McKinley, Leslie Budewitz, or Jessica Beck."
　　　　　　　　　　　　　　—*Library Journal*

"Marvelous . . . All the elements I love in a cozy mystery are there—a warm and inviting atmosphere, friendly and likable main characters, and a nasty murder mystery to solve . . . I highly recommend *Meet Your Baker* and look forward to reading the next book in this new series!"　　　　　　—*Fresh Fiction*

On Thin Icing

Ellie Alexander

St. Martin's Paperbacks

This is a work of fiction. All of the characters, organizations, and events portrayed in this novel are either products of the author's imagination or are used fictitiously.

ON THIN ICING

Copyright © 2016 by Kate Dyer-Seeley.
Excerpt from *Caught Bread Handed* copyright © 2016 by Kate Dyer-Seeley.

For information address St. Martin's Press, 175 Fifth Avenue, New York, NY 10010.

ISBN: 978-1-250-05425-8

Printed in the United States of America

St. Martin's Paperbacks edition / January 2016

St. Martin's Paperbacks are published by St. Martin's Press, 175 Fifth Avenue, New York, NY 10010.

10 9 8 7 6 5 4 3 2 1

To Luke, who makes everything in my world magic.

Acknowledgments

Nothing sends me into a panic more than attempting to thank the many people who've been a part of seeing this book into the world. Writing a book is easy compared with trying to sum up my gratitude. I'll try to keep it short and sweet.

To the libraries and book clubs who have invited me into their homes, wineries, and bakeshops, it's been such a delight meeting you and noshing on delectable treats this past year. To my PNW team, Erika and Candace, you rock! To my editor Hannah and everyone at SMP, thanks for loving Jules. To the book blogging world, thank you for helping connect readers to the series. To all of the independent bookstores that have championed the series and especially the staff at Vintage Books, thank you for providing a space for books and authors to live. To Cindy, thanks for providing information on the inner workings of a theater company. To the community of Ashland, Oregon, thank you for welcoming me into town and helping bring Torte to life. To you, the reader, thank you for coming into the kitchen with Jules and the team.

Chapter One

They say that you can't go home again. I'm not sure that's true. I'd been home for almost six months, and found myself settling back into a comfortable and familiar pace.

Working at our family bakeshop, Torte, had helped ease the sting of leaving my husband and the life I'd known behind. I didn't have any answers about what was next for Carlos and me, and the longer I was home the less it seemed to matter. Ashland, Oregon, my welcoming hometown, was the perfect place to mend. Being surrounded by longtime friends and family for the past few months had made me realize that while my heart may have been a bit broken, I wasn't. It was an important distinction, and hopefully a sign that I'd made the right decision.

I'd been so consumed with baking and growing our catering business at Torte that I hadn't had much time to reflect. Ashland is best known for the Oregon Shakespeare Festival. The world-famous theater company draws in thousands of visitors each year. From February through October our sleepy town transforms into a tourist hub. Theater enthusiasts, families, school groups, and travelers from every corner of the globe descend on our quaint streets.

The steady stream of visitors was great for business. During the height of the theater season it was nearly impossible to get a table at Torte, or any other restaurant in town. Shopkeepers make their yearly profits in the busy summer months. Torte had a booming summer and fall season, so much so that my only focus had been on the bakeshop. Now that winter had closed in and OSF had closed its doors for the season, it was as if the entire town shuttered in as well. I'd forgotten how quiet Ashland becomes in January—and how cold!

After spending ten years working as a pastry chef for a cruise line, I hadn't experienced a winter like this in a long time. My winters had been spent island-hopping in the Caribbean and sailing in the Mediterranean, where the sun sparkled on warm waters despite the fact that the calendar read January.

January in Ashland was a different story. The temperature had been dropping steadily since October. Fall's cool crisp mornings felt practically balmy compared to the icy layer of frost that coated the ground. I'd invested in a new collection of sweaters and wool socks. Despite pulling on heavy layers before leaving my apartment, I still shivered on my short walk to Torte.

Torte is located in the heart of downtown. The bakeshop sits in the middle of the plaza, nestled between shops and restaurants, with a front-row view of the bubbling Lithia fountains across the street. It's a prime location for grabbing a pretheater snack or a catching up on the latest gossip. My mom, Helen, had been running the bustling bakery solo since my dad died and I took off to see the world. Her delectable handcrafted pastries are legendary with locals and anyone passing through town. Not only do people find comfort in her sweet creations, they also seek her out for advice and her kind listening ear. Everyone who walks through Torte's front door is treated like family. That's the secret to Torte's longevity. Well, that and the binder of recipes passed down through generations of my family that Mom keeps locked in the office.

Keeping baker's hours means that I'm always awake long before anyone else. This morning as I hurried through a biting wind to Torte, the streets felt especially dark and gloomy. I quickly unlocked the front door, flipped on the lights, and cranked on the heat.

A large chalkboard on the far wall displayed a Shakespearean quote reading: "In winter with warm tears I'll melt the snow. And keep eternal spring-time on thy face."

My dad started the tradition of a revolving quote when I was a kid. He loved everything Shakespearean, hence his insistance on naming me Juliet. I prefer Jules. There's too much pressure attached to having a name like Juliet. But each time I glanced at thc chalkboard, I smiled at the memory of my dad's sparkling eyes and quick wit.

Torte's front windows had frosted overnight. I rubbed my hands together for friction and made my way to the kitchen. The bakeshop is divided into two sections. Customers can nosh on a pastry or linger over an espresso at one of the tables or booths in thc front. A long counter and coffee bar separates the dining space from the kitchen. It gives the bakery an open feel and allows guests to watch all of the action in the back.

I grabbed an apron from the rack and tied it around my waist. Our red aprons with blue stitching and a chocolate Torte logo in the center are as close as it gets to a uniform around here. Everyone on staff wears one of the crisp aprons that match Torte's teal-and-cranberry-colored walls.

My first task of the day was getting the oven up to temp. We'd been down an oven for a while. Managing with one oven was doable during the slow season, but

Mom and I had been tucking cash away in hopes of up-grading our equipment before things got busy again. I turned the oven on high, and leafed through the stack of special orders waiting on the kitchen island.

On today's agenda were two birthday cakes, a pastry order for the theater, and our normal bread deliveries. The tight-knit business community in Ashland diligently sup-ported and promoted each other, especially in the off-season. Wholesaling our bread to local restaurants and shops definitely helped with cash flow.

I washed my hands with honey-lavender soap and got to work on the bread. There's something so therapeutic about making bread. From watching the yeast rise to kneading the dough, I allowed my thoughts to wander as I went through the familiar steps. Some of my colleagues in culinary school had complained when they had to work early shifts. I remember one aspiring chef said that she always felt lonely in an empty kitchen. Not me. I like working in a quiet space with nothing more than the hum of a mixer and the scent of sourdough bread baking around me. That's not to say that I don't enjoy a vibrant kitchen with bodies squeezing past each other and a coun-ter chock-full of delectable treats. I guess, like so many things in life, it was finding the balance between solitude and socialization that counted.

With the first batch of bread rising, I quickly sketched out a menu for the day. Once the team arrived everyone would have an assignment. The cold weather had our cus-tomers hungry for hearty breakfast options. I'd have Stephanie, one of the college students I'd been mentor-ing, bake chocolate, cinnamon, and nut muffins. Mom could handle stocking the rest of the pastry case with an assortment of sweet and savory delicacies. That would give me time to focus on the special orders.

As I finished writing the menu and task list on the

whiteboard, the front door jingled and Andy walked in. He wore a puffy orange parka and knit stocking cap. His shaggy sandy hair stuck out from beneath the cap. "Morning, boss," he called, rubbing his arms. "Man, it's cold out there."

Andy had been working for Mom since he was in high school. Now he attends Southern Oregon University, and runs Torte's espresso bar whenever he's not studying. He's a genius when it comes to crafting coffee drinks. His creative flavor combinations have earned him a loyal following. There's always a line for one of Andy's expertly pulled shots or specialty lattes. He has an innate talent, and I've enjoyed watching him thrive.

He shrugged off his parka, stored it and his backpack behind the counter, and tied on an apron. Without missing a beat, he revved up the espresso machine. "You want to try something new?" he asked, pulling a canister of beans from underneath the bar.

"I'd love anything you want to make me," I said as I roughed out a sketch for one of the birthday cakes. The order form read: *Anything chocolate.* Talk about a dream client. Chocolate was wide open for interpretation. Since this was for an adult birthday, I thought it would be fun to work some childhood nostalgia into the cake. I'd make an Oreo mousse cake and slice it into four layers. Then I planned to fill each layer with chocolate mousse and fresh berries. I would top it with more berries, Oreos, and gold dust. It should give the cake a whimsical yet elegant touch.

While I whipped egg yolks and sugar in the mixer for the mousse, Andy plugged his phone into our sound system and blasted some tunes. I watched as he swirled steaming milk to the beat of the music.

Mom and Stephanie arrived a few minutes later. Stephanie had originally been hired to help at the front counter, but her introverted personality—and the fact that she could really bake—made her a much better match for the kitchen. When I first met her, I thought she was a bit sullen. I've come to realize that there's a kind and caring young woman underneath the layers of black eyeliner, purple hair, and her standoffish attitude. Mentoring Stephanie in the bakery had been one of the highlights of the last few months. She was a quick study and had an eye for design.

"Morning, everyone," Mom yelled over the music. She really needs hearing aids. "It's already hopping in here this morning."

I signaled for Andy to turn down the music. He nodded and turned the volume down.

Mom patted Andy on the shoulder in silent thanks as she walked toward the rack of aprons.

"You know it, Mrs. C. It's Monday. That means we crank up the tunes and the grinds." Andy grinned and drizzled white chocolate sauce over a steaming latte. "Order up, boss," he said to me.

"What is it?" I asked, grabbing the coffee from the front counter.

"I'm thinking of calling it a snowflake latte." He reached under the bar and pulled out a notebook that he uses to track coffee recipes and ratios of milk to espresso. "It's an almond latte with a little touch of white chocolate and whipped cream. Give it a try. I'm hoping it's not too sweet. It's my gift to the snow gods. We need some fresh powder on Mount Ashland. I'm dying to hit the slopes."

The coffee smelled heavenly. I caught a whiff of almond as I took a sip. The creamy latte was perfectly balanced with just the right touch of sweetness. Andy had succeeded once again. We make all of our sauces and syrups at Torte. Our white chocolate sauce is a customer favorite. It's much richer in flavor and texture than mass-manufactured sauces. I'm not a fan of sugary coffee drinks. Andy knew exactly how to add a splash of sweetness without letting the sugar overpower the drink.

"This is delicious." I held the mug up in a toast. "It's like winter in a cup. I think the snow gods will love it."

"That's what I was going for, boss." His cheeks reddened. "Anyone else want to give my snowflake latte a try?"

Mom and Stephanie raised their hands in unison. Andy laughed and started steaming more milk. I knew he appreciated the praise. It was well deserved. I could drink Andy's lattes all day. That is, until I started to shake from too much caffeine intake.

"This one needs to go up on the special board today," I said, cradling the warm mug in my hands.

Stephanie tucked her hair behind her ears. "What do you want me to do first, Jules?" She normally wears her dark hair with streaks of purple, but today it was dyed in a shockingly bright violet. The look was startling.

"You changed your hair," I noted.

She shrugged. "Yeah, I was tired of the black."

"It matches your gorgeous eyes," Mom said, returning to the kitchen and handing Stephanie a snowflake latte.

"Thanks." Stephanie looked at her feet as she spoke. She was dressed in all black, quite the contrast from her cheery red apron and purple hair.

"Can you start on the muffins?" I asked, pointing to the whiteboard. "We're going to need an extra dozen of each flavor for Lance's order."

Stephanie sipped her latte and studied the board. "What are you thinking for the cinnamon muffins?"

One of the many things that I appreciated about Stephanie was her willingness to ask questions. When I worked on the cruise line one of my biggest pet peeves with apprentice chefs was that they were afraid to ask questions. How are you going to learn if you don't ask? I'd much rather have a chef-in-training ask too many questions versus doing it wrong and having to dump an entire batch of pastries in the trash.

"What do you think?" I threw it back at her. "We could do cinnamon chips or a cinnamon crumble on the top."

"I'll do both," she said.

"Works for me." I returned to the mixer.

Mom squeezed between me and the butcher block island that sits in the middle of the industrial kitchen. She's shorter than me by a few inches. I inherited my height and lean frame from my dad. Even in her clogs, she has to stand on her toes to meet my eyes. "I see you've already got a head start back here."

"That's not a bad thing, is it?"

"Not at all. In fact, I might get used to this and start sleeping in." She winked.

I whipped the yolks and sugar together until the mixture turned a creamy lemon color. One of the things I've been trying to teach Stephanie is that each step matters when it comes to baking. The most common mistake novice bakers make is to dump all the ingredients in at once. For a light and airy cake, it's imperative that the egg yolks and sugar are slightly thickened before incorporating the chocolate.

Mom rolled up her sleeves. She cubed butter and measured brown sugar into a large mixing bowl. She chatted with Stephanie and Andy about their classes as she creamed cookie batter together by hand. Baking was in her DNA. Despite the fact that Torte has two industrial mixers, Mom was old-school when it came to making cookie dough. She prefers her large stainless steel bowl and wooden spoon.

"Mom, you know we have an industrial mixer, right?"

"How do you think I stay so fit?" She flexed her arm and raised the wooden spoon. "Who needs a mixer when I have muscles like these?"

I worried that the years of physical labor were taking their toll on her. Her pace had started to slow a bit, but not her enthusiasm, so I let it go.

I filled the double boiler with an inch of water and placed it on the stove. Then I measured dark chocolate chunks. I would melt the chocolate on a low boil and slowly incorporate it with the eggs and sugar. Soon the entire kitchen became infused with the delightful smell of cinnamon muffins baking in the oven, steaming coffee, and melting chocolate. I couldn't resist swiping a taste of the warm chocolate as it liquefied in the pan.

"Where's Sterling?" Mom asked, glancing at the clock on the wall. It was almost six. In a few minutes Torte would be bustling with locals stopping by for a coffee and pastry on their way to work.

"He said he'd be here by seven," I replied, wiping chocolate from my fingers. "He stayed late last night." Sterling was our newest staff member. Like me, he'd thought Ashland would be a temporary resting place, but had come to love our quirky small town. His piercing blue eyes, tattoos, and skater style had earned him quite the following among teenage girls. I wanted to tell them that they were wasting their time, while they stood in line, giggling and ordering hot chocolates. Sterling liked Stephanie. I wasn't sure where she stood. The chemistry between them was definitely palpable, but as far as I could tell that was where it ended.

Sterling and Andy made a dream team in the front. Their personalities complemented one another. Andy with his boyish all-American good looks, and knowledge of local sports, chatted up customers with easy banter. Sterling had a sexy edginess that customers responded to.

He discussed indie bands and dabbled in writing poetry. He reminded me of a young Johnny Depp.

After the holidays, Sterling asked me if I'd be willing to give him cooking lessons in the evenings. He didn't think baking was his style, but he was interested in learning his way around the kitchen. It was great timing for me, since Torte's catering business had been steadily increasing. Having an extra hand to help prep would be a huge help.

By the time Sterling arrived, Andy had sold a dozen snowflake lattes and packaged up pastries to go for our regular clients. A handful of locals occupied the tables in the front, but we were nowhere near as busy as we are in the summer months. I arranged the theater pastry order in a large white box with the Torte logo stamped on the side. Lance, the artistic director for the Oregon Shakespeare Festival, was hosting a breakfast for some local board members and requested pastries to be delivered before eight.

Mom and Stephanie had things under control in the kitchen. My chocolate mousse was cooling on the counter, so I zipped up my coat and balanced the box of pastries. "I'm off to deliver these to Lance," I called as I pushed open the front door.

A blast of cold air assaulted my face. *Hurry, Jules,* I thought as I quickened my pace. It's freezing. Little did I know things were about to get much, much colder.

Chapter Two

The Oregon Shakespeare Festival complex is just up the hill from Torte. This morning I opted to cut through Lithia Park and take the Shakespeare stairs. The staircase leads directly from the park's expansive grounds up through the tree line to OSF's theaters.

The park sat empty. Even the birds had flown south in search of warmer skies. I took the steps two at a time, as my breath frosted in front of my face.

Although the theater was shuttered for the season, OSF's senior staff work year round. It was odd to see "the bricks" (as locals refer to the brick plaza in front of the theater) deserted. The marquee read: "Thanks for Another Stunning Season! See Us Again in February When We Open with *Three Amigos*."

I smiled to myself as I hurried past. People tend to associate OSF solely with Shakespeare. The company is known for producing the Bard's works, but it also stages a variety of modern plays and even the occasional musical. Theater lovers from around the world return season after season for OSF's offerings.

Lance's office is located in the Bowmer Theater. I knew the way. Lance and I became friends last summer. He drives me crazy with his insistence that I should be on stage. Somehow word got out—that tends to happen in Ashland—that I'd dabbled in theater when I was younger. Lance had made it his personal mission to convince me that I should return. It wasn't going to happen. I had no interest in being on stage. Pastry was my medium.

I passed the dark stage. A single lamp with a glowing yellow bulb stood like a beacon in the otherwise vacant theater. It cast a ghostly shadow on the empty stadium seats. Lance had told me the practice of leaving a light on the stage was an old theater superstition. It gave me the creeps. I hurried past and walked down the back stairs to Lance's office. Balancing the box in one arm, I knocked on his door. "Lance, it's Jules."

"Juliet, darling, *entrez. Entrez,*" Lance said, waving me in with one hand and studying me through a pair of black wire-rimmed glasses that rested on the tip of his nose.

Lance's office was like a miniature museum showcasing the theater's success. Playbills and awards lined the walls. A stack of scripts sat in a pile on his desk. Against the far wall there was a couch with purple, gold, and black pillows. Behind the desk, a wall of windows looked out onto the theater complex and the dreary winter sky.

He removed his reading glasses and jumped to his feet when I came in. "Darling, let me take that." He placed the pastry box on his desk and kissed me on both cheeks. "Look at you, with nice rosy cheeks. I do believe that winter is becoming on you."

"Stop, Lance." I rolled my eyes, but my hand went to my ponytail. It's my typical style for working in the bakery. I can't stand it when hair gets in my eyes, or—God forbid—the food.

"What is it going to take to get it through that beautiful skull of yours that my makeup artists would die to work on your pristine palette?"

I ignored his comment.

He opened the box and waved his hands in front of his face. "As always your pastries look equally smashing."

Lance had a flair for the dramatic. He was perfectly cast as artistic director for the award-winning theater. He looked the part, too. Today he wore a pair of tapered jeans, a black turtleneck, purple scarf, and expensive shoes. "I'm so glad you stopped by," he said, taking a cheese blintz from the box and returning to his seat. "I have a favor to ask."

I handed him a stack of paper napkins. "Does this involve me and one of your productions? Because you know that my answer is going to be no."

"One day, darling. One day, I'll convince you. I'm good at getting what I want." He bit into the blintz for effect. Dabbing his chin with a napkin, he continued. "But no, this favor involves your culinary prowess."

"Okay, I like the sound of that."

"Have a seat." He motioned to the empty chair in front of his desk.

I sat and waited for him to continue. His large mahogany desk looked as if it had been built to intimidate. I could imagine a new actor gulping down fear as he waited for an audience with Lance. I could also imagine Lance flashing his signature Cheshire grin and enjoying every minute of watching an aspiring actor sweat.

"You may have heard that our quarterly board meeting is coming up." Lance set the blintz on a napkin. "Usually we have it here in town, but I want to do something more extravagant this year, so I'm hosting a weekend retreat for the entire executive board at Lake of the Woods Lodge next weekend."

"Okay." I glanced out the window. It looked like it was starting to rain.

Lance rifled through a stack of scripts. He removed a file folder and slid it across the desk to me. "I want *you* to cater the weekend. The theme is 'cozy cabin.' I've rented the lodge for the entire weekend. I'm pulling out all the stops. I want the board to feel pampered and dazzled by the food. We have a huge giving campaign that we're going to kick off next month, and I need them feeling ready to get out there and raise new funds and friends for the theater."

I opened the file folder. It contained an agenda for the board retreat which involved breakfast, lunch, dinner, and snacks for forty people over the course of a three-day weekend. Wow. Even though I'd served tens, if not hundreds, of thousands of guests while working on the cruise ship, I'd specialized in pastry and I had a team of sous chefs and dishwashers. An entire weekend of meals would definitely be a new challenge.

This is what you've been hoping for, Jules, I told myself as I returned the agenda to the file folder. "Thanks for thinking of us," I said to Lance. "There's not a lot of time to prepare. Your event is in just over a week. I'll have to call our suppliers right away and make sure they have enough in stock."

He waved me off. "Darling, you're the best chef in town, you'll figure it out, I'm sure. That Sunday supper last weekend was like stepping back in time or into the pages of a storybook. I know you won't disappoint."

Mom and I had started hosting Sunday suppers at Torte. For twenty dollars, diners were treated to an appetizer, entrée, and a signature Torte dessert. Each course was served family-style in the dining room. We pushed tables together to make an inviting space for everyone to gather. The concept had been a hit with locals. The last two suppers had sold out.

Without asking whether or not I was going to take the job, Lance launched into a list of details. "I'll need you to coordinate with my new assistant, Whitney. She'll order anything you need. I've already tasked her with ordering extra booze. I want the wine to flow freely, if you know what I mean."

I started to ask for clarification about the menu. Lance pushed to his feet. "Must run, darling." He kissed me on both cheeks. "Talk to Whitney. I'll see you at the lodge next weekend."

Before I could say anything else, he snatched the box of pastries from his desk and walked away.

I sat for a moment, lost in thought. Catering OSF's executive board retreat might push me out of my comfort zone, but it was exactly what Torte needed.

What a welcome surprise, I thought as I hurried back through an icy rain to the bakeshop. I couldn't wait to tell Mom and the rest of the team. A new corporate account would certainly give our bottom line an extra boost.

Torte was humming when I returned. The heat from the oven had significantly raised the temperature. The ice on the windows had begun to melt, and dripped down the single glass panes. I needed to remind Stephanie to wipe them down soon.

"Hey, Jules, you look excited," Sterling said, as I stepped inside and shrugged off my coat. He wore a gray hoodie that matched the sky outside.

"I am." I grinned, and glanced around the bakeshop. A couple sat at one of the booths in front of the windows, and two of the bistro tables were taken. Otherwise the shop was quiet. "You two want to take a quick break, and come hear my news?" I said to Sterling and Andy.

They agreed and followed me into the kitchen. Stephanie stopped the blender, and Mom turned the sauce she was simmering on the stove to low. "Look at the gig we just landed, you guys," I said, placing Lance's agenda on the island.

Andy snagged a cinnamon muffin from the cooling rack. He ate nonstop. Playing football for Southern Oregon University had him burning calories around the clock. No wonder he likes working here, I thought, as he devoured the muffin in two bites and grabbed another. Mom has always had an "eat whatever you want policy" for staff. We used to joke on the ship that you could tell who the newbie baker was by how much they ate. Once you've been around a bakeshop for a while, the lure of consuming every tasty morsel in front of you tends to dissipate. That wasn't the case for Andy.

"Lance wants us to cater an executive retreat at Lake of the Woods next weekend," I said, passing around the file.

Mom dusted her hands on her apron. Her walnut eyes lit up as she read the agenda. "This is great news, honey!" She paused and looked concerned. "But this is a big order. You can't do it yourself."

I nodded. "It's a big order. It'll mean preparing every meal for all forty guests."

"And more dough, right, boss?" Andy said through a mouthful of muffin.

"Right, and I have a plan." I turned to Sterling. He stood next to Stephanie, their arms almost touching. "I'm wondering if you want to be my sous chef for the weekend?"

Sterling took a step back. "Sure. I can do that."

"Perfect!" Mom clapped. "Andy, Stephanie, and I will keep Torte in tip-top shape while you two are away."

"You better." I pointed my index finger at her.

She grabbed a dishtowel and flicked me with it. "If our

fearless captain here will let us little people help, who has suggestions for the menu?"

I found a pad of paper in the top drawer by the whiteboard and started taking notes as everyone started talking at once. Mom is a genius at collaboration. I loved that she had instilled that in our young staff. It was something I tried to model, too.

"Breakfast is easy," Andy said. "You guys can just do all our standard morning pastries, right?"

"Yes, but you know Lance. His exact words were that he wants us to *dazzle* the board members with our food." I mimicked Lance's dramatic speech pattern.

"But he wants comfort food?" Sterling asked. "Dazzling and comfort don't exactly go together."

Mom picked up the dishtowel again and flung it at him. "Sterling, how can you say that? Isn't dazzling comfort exactly what we make here at Torte?"

Sterling held up the towel in surrender. "You've got me there, Helen."

"I heard good things about your lasagna last weekend," Stephanie said.

"Okay." I scratched notes on the paper. "We start with morning pastries. Maybe one day we can do a warm egg dish. Lunch should be easy. We can do sandwiches on homemade bread."

"And stew," Mom said.

"Yes, and definitely stew." I made a note, as we mapped out a menu and supply list.

I spent the remainder of the morning feeling the familiar jitter of a new challenge. I hadn't been to Lake of the Woods since I was a kid. Spending the weekend at a remote high-mountain lodge and putting my culinary skills to the test sounded perfect.

Only I would soon come to learn that much more than pastry was on the menu for the weekend.

Chapter Three

The next week passed quickly. I had plenty to do with getting ready to cater Lance's retreat and managing Torte. Mom promised that she had things under control. I knew she did. I just didn't want to burden her. One of the best things about coming home had been that I was able to lighten her load a little. During some of the leaner years after the recession hit, Mom had struggled to keep Torte afloat. Her kind heart and generosity were a strength, but they could also be a weakness when it came to money.

I had learned last summer that Mom had lent money to half of the town. I appreciated how much she cared about her friends and fellow business owners, but I also knew that if we wanted Torte to see another thirty years it meant that we had to cinch our purse strings a bit tighter. Catering clients and Sunday suppers were both helping to put our profit margin back in the black.

Sterling took an active role in preparing for the weekend. I took him along to meet with our vendors so he could get a feel for the business side of running a bakeshop. By the end of the week we had amassed enough fresh fruit, vegetables, herbs, meats, and cheeses to pack the back of Mom's car. I did one final check of our supply list, before taking Mom's keys. She sent us on our way with a bag of hot-from-the-oven snickerdoodles, and Andy made us snowflake lattes to go.

I offered to drive. It had been years since I'd taken a road trip. I remembered the winding route to Lake of the Woods from my childhood. My parents used to bring me to the resort every Labor Day weekend. They would arrange for friends to run the shop for the weekend, and we'd pack our station wagon and head out to the lodge for the final days of summer.

Lake of the Woods sits at almost five thousand feet above sea level. The lake was formed from a volcanic eruption thousands of years ago. Getting to the high-altitude lodge was an adventure in itself. The most direct route from Ashland would take us on Dead Indian Road. I told Sterling to buckle up as we pulled out of town and made our way toward the winding road. The road cuts through the Siskiyou National Forest, twisting past sharp corners and down curves without a shoulder. Its name pays homage to the Native Americans who belonged to the land long before white settlers made their way west. I couldn't help wonder as I navigated the dangerous road if there was more to its meaning.

"This is a crazy ride." Sterling broke my concentration as I slowed around a hairpin turn.

"I know. I'd kind of forgotten how scary it is." My fingers clenched the steering wheel. They were all bare, even my ring finger. I hadn't worn my wedding ring for months, but I still caught myself feeling for it sometimes.

"You want some tunes to distract you?" he asked, removing his phone from the front pocket of his hoodie. Sterling's wardrobe consists of hoodies and jeans no matter the weather.

"That would be great." I couldn't imagine driving the narrow road at night. Towering evergreen trees barricade the sun from view. There were no streetlights, cabins, or even signs of movement as we twisted our way up the mountain. Sterling plugged his phone into the car's sound system and chose a melodic mellow band. It helped relax my nerves.

"Who is this?" I asked. I appreciate music, but I'm far from a connoisseur. On the ship I used to listen to Carlos's Latin rhythms. I'd given that up, along with any thoughts of trying to figure out where he and I stood.

"It's a band called Orange. They just released this demo. I think it has a good vibe. Listen to the lyrics. It's really powerful stuff."

We listened in silence as I kept my focus on the road. My ears popped as we climbed higher and higher. The landscape transitioned from forest to high grasslands. Open-range cattle farms occupied the space on both sides of the highway. Signs warned of cattle crossing.

"I like them," I said to Sterling, pointing at the radio.

"Yeah, I thought you would." He caught my eye. I've never gotten used to Sterling's startling blue eyes. They look like bright blue ice, yet are equally warm and welcoming. It's a unique mix, and just one of the reasons he has a following among Ashland's teen girl set.

"How's your poetry coming?"

He shrugged. "I don't know. I'm not sure I have anything to say."

"Of course you do. You're one of the wisest twenty-two-year-olds that I know. Mom calls you an old soul."

"I love your mom." Sterling sighed and looked out the window. He had lost his mom young, and went through a period of turmoil after her death. I didn't know him then, but I did know what it was like to lose a parent. Sterling and I had bonded over our lingering grief. I was impressed that he'd found a way to overcome his struggle and turn his life around. Especially because he'd done it all on his own.

"She loves you, too." I reached over and touched his arm. "Really. She does."

"I feel that." Sterling met my eyes. "I'm really glad things worked out, and you guys took a chance on me."

"Me, too." I returned my gaze forward as we passed snowmobile trails like "Old Baldy." The higher we climbed, the more snow was piled on the sides of the highway. Fortunately the road was clear. I hoped that didn't change. Mom told me there were chains in the back of the car, but I had no idea how to put them on and I was pretty sure that Sterling didn't, either.

"Have you given any thought to going to Southern Oregon for writing?"

"I don't know." Sterling flipped to the next song on his phone. "I guess I'm good for the short term. I'm grateful I get to do things like this. I really appreciate you giving me a chance."

I glanced to my left as an eagle circled above us. "Of course. But don't sell yourself short. I know how talented you are, and if you decide you want to pursue writing Mom and I will do whatever it takes—write you a letter of recommendation, work around your schedule, whatever."

"Thanks." Sterling smiled. "You're the best, Jules."

There was another subject I wanted to broach with him—Stephanie. Things hadn't been the same with them since last fall when Stephanie developed a crush on a Pastry Channel chef in town for a baking competition.

I decided to try a tactic that I'd learned from Mom, and ask a global question. "How's everything else?" I asked, keeping my eyes on the rearview mirror.

"Good." Sterling paused. I thought he was going to open up, but instead he tried the same trick on me. "What about you, Jules?" His voice was sincere.

"I'm fine." I probably replied too quickly. "I mean, I'm

still adjusting to being home, but for the most part it's good. Weird sometimes, but good."

Sterling paused for a moment. "Do you know anything about the Greek philosopher Heraclitus?"

"Not at all." I laughed. "Let me guess, you do."

He smiled. "Yeah, he's known best for being the first philosopher to understand that change is a constant in the universe."

"That sounds like my life."

"Yeah, mine too." Sterling gave me a sympathetic smile. "One of my favorite quotes is attributed to him. He says something like, 'You cannot step twice into the same rivers, for fresh waters are forever flowing in upon you.'"

I inhaled deeply. "Wow. I love that so much."

Sterling tugged at the strings on his hoodie. "It kind of seems like where you're at. You know, you're home, but you can't really ever go back to things as they used to be."

I placed one hand on my stomach, and drew in a long breath. "Yes! That's exactly how I feel." I couldn't believe that he'd so eloquently voiced what I'd been struggling with. "You're a decade younger than me, how do you have things so figured out?"

"I don't, Jules. I just know where you are," he said softly.

We both became lost in our own thoughts again as we sped past a fire station. In the summer months the station serves as a lookout and gathering point for firefighters battling forest fires, but it sat in a lonely winter slumber today. Next, expensive cabins came into view. We were only about five miles from Lake of the Woods now.

Sterling was right. I was home again, but I was an entirely different person. Fresh and salt waters had been flowing in upon me for years. That was it. Change. The universe was alive with change. I had changed. Home had changed. Neither of us were the same. And for the first time since I'd been back, I understood that was exactly as it should be.

Chapter Four

Lake of the Woods Resort was originally built as a fishing retreat in the 1920s. At just under five thousand feet in elevation, the natural lake is a popular destination all year round. During the summer months vacationers swim off the lake's shallow banks, fish for rainbow trout, and tool around on party boats. In the winter the lake freezes over, making it a prime location for ice-fishing.

I navigated off Dead Indian Road and over a bumpy one-lane road toward the resort. A fresh blanket of snow coated the tops of the evergreen trees. They looked as if they'd been frosted with buttercream. Mounds of dirty snow had been pushed to both sides of the road. As we rounded a bend the lake came into view. The midmorning sun cast a warm glow on the frozen lake. It was hard to imagine that there was water under its smooth surface.

Sterling pulled a knit cap from his backpack and positioned it on his head. "Looks like it might be colder up here."

"You think?" I laughed as I maneuvered the car over the snowy road. Spaces in front of the rustic lodge had been plowed. I parked in one of them and we both got out. Sterling was right. The mountain air was much cooler here than in Ashland. Good thing I packed extra layers, I thought as I took in the view.

The lake sat directly in front of us. To the right, smoke puffed from the lodge's chimney. A deck wrapped around the two-story lodge. Its exterior was painted brown to blend in with the forest. Snow covered its slanted green metal roof. Note to self, don't stand underneath the overhang. I could imagine an avalanche of snow landing on my head.

The general store, to the left, looked like a miniature version of the lodge. It was closed for the season. Behind us, dirt trails, partially covered in snow, snaked from the lodge up into the woods. Cute cabins, each with a peekaboo view of the lake, were tucked into the trees.

Sterling took a load of supplies from the back of the car. I followed behind with a box of my baking gear, feeling grateful that I'd opted to put my winter boots on before we left Ashland. I hadn't seen this much snow in years. It made me want to grab a ball of it and toss it at Sterling.

The smell of a crackling fire greeted us as we stepped inside the cheery lodge. A familiar memory washed over me. The lodge was exactly as I remembered it. Its knotty-pine walls were adorned with antlers, hunting trophies, and Native American artwork. Giant picture windows offered a spectacular view of the lake. The open communal dining room had one long wooden dining table in the middle and an arrangement of smaller two- and four-person tables throughout the room. There was a roaring fireplace with a well-worn leather couch, comfy chairs, and vintage travel magazines in the front corner. An attached bar stood to the left and the kitchen where Sterling and I would spend our weekend was in the back.

"This is cool," Sterling said, resting the boxes on the

main dining table. "It's like a retro cabin. Kind of like stepping back in time."

"Exactly." I set my box with my marble rolling pin and pastry knives next to the supplies. "Lance said he was going for a theme of rustic elegance. I'd say that pretty much sums up this space, right?"

"Right." Sterling wandered toward the fireplace and picked up an old issue of *Life* magazine. "Nineteen fifty-five." He held up the magazine for me to see. "Is that when this place was built?"

A woman's voice answered before I could. "No. The lodge was built much earlier, but we're trying capture the spirit of that era here." She strolled toward us, and extended her hand. "I'm Mercury Rule, owner and manager of Lake of the Woods. You must be Jules."

I shook her hand. "Nice to meet you. This is my sous chef, Sterling."

Mercury shook Sterling's hand and then stepped back and waved her arm toward the frosted windows. "What do you think?" She was dressed in a casual pair of jeans, black snow boots, and a comfortable fleece with a Lake of the Woods logo embroidered on the front. While her look was casual, her demeanor was very businesslike. I'd guess her to be in her early fifties, probably a little younger than Mom. Her graying hair was twisted in a tight bun.

"Cool vibe," Sterling replied.

"Good. That's what we're hoping for. There's no cell service, cable, or Internet access in any of the cabins. We want our guests to completely detach from the outside world while they're here."

"So no texting, then?" Sterling pulled his phone from his pocket.

"I'm afraid not." Mercury pointed toward the lake. "You can try down by the marina, but we don't have cell towers out this way. We have a landline in case of emergencies, but otherwise we're off the grid up here."

Sterling shrugged. "That's cool. She probably wasn't going to text me back anyway." He winked at me and tucked his phone back in his pocket.

Not having cell service wasn't a big deal for me. I was still getting used to my phone beeping and dinging all the time. We didn't have service on the cruise ship, so being constantly attached to a device was new to me. It had been strange, even in a small town like Ashland, to see how dependent people had become on their smartphones since I'd been away. Even Mom texted me all the time, just to check in.

Mercury reached into her pocket and handed me a heavy set of keys. "Before I forget, these will open the lodge and the marina. I'll get you both keys to your cabins later." She glanced toward the front door and frowned. "We're short-staffed and the cleaning crew is still getting the cabins ready."

"Don't worry about it," I said. "We've got some serious cooking to do."

"Well, in that case let me to show you the kitchen." Mercury smiled. "I appreciate your flexibility. Usually guests get very upset if their cabin isn't ready. It's one of the many things I've been trying to fix up here."

"Really, it's no big deal." I picked up my box of baking supplies.

Mercury walked us to the kitchen. "When my husband and I bought this place two years ago you should have seen what a disaster it was," she said over her shoulder. "We've been remodeling one building at a time. We started in here because we figured having a quality kitchen was critical when we reopened to the public. It's been a real labor of love." She sighed.

The kitchen definitely looked like it had been updated. I was impressed with how Mercury had managed to maintain a rustic vibe. The natural maple countertops blended seamlessly with the knotty-pine walls. They were ideal for chopping and slicing. All of the appliances were new, including an eight-burner gas stove. My eyes focused in on a wood-fired brick oven and stack of apple wood waiting to be burned.

"Did you put that in?" I asked, pointing to the oven. Terra-cotta-colored bricks ran from floor to ceiling. A stainless steel ash rake, shovel, and pizza peel were mounted to the bricks. Between the oven and the picturesque snowy windows, I felt like I was in the Italian Alps.

Mercury smiled, making the wrinkles around her mouth crinkle. "We did. Isn't it gorgeous? I don't cook, or claim to know anything about cooking, but I love having a fireplace in the kitchen. It was my husband's idea. He's the chef."

"It's amazing." I ran my hand over the bricks. My head was swimming with ideas of things to fire, from bread to pizzas. I wondered how expensive adding a wood-fired oven would be at Torte. I'd have to add that to our dream list of potential upgrades.

"Customers seem to love everything that comes out of it," Mercury said. "I don't know if Lance told you, but my husband is in California right now. I think we finally have an offer on our house there. We've been trying to sell it ever since we bought this place. It wasn't a good time to sell, and let me tell you I cannot wait not to have a mortgage payment on top of all the bills we have here. No one told me running a lodge was going to cost so much, and I'm determined not to lose this place."

I nodded. Ashland had seen a number of established business succumb to the recession.

"He said to tell you to make yourselves at home here. Use anything you want, and just let me know if there's anything you need. Like I said, I'm not a chef, but I know my way around the property now, and I can call Gavin Allen. He's the marina manager. He knows everything about this resort. He's been working here since he was in high school. I don't know what I would do without him. He can fix anything, which is a good thing right now since everything seems to be falling apart." She paused. "Anyway, you don't need to know that. Gavin is a great guy. He's rough around the edges, but a teddy bear. The store is closed, but Gavin has extra supplies in the marina if you need anything."

"Great." I surveyed the kitchen. "I can't think of anything we need now, but I'll let you know."

Mercury snapped her fingers. "Oh, and—if he actually shows up anytime soon—I'll introduce you to Tony. He's our bartender." She sighed. "And a total flake, but that's not your problem, either." She walked toward the door. "Like I said, let me know if you need anything. I tried to make room in the fridge and cupboards. You can store extra supplies in the marina if you need to. Make yourselves at home."

"A flaky bartender—that sounds about right," Sterling said as he began unloading boxes with pastry flour, sugar, and yeast. "Where do you want this?"

"Good question." I surveyed the kitchen. Mercury had cleared two shelves in the large stainless steel refrigerator, and emptied two cupboards near the sink. "Let's get all the perishables put away first," I said to Sterling. "Then we can make a game plan for everything else."

"That works for me. You want me to unload the car first?"

"Absolutely!" I grinned. "Especially if that means I get to stay inside and fire up this baby." I massaged the bricks.

"Go for it." Sterling pulled his hoodie over his knit cap and headed for the car.

I arranged the meats, cheese, vegetables, and other perishables in the fridge. This was by far the nicest kitchen I had worked in. Red gingham curtains were tied back on the window, allowing for a glimpse of the icy lake. It did feel like I was stepping back in time, but with all the perks of a modern kitchen. While Sterling unpacked the car and organized our baking supplies, I loaded the brick oven with apple wood and lit a fire.

Soon the snug kitchen smelled like the fruity, sweet wood. "This is going to be a great weekend," I said to Sterling.

He tossed me a Torte apron. "You know it."

We mapped out our plan for the day. The board members would be arriving sometime in the late afternoon. Dinner was our first official meal, but I wanted to have some appetizers and snacks prepared for guests to nosh on while they waited. Sticking with Lance's theme of rustic elegance wouldn't be difficult. That was my philosophy on food. I love creating meals that are simple and comforting.

I had already planned on making roasted chicken for tonight's meal. But baking the chickens in the brick oven would elevate the dish and add a lovely smoky flavor to the meat. I wanted them to roast slowly.

Sterling rough-chopped carrots, celery, onion, and garlic while I showed him how to assemble the birds. I drizzled olive oil over the skin and massaged it in. Then I poked holes in clementines and lemons and stuffed them into the bird along with a handful of fresh rosemary and sage. I drizzled more olive oil in the bottom of an oven-safe baking dish, layered the bottom with the vegetables, and added a splash of homemade chicken stock. Then I placed the bird on top and finished it with a healthy shake of sea salt and cracked pepper.

"Oh man, that smells good already." Sterling swept onion peel into the garbage. "Looks easy enough. You want me to take it from here?"

"It does, doesn't it?" I fanned my hands over the pile of vegetables and herbs on the counter. "Just wait until we get these beauties in the oven." Roasting the chickens with the vegetables should infuse them with flavor. The lemons and clementines would give them a hint of citrus and ensure that the meat would be moist. We would use the vegetables to make a hearty gravy and serve the roasts with smashed garlic and rosemary red potatoes, whole-grain bread with whipped honey butter, and a green garden salad. I practically salivated as I reviewed the menu in my mind.

With Sterling focused on the chickens I turned my attention to appetizers and dessert. I'd brought some day-old baguettes from Torte. They should make a nice crostini that I could top with pesto, parmesan cheese, bruschetta, and a bean spread. I sliced the baguettes into quarter-inch pieces and brushed them with olive oil.

Sterling grabbed his phone. "No service, but at least I can play some tunes." He turned the volume as high as it would go and blasted Irish funk music.

I tapped my foot to the beat, and set the baguette slices aside. We could grill them in the oven right before we served them. Next I chopped basil and pine nuts for the pesto, and diced tomatoes and red onions for the bruschetta. Lance hadn't ordered appetizers. I wanted to surprise him with a little bonus for any guests who arrived early.

The heat from the brick oven continued to rise. Sterling

removed his knit hat, and wiped his brow. "That thing cranks out the heat."

"I love it," I said. "This is the first time I haven't felt cold since October."

"And you call yourself a native Oregonian." Sterling shook his head. "Hardly."

"Hello?" a voice called from the doorway.

"Come on in," I replied.

A young woman with frizzy brown curls pushed the door halfway open and peered into the kitchen. She looked as frazzled as her hair. "Is Tony in here?"

"Nope, just us." I pointed to Sterling and then back to myself. "Can we help you with something?"

She sighed. "Not unless you happen to have a couple cases of booze back here."

"Yikes." I glanced at the clock above the sink. "It's not even noon, and you look too young to be hitting the bottle this early."

"It's not for me." She came into the kitchen. "Wow, it smells amazing in here." Her hair frizzed in all directions. It looked like she'd stuck her hand in a light socket.

"I'm Jules." I held up my hand which was green from the basil.

She held a tablet under her arm. "I'm Whitney, Lance's new assistant."

"Right, we spoke on the phone. Nice to meet you in person."

"You, too." Whitney scrolled through her tablet. "You're the caterer?"

"That's me."

"Please tell me you have everything you need."

I looked at Sterling. "Yep. We're all set. Why?"

She didn't look up from her tablet. "Everything is a mess. Everything. I just flew in from California last night. Now they're predicting a snowstorm. Some of the board members are scared to drive up here, and have canceled. There's no Wi-Fi. I have no idea how I'm going to get anything done without an Internet connection." Her voice was breathless. She looked like she'd just arrived from California. Hopefully she'd packed warmer clothes. I couldn't imagine traipsing around the resort in her outfit—skinny jeans, a peasant blouse, and a pair of pumps without socks. She had to be freezing.

"Don't stress," I tried to reassure her as I continued to chop the fragrant herbs. "Everything seems great to me."

Sterling walked to the sink and washed his hands. "I'm originally from California, too. Where are you from?" I could tell he was trying to get Whitney to relax.

"The Bay Area." Whitney slid the tablet off. "Well, at least we'll have food." She looked up for a minute. "There's not any alcohol hiding somewhere in here is there?"

I shrugged. "Not that I know of, but you're welcome to take a look around."

She ran her fingers through her hair, making it look even more disheveled. "I don't know what to do. Lance is going to kill me."

Grabbing a red gingham towel from a hook, I wiped my hands on it. "Lance won't kill you. He's all bark and no bite, trust me."

"But we don't have any alcohol." She chomped on her fingernails. "Tony never ordered it and now he's telling me that if we use what he has stocked here, he's going to charge me double."

"That doesn't seem right." I looked at Sterling. He gave a nod of agreement.

Whitney opened two cabinet doors and stood on her tiptoes. "I don't know what else to do. We can't have a weekend retreat without any alcohol."

She was probably right. Not that Lance or any of his

board members were prone to getting drunk—I mean, maybe they were—but a cozy weekend at a remote mountain lodge really did pair perfectly with bottles of Oregon's Pinot Noir and spiked after-dinner coffees.

I started to tell her as much, but was interrupted by the sound of an argument in the dining hall.

"Whatever, Mercury!" a man's voice bellowed.

"That's him." Whitney put her finger to her lips and pointed to the hallway. She mouthed the word "Tony." Her petite frame and short statute made her look even younger than she was.

We couldn't hear Mercury's response. Tony hollered back to whatever she said with, "What? Like you're going to find another bartender up here? Good luck with that."

Had she just threatened to fire him? Yikes. No alcohol and no bartender weren't exactly a great way to start the weekend.

Tony huffed into the kitchen. He stopped mid-stride when he spotted us. I recognized his type immediately. Ashland may be a mecca for lovers of literature, but the surrounding areas of the southernmost part of the state are known for farming, hunting, and fishing. Tony looked like he would blend in with the outdoor crowd in his faded jeans with patches on the knee and work boots. A Budweiser T-shirt stretched across his belly, which looked as if it had consumed its share of beer over the years. He finished off the look with an unbuttoned flannel shirt. His balding blond hair was combed over to one side.

"What's going on in here?" he asked, letting his eyes scan my entire body.

"Not much, just prepping for dinner," I replied, making sure to use my authoritative chef voice.

"No wonder it's so hot, you're smokin'." He winked and clicked his cheek.

Great. Just what I needed. Sterling tried to stifle a laugh.

"I'm Jules. I'll be running the kitchen this weekend." I pointed to Whitney. "I hear there's some kind of problem with the alcohol."

Tony puffed out his chest. "Nope. No problem. I told the girl that I'd take care of her. I'm pretty good at taking care of the ladies, if you catch what I mean."

I caught Sterling's eye. He puffed out his chest like Tony. He was enjoying this way too much.

Whitney closed the cabinet doors. "So you have enough wine and beer in stock?"

Tony helped himself to a slice of baguette. It couldn't taste good since it had yet to be toasted. He ate it in one bite anyway. With his mouth full he said, "Yep. I've got a stocked bar, like I told you."

"But you said I'd have to pay double." Whitney bit her thumb.

"That's right. It's expensive to get booze delivered all the way up here. I'm going to have to charge you for the delivery fees." He grabbed another slice of bread.

It must be hard to get good help, I thought. Mercury hadn't sounded thrilled about Tony when she spoke of him earlier. I wondered if she was seriously trying to find a new bartender. I couldn't blame her.

Tony gave Sterling a nod. "Cool tats."

Sterling glanced at his forearms. He had pushed up his sleeves, revealing tattoos that covered his skin. "Thanks."

Tony pulled back the neck of his T-shirt. "I've got one right here." He showed off a tattoo of a hunter holding up a dead deer on his chest.

Wow. Sexy.

Sterling didn't respond. Whitney grimaced.

"Man, this one really hurt." Tony massaged the tattoo.

He held my gaze. "I won't show you where my other tat is. I'll save that for later."

"Please don't." I picked up a spatula and unwrapped cubes of butter. I wanted Tony out of my kitchen. If he didn't get the message soon, I'd have to kick him out.

Surprisingly, he took the hint. "I've got to get the bar ready for action, but don't you worry, I'll be right up front if you need me." He turned to Whitney. "You wanna come see what I've got in store for you?"

She tucked her tablet under her arm and followed him toward the dining hall. I felt sorry for her.

"Do you think we should go help her?" I asked Sterling once they were out of earshot.

He pulled his hoodie from his chest. "Want to see my tats?" He winked.

I flung the dishtowel at him. "Stop."

"Now that is something you don't see every day in Northern Cal," he said, catching the towel. "Talk about redneck."

"Welcome to Southern Oregon."

He shuddered. "You know, everyone said that Southern Oregon had a big redneck population, but I guess I've just never seen it in Ashland."

"Yeah, we're kind of in a bubble."

"I guess." He wiped his hands on his apron. "You want me to go check on her?"

"He's probably harmless, but yeah, why don't you."

"These are ready to go." He pointed to beautifully assembled chicken roasts.

"I'll stick them in," I promised as he went to check on Whitney.

A blast of hot air hit my face, as I opened the metal doors on the front of the oven. Heat radiated from the bricks. I couldn't wait to taste the end result of slow-cooking the chicken over apple wood. I pulled on a pair of oven mitts and carefully slid each roast into the oven. They should infuse with the flavor of the smoldering wood as they baked. Sterling and I would need to keep close watch on them. I hadn't baked in a brick oven since my days in culinary school, and didn't want to burn them.

With the chickens complete and the appetizers prepped, I started on the final and—in my humble opinion—most important part of the meal, dessert. Lance hadn't specified any special requests when it came to dessert. I wanted to make something that would pair well with the chicken and fit with his theme of rustic elegance.

We had overprepared for the weekend. I had packed extra staple ingredients. Inspiration tends to strike when I'm baking and I wanted to be sure I had everything I might need on hand. I took a quick inventory of our supplies and decided on preparing individual bread puddings. We could bake them in the brick oven and serve them warm. In fact, we could create a grown-up bread pudding bar with an assortment of toppings. I could whip up caramel and hot fudge sauces, and have Sterling arrange a tray of fresh berries, nuts, cream, toasted coconut, and dates and golden raisins.

Bread pudding is the ultimate comfort food. I cracked eggs into a mixing bowl and whisked them together. Fortunately, I had asked Sterling to toss in all the extra bread we had at Torte right before we left. Usually Mom donates anything that doesn't sell to the homeless shelter—which usually isn't much. I'd been saving day-old bread for the past few days knowing that it might come in handy this weekend.

Sterling returned as I cut stale bread into cubes. "Everything okay up there?" I asked.

He nodded, and walked to the sink to wash his hands. I smiled to myself. We had trained our staff well. "Yeah, it's under control. Mercury is up there and Lance just arrived. Tony's something, though."

"You can say that again." I tossed the cubes of bread into a separate bowl.

Sterling put his apron back on. "What should I do next?"

"You want to cube this bread, and I'll keep working on the base for the pudding."

"Sure. What kind of pudding are you making?"

"Bread pudding. I'll make a simple vanilla cream pudding and we'll bake them in individual ramekins in the pizza oven."

"You're in love with this thing, aren't you?"

"Is it that obvious?" I put my hand to my chest and batted my eyes.

Sterling rolled his eyes.

I turned and moved toward the stove. Making pudding requires constant attention. I whisked eggs and milk on medium heat, paying careful attention not to let the eggs scramble. "You have to whisk this like you mean it," I said to Sterling. "If this gets too hot, you'll end up with scrambled eggs."

"Maybe you're onto something, Jules. Scrambled-egg pudding."

"Ugh." I grimaced. The pudding was starting to thicken. I added vanilla and cream and continued to whisk until my arm ached.

I was just about to take the pudding off the stove, when the kitchen door swung open. I froze in mid-whisk. I recognized the face and familiar Latin accent immediately. "Julieta," Carlos, my estranged husband, said as I dropped the whisk on the floor.

Chapter Five

My knees buckled. I grabbed the counter to steady myself. The altitude must have been going to my head. Was I hallucinating? That couldn't be Carlos standing in the doorway. Could it?

"Mi querida." Carlos looked concerned as he came closer. "Are you okay?"

Sterling picked up the whisk and grabbed the pudding from the heat. I could feel my body start to sway. My heartbeat pulsed in my head. This couldn't be happening. Carlos was supposed to be on a ship somewhere in the middle of the Mediterranean, not standing in the middle of nowhere in Oregon, wearing a thick high-neck cobalt cable-knit sweater that brought out the gold specks in his eyes.

His relaxed cadence was so familiar. I wanted to rub my eyes.

Sterling cleared his throat. "I've got to check on how things are going at the bar. I'll be back in a minute." He nodded a curt greeting to Carlos, gave me a knowing look, and left me standing with my mouth gaping open.

Carlos's cheeks were bronzed with sun. His eyes burned with a look of longing. He strolled to me and enveloped me in an embrace.

I let my body collapse into his, breathing in the scent of his aftershave.

His lips brushed my forehead. My knees went weak again. Carlos wrapped me tighter in a hug and stroked my hair. "Did you get my messages?"

I shook my head. What messages? Carlos had been sending me letters for the past few months, but I hadn't opened any of them. I wasn't ready, but maybe I should have. I never expected that he'd just show up.

"*Querida,* I have missed you," he whispered in my ear.

My heart pounded so hard I thought it might explode from my chest. Keep it together, Jules, I warned myself.

Carlos released his grip on me and took a step back, still clasping both of my hands. He caressed my ring finger, then paused, and looked at me with a pained expression. "You are not wearing your ring?"

The question lingered between us. Carlos glanced at the brushed silver band on his left hand. I thought about trying to explain, but he met my eyes and nodded in understanding.

"You look even more beautiful than when I last saw you," he said quietly.

"You look good, too." I swallowed, trying to steady my breath.

"It has been too long, *querida.*" He leaned closer and rested his lips on my forehead.

I closed my eyes. I'd been dreaming of this moment for the past six months, imagining what I might say when I saw him again. Now here he was, and I couldn't find a single word to say. It was like my brain and mouth had been disconnected. There were so many things I wanted to say but nothing would come out.

Our bodies swayed in rhythm to Sterling's music playing in the background. Everything felt fuzzy and surreal. Carlos's lips remained locked on my forehead as his hands massaged my hips. We were both lost in the moment.

We may have stayed that way indefinitely, but our minireunion was interrupted by Lance. He flung the kitchen door open with his usual dramatic flair.

"Juliet, darling, I can smell your divine cooking from . . ." He trailed off and gasped. "Well, well, well, who do we have here?"

Carlos stepped to the side and placed his arm around my shoulder.

I wasn't sure how to introduce Carlos. Should I call him my husband? My estranged husband?

Carlos was the easy answer. Plus, I knew that Lance would know exactly who Carlos was. "Lance, this is Carlos."

Lance massaged his goatee. "Ah, so *this* is Carlos." He strolled over and extended a bony hand. "No wonder Juliet has been so hush-hush about you. I'd want to keep you all to myself, too."

I shot Lance a look, begging him to knock it off.

Carlos grinned and shook his hand. "That's what I say about Julieta."

"Julieta?" Lance looked to the ceiling and clasped his hands together. "Oh, this is too much, Julieta and her lovely Latin leading man here at this little lodge for the weekend. I couldn't script this."

"Lance." I furrowed my brow. "Did you need something?"

"No, no, not a thing, darling. I just wanted to see how things were coming along in the kitchen." He appraised Carlos from head to toe. "I can see they're heating up quite nicely. Quite nicely." Turning toward the door, he blew me a kiss. "I don't want to keep you from whatever it was you were in the middle of, ta-ta."

"He is in the theater, yes?" Carlos asked, watching Lance prance away.

"How did you guess?"

Carlos's eyes sparkled. "He knows beauty when he sees it."

A lump formed in my throat. I'd forgotten—more like pushed from my mind—how romantic Carlos is, and how often he comments on my looks. It was unsettling.

I had to do something. I needed to bake.

"What are you doing here?" I asked as I picked up a clean whisk and began beating pudding that didn't need any beating.

Carlos peered over my shoulder. "What is that that you are making?"

"Bread pudding."

"Ah, yes, I remember when you made this dish on the ship." He picked up a vanilla bean. "I will help, yes?"

I beat the pudding so fast that it sloshed out of the bowl. "Carlos, what are you doing here?"

He pushed up the sleeves of his sweater and peeled the vanilla bean. The sweet scent permeated the kitchen. "I had to see you, *mi querida*. It has been six months now. We agreed. Six months, yes?"

"Yeah, but I didn't think you were going to *show up* here in six months." I wiped pudding from the counter. "I thought maybe we'd talk on the phone or something." Carlos and I agreed to take a break for a few months after I left. He returned to the ship, and I started my new life in Ashland. It had been easier for me to compartmentalize my worlds. With Carlos sailing oceans away, I immersed myself in Torte. The busy bakeshop had been the perfect place to disappear, and to Carlos's credit, despite sending me a handful of letters that I never opened, he gave me my space. Until now.

"No. The phone is no good. We have much to say to

each other in person." He kept his eyes locked on mine as he scraped vanilla seeds from the pod.

I reached for the sugar. "But how did you know to come up here?"

"Your mother."

"My mom?"

"Yes, she told me I could find you here. Please do not be angry with her."

I added more sugar. "I'm not mad at her. I'm just having a hard time believing you're really here at Lake of the Woods. This is crazy."

"Julieta, I would sail across seas for you."

"Carlos, don't." I shook my head. "Really, don't."

He gave me a wistful look as he added the vanilla to my pudding without even needing to ask. This is how it used to be. We worked in perfect rhythm in the kitchen. It was like one of Lance's well-choreographed productions. Carlos and I knew exactly where to move, what ingredient came next, how to plate a dish. We were like beautiful dancers on stage in the kitchen. Real life was where we stumbled.

"I can't do this right now." I waved to the countertop with baguettes, sauces, and cubed bread. "I'm catering dinner tonight."

He kissed my forehead again. My body stiffened. "It's okay, I will stay. I will help for the weekend, yes?"

"I guess." I couldn't say no. I didn't want to say no. Seeing Carlos again had sparked something that I had buried deep inside myself, but I was still angry and confused about why he had lied to me about having a son. How was I going to concentrate on catering Lance's retreat with Carlos in the kitchen? Just having him stand next to me had my pulse rate on high.

He walked to the sink, washed his hands, and wrapped an apron around his muscular torso. I wanted to pinch myself. Carlos was here, in the flesh, wearing a Torte apron and looking so incredibly sexy that I had to keep my eyes focused on the bread pudding. You can do this, Jules, I told myself.

Yeah, right.

Chapter Six

Sterling returned a few minutes later. I mouthed, "Thank you." He shrugged and introduced himself to Carlos.

Carlos took an instant liking to Sterling. He asked about Sterling's Irish dance music and taught him his special trick for peeling garlic.

"Watch this," Carlos said, placing an entire bulb of garlic between two small stainless steel bowls. He pushed the lids of the bowls together and held them on both ends. "You shake and shake and the skin it peels off like magic." He shook them like a maraca to demonstrate. It sounded like he was playing the kettle drums.

"Come closer. Come see." Carlos motioned for Sterling to get a close-up view of his trick. He shook the garlic into one of the bowls and placed it on the counter. All of the peels had been removed, leaving beautiful cloves of garlic ready to be diced. "It is the friction. It works every time and no sticky peel on your fingers." Carlos rubbed his fingers together.

"That's amazing." Sterling held up a clove of garlic. "Have you seen this, Jules?"

I nodded.

Carlos grabbed another bulb of garlic and handed it to Sterling. "Now you try. It's easy and you do it to the beat of your music, yes? That's cooking. Feel it. I always say to my new student chefs that food is *love*. You must infuse the food with love. You cook angry—the food, it will know."

Sterling tried the trick. Carlos grinned and clapped as Sterling shook the bowls like a maraca.

"Yes! That's it. He's good, yes?" Carlos said to me.

"He's the best," I replied, as I added equal parts of cream and milk to the pudding.

"Impressive," Sterling said. He held up his bowl of garlic. "It really works."

"I'll show you more like this." Carlos grabbed a knife and chopped the garlic at lightning speed. Sterling watched in awe. I was used to people being impressed with Carlos's talent. "You must curl your fingers like this, so you do not chop them off," Carlos said, demonstrating the proper cutting technique.

While they topped the baguettes with olive oil, garlic, pesto, bruschetta, and bean spread, I arranged the cubed bread in ramekins, and returned my pudding to the stove. It wasn't thick enough, and for some reason it was taking forever to bring it to a boil. I blamed it on the fact that I'd been distracted by Carlos's surprise appearance.

Sterling slid the appetizer trays into the oven. I would wait until the chickens had finished roasting before baking the bread pudding. I didn't want to run the risk of infusing any of the scent of the herbs into the sweet dessert.

Sterling set appetizer plates and cocktail napkins on the communal table. I went to check on what wine Whitney was planning to pour with dinner. Carlos followed after me.

Tony leaned against the long walnut bar. The far wall displayed hunting trophies and stuffed animal heads. There were vintage ski posters, a bulletin board with announcements about ice-fishing and skimobile meets, and old photos of the lodge hanging throughout the room. Soft dainty flakes fell outside the long narrow windows. It looked beautiful, but I was thankful we made it to the lodge before the snow started.

A man in his early sixties sat at a high bar stool with a glass of whiskey in front of him. He looked up from his drink when we came into the bar. I smiled.

"What can I do for you, pretty chef?" Tony slid his elbows on the bar.

I could feel Carlos's energy shift behind me. Without looking at him I knew that every muscle in his body had tensed. I wanted to handle Tony on my own.

"I need to see what wines you have for dinner tonight. I want to pair them with the food."

Tony reached under the bar and heaved two boxes up. "Who cares about hoity-toity pairing? Booze is booze if you ask me."

I didn't ask you, I thought.

Carlos squared his shoulders and removed a bottle of wine from the first box. He studied the label and held the bottle to the light. "You know this vintner?" He handed me the bottle.

The label was from a small vineyard just outside of Ashland. They produced award-winning artisan red blends. I was impressed that Tony had stocked the label. I was expecting grocery-store wine. "This is a great blend."

"Can we taste?" Carlos asked.

"He's with me." I tensed slightly, not because of Tony. I didn't appreciate Carlos jumping in.

Tony glared at Carlos, but proceeded to open the bottle of wine. He poured us both a taste.

The older gentleman finished his whiskey in one shot. "If you're pouring, I'll take a glass of that, too." His words ran together as he spoke. I wondered how many shots he'd already had.

"You must be the chef." He wobbled slightly on the stool as he extended his hand. "I'm Dean Barnes, board member." His British accent came through despite his impaired speech. I wasn't surprised that he was a board member. Lance could have cast him in a production of Sherlock with his trousers and corduroy checked cap.

"Nice to meet you, Dean," I replied, raising my eyes at Carlos. "I'm Jules, I'll be catering the weekend, and this is . . ." I paused. "Carlos—another chef."

"I noticed the aprons. What's Torte?" Dean asked.

"It's my family's bakeshop back home in Ashland."

"I believe I know the place. On the plaza?" Dean took a large swig of the wine that Tony placed in front of him. "I've been there before. Yes, yes, I had excellent homemade crisps. Quite nice."

"Thanks." I sipped the wine. It tasted like berries with a hint of tobacco. The finish was smooth. It should pair well with the hearty meal we had planned.

Carlos swirled the burgundy liquid in his glass.

Tony glared at him. "What, are you going to stare at it, or drink it already?"

"You know Galileo?" Carlos asked.

Tony continued to glare at him.

Carlos pretended not to notice. "He said 'Wine is sunlight, held together by water.' This you drink slowly." Carlos raised his glass higher in the air and swirled it again.

"Knock yourself out, man." Tony filled a wine glass to the top and chugged it. He challenged Carlos with a sneer as he emptied the glass. A bartender drinking on the job is strictly prohibited. It would be a fireable offense on the cruise ship. My girlfriends used to say that Carlos was a lover not a fighter. I think it was due to his Spanish roots, and his passion for food. Like most executive chefs, Carlos could be a bit of a snob when it came to food and wine. Not that I blamed him. Chefs are supposed to have superior palates, but Carlos's dedication to his craft had gotten him into disagreements with guests in the past.

I remember one incident when a passenger complained that his hamburger was too pink. Carlos was having a particularly bad day. He stormed out of the kitchen with a charred hunk of beef. The overweight sunburned guest didn't have time to blink when Carlos dropped the blackened burger that looked more like a hockey puck on his plate and said, "Is this too pink?" He stormed away before the poor guest had a chance to respond.

Carlos was so well loved by all the staff, and the vast majority of passengers, that he barely got reprimanded for the event. He tossed and turned that night. I remember him sitting up in bed at four o'clock in the morning. "Julieta, why do I let these things get under my skin?"

"Because you love what you do. That's a good thing." I massaged his back.

He rested his head on my chest. "Yes, and it also makes me do stupid things sometimes. It is time for us to leave this life, and build our own dream, don't you think?"

I did. Carlos and I had been planning to leave the vast ocean behind for dry land. We'd been tucking away extra cash, which was easy to do since life on the ship included everything we needed from our meals to our tiny cabin. We didn't partake of extravagant adventures while docked. We preferred to find hidden local gems off the beaten path, like a little cottage on the Irish coast where the owner served us eight courses on her great-grandmother's china. Or the bistro we discovered in a French alleyway where the chef brought up four bottles of wine from his private cellar. We noshed on small plates and drank so much wine that Carlos and I both stumbled back to the ship.

Those plans were distant memories now.

Tony's burly voice shook me back into the present. "So, hot chef, how's the wine?"

Hot chef. That was a new one. "It's nice," I replied.

Carlos stepped in front of me. "That is no way to address Julieta."

"Hoo-lee-what-a?" Tony walked around the front of the bar. "Come find me later. We'll go someplace quiet, if you know what I mean." He pinched my waist.

I smacked his hand away.

Carlos jumped between us and held his arm in front of me. "You do not speak to my wife like that." He poked Tony in the chest.

Tony arched his back. "You wanna go, man?"

I shot Carlos a warning look and ignored Tony's overt advances. The best way to handle guys like Tony was to stay professional. "Make sure the wine is ready to go in the next thirty minutes. We're getting ready to put the appetizers out now," I said.

"Whatever you say." Tony slugged more wine and returned to the other side of the bar.

Why had Mercury hired him? Or maybe the better question was, why hadn't she fired him? A drunk bartender was going to make for a potential disaster.

I turned to leave, but Whitney scurried in at that moment. She bumped into me and almost dropped her tablet. "Oh, sorry. I didn't see you." Her hands shook as she repositioned the tablet under her arm.

A man wearing a Lake of the Woods fishing hat, one of the lodge's sweatshirts, camo pants, and work boots stepped in behind her. He had a can of WD-40 clipped to his tool belt. "I heard there was a problem up here?"

Whitney shuddered. "No. No problem."

"I was talking to him," the man said, twisting his head toward the bar.

"Yeah. Generator's not working." Tony sneered. "You better get back outside and fix it, Gavin."

Gavin's hand went to his tool belt, where he patted the canister of WD-40. "Yep, that's what I do around here. I *fix* things." His meaning was clear. Mercury must have asked him to step in.

Tony slugged more wine and laughed. "Sure you do."

Dean held out his wine glass. "I'll take a splash more, if you don't mind, old chap."

"I do mind, old man. You're cut off." Tony yanked the wine bottle from the top of the bar.

Gavin stomped to the bar. His heavy boots thudded with each step. "If the man wants another drink, give him another drink."

"This is my bar." Tony pounded his fist on the counter. "I decide who drinks."

I caught Carlos's eye. What was happening?

"It's Mercury's bar." Gavin hunched his shoulders. "Give the man a drink."

Tony reached for the bottle and slammed it on the bar. "You want a drink? Take it." He flung the bottle and knocked Dean's glass off the bar. It shattered on the hardwood floor and splattered on Dean.

"Maintenance." Tony snapped his fingers at Gavin, and pointed to the shards of broken glass.

Dean's reflexes were surprisingly quick for his age and how much he'd had to drink. He sprang from his stool and yelled at Tony. "Do you know what you've done? These are Balmoral leather-lined royal hunting boots. They cost five hundred pounds."

Tony scoffed. "Five hundred pounds. What is that? Like five bucks?"

Gavin walked behind the bar and handed Dean a

towel. Dean mopped his trousers and glared at Tony. "You will be replacing my boots and trousers."

Tony grabbed the bottle and pushed past Gavin, completely ignoring Dean's fixed stare. "Time for my smoke break." On his way outside he paused and winked at me. "Don't forget our date later, hot chef."

In your dreams, I said to myself.

"Sorry about him," Gavin addressed all of us. "Mercury said he was in rare form today. She wasn't kidding." He wiped the counter and looked up at me. "Don't think we've met. You must be the caterer."

"Yeah, Jules," I replied. "And this is Carlos."

"Welcome to LOW. You met our friendly bartender, I see." Gavin tossed a wine-stained towel in the sink.

Carlos shook his head. "This is no way to run a bar."

Gavin removed a broom and dustpan. "Tell me about it. Mercury has to get rid of him."

Dean stood to make way for Gavin to sweep the floor. He swayed slightly. Whitney raced to help steady him. "I believe I need a new pair of trousers," Dean said. "Can't show up to dinner looking like this, can I? I'll be speaking to your boss about being reimbursed for the damages that bartender did to my clothing."

"I'll help you to your cabin," Whitney said. She seemed much calmer. "You said you're working on a generator or something?" she asked Gavin.

He nodded.

"Does that mean my e-mail will work again?"

Gavin swept glass into the dust pan. "Nope. There's no service up here. The generator is backup for when we lose power."

"When we lose power?" Her eyes widened.

"Yep. Count on it." He nodded to the bay window where fat flakes of snow cascaded to the ground. "This is just a warm-up. Mother Nature has a big show brewing."

Whitney's shoulders sagged. She took Dean by the arm and led him away.

Gavin dumped the glass in a garbage pan. "I've got a date with a generator. Anything else you need?"

"We're good, thanks," I said.

He tipped his fishing cap and headed out into the snow.

Carlos and I walked to the kitchen. "That was weird."

"I do not like that man," Carlos said, holding the door open for me.

"You made that clear," I replied. "You don't need to do that, you know.

"Do what?"

"Try to protect me like that. I can handle myself. I've dealt with much worse than Tony over the years."

"I know you can." He waited for me to go in first.

I pushed past him. He wasn't wrong about Tony. The guy was a first-class jerk, but there was something about Carlos stepping in to protect me that triggered my anger. Had he always done that? Swooped in and taken over?

I didn't have time to dissect it at the moment. I had a dinner to serve.

Sterling was assembling the beautifully toasted baguettes on silver trays. "Hey, how's everything up front?"

"Tony's a real winner," I replied, walking to the sink to wash my hands. "Those look great and smell even better."

Carlos removed a bruschetta slice from the tray and took a bite. "It's good." He nodded. "But maybe it needs a little more balsamic." He picked up a bottle of the vinegar and covered the top with his thumb. "See, do this." He showed Sterling how to shake the vinegar so that it speckled each colorful slice of charred toast with a splash of rich liquid.

"Got it." Sterling took the bottle from Carlos and practiced the technique. Carlos gave Sterling a look of approval.

I opened the oven doors to check on the roasts. The smell of citrus, herbs, and golden chickens escaped from the bricks. Each chicken had a lovely buttery skin, but when I cut into one its juices still ran slightly pink. They needed a few more minutes. Why was everything taking so long to bake?

I sent Sterling out with the bruschetta while I gave the chicken more time to bake. Carlos sensed my anxiety. He rubbed my back. "It will be fine, relax, Julieta. The food, it has a mind of its own. It will be done soon."

"They're loving the appetizers, Jules," Sterling said, returning with an empty tray.

"See, relax." Carlos released me.

I directed Sterling to assemble the garden salad. He tossed butter leaf and romaine lettuce in a large mixing bowl and then added shredded carrots, cherry tomatoes, olives, snap peas, and homemade croutons. Right before we served the salad, we would dress it with a light olive oil and citrus vinaigrette to pull out the fruit flavor in the roasts.

Carlos rolled up his sleeves and started mashing potatoes without a word. He always knew exactly what needed to be done. That bugged me, too. Was he always this perfect?

Pulling on the thick gloves, I removed a pan from the oven and said a prayer as I cut into it. This time the juices ran clear. Thank goodness they were finally done. I removed the remaining birds and placed them on the counter. Then I covered them with foil. I'd let the juices settle while Sterling served appetizers. After they'd rested for a few minutes, we would make a vegetable gravy.

We could hear board members mingling and chatting over wine as we put the finishing touches on the meal. I transferred the roasted vegetables to the stove and added white wine. I'd let them reduce and add some flour to help thicken them into a gravy.

Lance had requested that all meals be served family style in order to match his cabin theme and encourage the board members to get to know each other. That was great with me. It was much easier to serve the meal in large dishes, rather than individually plating each serving.

I ran the gravy through a sieve and poured it into a silver gravy boat. Carlos sprinkled the smashed potatoes with sea salt, pepper, and a little fresh rosemary. Sterling tossed the dressing on the salad and took it out to the dining room. I followed behind him with the potatoes, as Carlos expertly carved the juicy roasts.

Lance jumped to his feet as I entered the dining room. "May I introduce the lovely Juliet, our chef for the weekend." He dinged on his wine glass with his salad fork. "We're a bit shorter in numbers than expected thanks to Mother Nature. I've counted twenty-five of us which means that we'll have a majority for any voting, and it also means that you brave souls who have ventured out in the storm will have more of Juliet's divine cooking all to yourselves."

I could feel my cheeks warm as I balanced a piping-hot ceramic bowl of potatoes. It's an annoying habit that I can't control.

Dean and Whitney sat next to one another on the opposite side of the table. Dean had changed out of his wine-stained clothes. Whitney smiled at me as Lance gushed about my talent.

"Juliet's baking is to die for, isn't it, darling?" His playful eyes shimmered with delight. "You are all in for a treat this weekend." He waved at the food Sterling and I delivered. "Don't be shy, dig in, everyone, dig in."

I made my escape to the kitchen before Lance could embarrass me more. I needed to get the bread pudding in the oven to give it enough time to bake before the guests finished dinner. Knowing Lance, I had a feeling we didn't need to rush. He had a tendency toward long speeches and making sure wine was constantly flowing.

"The puddings are already in," Carlos said, as I returned to the kitchen.

"Thanks." I tried to silence my head as I rinsed blackberries and raspberries. Had I really changed this much since I'd been home? I knew I was different, but having Carlos here made me feel like an entirely different person and the same all at once.

Before I had time to dwell on it, a commotion broke out in the dining hall. I knew immediately who was to blame—Tony.

Chapter Seven

Carlos grabbed a wooden spoon and sprinted to the dining room before I could even react. Sterling removed warm caramel sauce from the stove. "What is that guy's problem?" he asked over the sound of Tony's bellowing voice.

"I don't know, but I better go check."

"It seems like Carlos is on it."

"Yeah." I sighed and wiped my hands on my apron. "He is."

Sterling looked puzzled. "Isn't that a good thing? He's great. And he's obviously in love with you, Jules."

Tony's voice was getting louder. "Anyone else want a piece of me?"

I shook my head and hurried out of the kitchen. "How about you, old man?" Tony bellowed at Dean Barnes. "You wanna stop following me around? What? Are you so desperate for a drink, you gotta follow me?"

"No. I want you to reimburse me for ruining my hunting boots and best trousers." Dean held his full wine glass in a challenging toast, egging Tony on. Not a wise move. Tony was clearly drunk. His ruddy cheeks and nose were bright red. He rocked from side to side.

Mercury jumped to her feet. "Tony! Enough—get

outside." She waved frantically to Gavin Allen, who was tinkering with the thermostat.

Gavin shoved his screwdriver in his tool belt and stomped toward Tony.

Tony swayed in a circular motion. He tried to raise his arm and point at Mercury, but it danced with the motion of his body. "I know things. Important things."

"What this chap doesn't seem to know is how to pour a glass of wine or control his liquor," Dean said to Mercury. "I'll have you know that he ruined a very expensive pair of boots. Not a good impression for your guests."

"I'm so sorry," Mercury replied, keeping one eye on Tony as she spoke. "I'll make sure that we get everything straightened out."

Tony pantomimed her speech as she tried to reassure Dean.

Mercury pursed her lips and wrapped her arms around her body, standing her ground. "Outside—now!"

"Who's gonna make me?" Tony slurred.

Gavin came up from behind him. He grabbed Tony's arm but Tony was surprisingly quick. He swung his elbow and punched Gavin on the side of his forehead. Gavin stumbled backward.

Mercury looked to Lance for help. He caught her eye and nodded. Then he threw back his chair and poised as if he were pacing out a fight scene for the stage. Tony lunged at him. Carlos jumped between them just as Tony took a swing. His fist hit Carlos square in the jaw.

I heard the sound of a crack, and threw my hand over my face.

Carlos ducked as Tony took another swing. He missed.

Lance jumped into position. He grabbed Tony from behind, as Carlos avoided another punch and managed to yank Tony's arm to his side. He held the wooden spoon in his other hand like a sword. I had to stifle a laugh. What was Carlos going to do with a wooden spoon?

Gavin had recovered from the hit he took to the head. He flipped his fishing cap backward and stormed toward Tony. Two other board members sprang into action. In a flash they wrapped Tony up. Tony tried to free himself from their grasp, as they escorted him out. I watched as Gavin kicked open the front door to the lodge with his heavy work boot. Tony stumbled into the cold. Mercury followed and stood in the door frame. He yelled, "I know things!" Then he disappeared into the darkness.

The dining hall went silent. There were no clinking forks or conversations. Everyone stared at Lance as he tightened the scarf around his neck and addressed the board. "Well, who knew that even in this remote location, we'd have a chance to witness such dramatic flair? I want to cast him as Brutus. Who's with me?"

Board members chuckled. Lance had broken the tension. "I think this is a good time for dessert," he said to me, as he took his seat.

"I'm on it."

Carlos started to follow after me. Lance reached out and grabbed his wrist. "Oh, do wait." He raised his wine glass in the air. "A toast to our dashing hero. Thank you for swooping in and saving the day."

Carlos gave a little bow. Bad idea. That fueled Lance. He rested his glass on the table. "A round of applause for our new leading man."

The room erupted in laughter and applause as Carlos took another exaggerated bow with his wooden spoon.

"Put a steak on that chin. We wouldn't want that chiseled jawline to see any permanent damage."

"I am fine," Carlos protested and followed me into the kitchen. I knew he was in more pain than he was letting on. He massaged his jaw, and kept twisting his mouth from side to side.

I went straight to the freezer, pulled out an ice pack and tossed it to him. "Lance is right, you better ice that before it swells."

"It's nothing," he replied, placing the ice pack on his chin.

Sterling had finished assembling the bread pudding toppings. A tray of beautiful colors and flavors sat on the counter. "What happened out there?"

"Tony happened." I stretched the leather oven mitts over my arms. "I don't know what his deal is. I'm not sure if he was drunk, or just intentionally trying to pick a fight."

"The second," Carlos said.

"Why?" I asked.

"Some men are like that."

Sterling nodded in agreement. "I know the type."

"I don't get it." I removed a bread pudding from the oven and tested it. The center jiggled. Drat. They weren't quite ready, either. "Women don't do that."

"No, women do other maddening things, no?" Carlos asked Sterling.

Sterling laughed. "No comment."

"We need to get this dessert out." I changed the subject. After a few minutes I removed another ramekin from the oven. The vanilla scent of the warm pudding was heavenly. The top of the pudding had crisped to a light brown color. That was a good sign. Now for the moment of truth. I carefully tested it with a fork. I squinted as I pulled the fork from the center. It came out clean. Whew. I removed the rest of the puddings, thankful that this was our last item of the evening.

If the pudding tasted as good as it looked and smelled, Lance's guests should return to their cabins with happy bellies. Carlos and Sterling delivered the toppings to the guests while I carefully placed the puddings in front of each guest, with a stern warning not to touch the side of the ramekins.

"Impeccable timing, darling," Lance whispered as I set a steaming bread pudding on his plate. "Any chance you have some coffee on back there?"

Coffee. Shoot. I'd totally forgotten to start coffee with the scuffle between Carlos and Tony. "No, but I'll get right on it," I replied.

Sterling removed the dinner dishes. I hurried to grind beans. There's no comparison to using fresh ground beans in my opinion. We store our beans in airtight containers at Torte. When a customer places an order for coffee, they know they are getting the absolute freshest experience.

Carlos poked at the fire as I dumped beans into the grinder. A fruity chocolate aroma filled the room. I found myself acutely aware of my posture as I poured water into the coffee maker and added the coffee grounds. I could feel Carlos's eyes on my back as I moved through the kitchen. If I had known he was coming I would have put a little more thought into what I was wearing.

The coffeepot hummed to life. I could use a cup of the rich brew right now, I thought. Sterling filled the sink with hot soapy water and rinsed the dishes. Fortunately the kitchen had a large industrial dishwasher. We'd need all the dishes for breakfast. I had a feeling the next two days were going to be a constant cycle of bake—serve—wash—repeat.

"You want me to run this yet?" Sterling asked as he loaded the last plate into the dishwasher.

"Is there enough room for the ramekins?" I asked, stacking coffee cups on the counter. The coffee was almost finished. I filled one of the mugs with water and stuck it in the microwave. Mom says that I'm a coffee snob. I say I have a ritual when it comes to drinking java. My ritual always begins with a warm mug. It makes a difference, trust me.

"I think I can squeeze them in the top." Sterling rearranged the wine glasses.

Carlos had successfully tamped down the fire. The blackened wood burned low, a sign that the evening was officially winding down.

The microwave beeped.

"I believe this is for you." Carlos removed my mug, dumped the hot water in the sink, and poured exactly the right amount of cream into the bottom of the cup.

"Thanks." I poured the dark coffee over the cream. It stirred together into a delicious walnut color. I indulged in a taste before I sent Sterling to the dining room with the coffee service.

The rest of cleanup was a breeze. Sterling was an efficient worker. He had the counters wiped down and the pots scrubbed before the guests had finished dessert. Lance popped into the kitchen on his way out.

"As always, everything was absolutely divine, darling." He blew air kisses in my direction. Then he turned and gave a little bow to Carlos. "And you, dear boy, are the most exciting thing to happen around these parts in years. We will have to have a little tête-à-tête in the morning. Until then, keep icing that bruise and sleep tight!"

Sterling finished clearing the dessert plates, and started the dishes. I served the three of us leftovers. We gathered around the island and devoured a late-night dinner. That's the way it goes in a professional kitchen, chefs eat last. I practically inhaled my food. I couldn't believe how famished I was. Probably stress, Jules, I told myself.

Carlos ate at a more leisurely pace, regaling Sterling with stories of our escapades on the ship. Like the night that Carlos had me sneak in the kitchen with him and fill two buckets with water. He took all of the paring knifes and dropped them in the buckets. Then he hid them in the freezer. The next morning, staff arrived for line prep to find their knives frozen solid. Carlos was notorious for playing pranks in the kitchen. He said it helped lighten the mood.

"Jules, I've never seen this side of you." Sterling grinned as he stacked our empty plates and walked them to the sink.

"Julieta has a devilish side," Carlos said.

"I do not," I protested, and tossed him a fresh bag of frozen peas. "You are the troublemaker."

"Is there anything else you need me to do, Jules?" Sterling asked as he loaded our dinner plates in the dishwasher. "I want to get out of here before the pranks begin."

I surveyed the kitchen. Everything had been put away. "It looks great. You've been amazing. Go get some sleep. I'm going to sketch out the plan for tomorrow."

He removed his apron and hung it on a hook near the sink. "Are you sure?"

"Absolutely. I've got it from here. Thanks for all your hard work. I could not have done it without you."

"Not a problem. I had fun." Sterling smiled at both of us and pulled his hoodie over his head. "See you bright and early."

I tried to busy myself with tomorrow's schedule after Sterling left. It was hard to concentrate. Carlos poured two glasses of wine and pulled a chair on the opposite side of the island from me. He rested his hands on his chin. "You are so lovely when you're thinking, Julieta."

"Stop." I shook my head, and focused my gaze at the notebook in front of me, acutely aware that Carlos was staring at me. "You can't just waltz back in my life and pretend that nothing happened."

"*Sí*, I know, and now we are alone. Can we talk?" There was longing in his voice.

I drew in a breath and rested the pencil on the notebook. "Where do we even start?" I met his eyes.

"Let's take our wine and have a seat by the fire." He nodded toward the dining room.

"There's so much I need to do for tomorrow." I protested.

"That can wait. We cannot." Carlos held my gaze. The intensity in his eyes made my heart thump again.

"I don't know." I motioned to the notebook. "I still need to map out tomorrow's plan." I could hear the timidity in my voice. There was nothing I wanted more than to curl up in front of the fire and have Carlos wrap his arms around me.

Carlos knew he'd won. He slid from the stool and picked up his wine glass. I closed the notebook and followed him.

Keep it together, Jules.

Chapter Eight

The lights in the dining room had been turned off. We only had the glow of the embers burning low in the fireplace in the far corner of the room to guide us.

I could feel my breath coming fast and unsteady. I'd waited so long for this moment. I was filled with equal parts of excitement and dread. Whatever Carlos had to say would affect my future for better or worse. That's what you said when you got married, Jules, for better or for worse.

A shiver ran down my spine. I wasn't sure if it was because the dining room had cooled significantly with the falling snow outside or it if was my nerves.

Carlos started as he got closer to the fireplace. "Sorry. I did not know that someone was here."

Someone was here? So much for a quiet conversation.

Mercury jumped to her feet from the couch. "Oh, my goodness, I must have fallen asleep. What time is it?" Her light gray hair spilled from a loose ponytail.

Carlos shrugged. He looked at me.

"No idea." I don't wear a watch. I don't wear any jewelry when I'm baking. It gets in the way.

Mercury glanced at her wrist. "It's after eleven. How did that happen? How long have I been asleep?"

"I'm not sure," I said. "We finished cleaning up."

She rubbed her eyes. "I can't believe I slept through that. I don't know what came over me. Well, actually I do—Tony." She grabbed a fire poker and hit the coals. "You must be exhausted," she continued without noticing our full wine glasses. "I'm so sorry about this. About everything. I've never seen Tony that bad."

"That was quite the scene," I said.

"He better be sleeping it off tonight, because tomorrow he and I are going to have words. He's not going to ruin everything that we've worked for up here. Our staff are the first impression guests have of the resort." She looked at Carlos and winced. "How's your face?"

"It will be fine," he said, patting the growing bruise on his cheek.

"I'm so sorry." She placed the poker in its holder. "And you need your cabin keys, don't you? Oh my goodness. I'll grab them from the desk."

"Don't worry about it." I made eye contact with Carlos. "Let me make sure everything's off in the kitchen, and we'll meet you up front." I thought about Mercury's words. Staff were a reflection of the lodge. I was so thankful to have the staff we did at Torte, but I couldn't help but wonder why Mercury had kept Tony on.

Carlos looked defeated as we returned to the kitchen. He took a long sip of wine and placed his glass in the sink. I dumped mine. I needed a clear head to survive this weekend anyway.

"All set," I said, returning to Mercury.

Mercury handed a large gold key to me. "You're in cabin number five." She pointed behind her. "Follow the path up the hill and it's the first cabin on your left."

"Got it." I tucked the key in my pocket.

"You'll need a flashlight to see." Mercury reached under the desk and handed me a small flashlight. "It's really coming down out there, so be sure to stay on the path." She paused and stared at Carlos. "What about you? What cabin are you in?"

Carlos placed his arm around my shoulder. "I'll be staying with my wife."

"Wife?" Mercury raised her eyebrows. "I didn't know you two were married."

"We're not, exactly," I said at the same moment that Carlos said, "Yes, we are."

Mercury looked confused, but said, "Stay on the path," as we left.

She wasn't kidding about the snow. It fell in giant clumps as if the sky were launching handfuls of snow-balls at us. What path was Mercury talking about? At least six inches of snow covered the ground. I couldn't believe how much had fallen since Sterling and I arrived.

Carlos shined the flashlight in front of us. "I think we go that way."

We tromped to the parking lot to grab our bags. Carlos hoisted both of them over his shoulder and handed the flashlight to me. Darkness had descended over the resort. The flashlight cast eerie shadows on the trees, as I beamed it toward the cabins. Heavy, wet snow fell at a furious pace.

I moved as fast I could through the gusting wind. It shrieked through the top of the evergreen trees, rattling their branches and echoing into the dark night. Cold air burned my lungs as we struggled up the small hill toward the cabins.

"It is up ahead!" Carlos shouted, and pointed toward one of the cabins tucked into the hillside.

We were just a few feet away when the sound of a loud bang stopped us in our tracks.

"What was that?" I glanced from my left to my right.

Carlos stopped and waited. "The wind?"

"It's crazy out here."

"Keep moving." Carlos nudged me forward.

We made it to the cabin. I climbed up a small set of steps that led to an enclosed porch. The screen door was unlocked. I opened it and stepped inside. Carlos followed. We kicked off our boots.

"Can you shine the light right here?" I pointed to the sliding glass door.

Carlos held the light for me to see as I unlocked the door.

I flipped on the lights and stepped inside. My breath evaporated into fog. The heat was obviously off. I found the thermostat and switched it to high.

The cabin was the textbook definition of cozy and snug. It had wood floors, knotty-pine walls, and red and white gingham curtains (just like the ones in the lodge) tied with twine on the windows. The front room had a woodstove, rocking chair, and futon couch that look liked it doubled as a bed. That was good. Carlos could sleep there tonight.

A small kitchen was attached to the living room. Above us there was a loft with two-foot-high ceilings and a wooden railing. I dropped my bag by the front door, and walked to the back of the cabin. There were cupboards with board games, a collection of old movies and books, and popcorn. A small bathroom with a standalone shower and sink and a bedroom took up the space in the back of the cabin.

"This is so romantic, no?" Carlos lit a candle on the kitchen counter.

"It's adorable," I agreed. I still couldn't wrap my head around the fact that Carlos was actually here.

"You want a glass of wine, and we will curl up by the fire and continue?" Carlos stuffed wood and kindling in the woodstove.

"I didn't bring any wine."

"This is no problem. I will go get some. You stay here." He lit the fire and zipped his coat.

"But it's terrible out there."

"It's nothing. I will be back very soon." He started to open the sliding door. "Do you have the key?"

"Yeah." I reached into my pocket and tossed him the keys to the lodge and marina. "Are you sure you really want to go back out there?"

"Of course. For you, Julieta, I would do this and much, much more."

"You don't need to do this for me. I don't need a glass of wine. I'm fine." On the ship when Carlos spoke to me like that I remember feeling almost dizzy with love. Now on land, his words felt different.

Carlos shook his head. "No, no. This is good. I will be back. You stay warm by the fire." He slid the door open and stepped onto the porch before I could protest more.

Did I look like I needed a drink? Come to think of it, how did I look? The afternoon and evening had been such a whirlwind of activity and cooking that I hadn't had a chance to slow down. Carlos heading out on a late-night wine run meant that I could hop in the shower. There's nothing better than a cleansing shower after a long day in the kitchen. Apron or no apron, my skin always ends up with a layer of flour. It's impossible to avoid.

I turned the shower on its hottest setting and let the small bathroom fill with steam as I unpacked a pair of black fleece sweats, wool socks, and a soft ivory-colored sweater. I might as well be comfortable if Carlos and I were going to share a bottle of wine. The bathroom was stocked with travel-sized oatmeal soaps, shampoo, and conditioner as well as mouthwash, toothpaste, and razors. It reminded me of our tiny cabin on the ship.

Life on the sea was like living in a magical storybook.

Things like toothpaste and bars of soap were delivered to our cabin on a weekly basis. We didn't cook for ourselves, except when Carlos would close the kitchen in the evening and whip up something special for the staff. We were responsible for thousands of meals, but not much else. It was an extension of youth—drinking wine at two o'clock in the morning, dancing under the stars, meeting new people from every corner of the globe. It wasn't real life. Was that the root of the problem between Carlos and me? We never had to grow up?

I sighed and stepped into the steamy shower. As the water ran over my skin I lathered oatmeal shampoo into my hair. It smelled like the kitchen. The heat felt rejuvenating. I became lost in my thoughts as the water swirled down the drain.

After a while, my skin was two shades pinker. Probably time to get out. I dried off and applied a thick layer of lotion. My skin practically glowed. I pulled on my comfy clothes and ran a blow-dryer on my hair. It takes forever to get my hair dry. One of the major disadvantages to having long, thick locks. I just wanted it dry enough to tie up in a ponytail.

Then I put on a little lip gloss. It was silly, but I couldn't help myself.

I clicked on the overhead fan and returned to the living room. The cheery room had warmed up nicely. I plopped onto the couch and covered my legs with a Pendleton wool blanket. The blanket matched the country vibe in the cabin. It was a deep red with patchwork Native American geometric designs woven in.

Where was Carlos? What was taking him so long?

A digital clock on the white stove in the kitchen read twelve-ten. How long had I been in the shower? Twenty minutes, maybe? He should be back by now. It was only a five-minute walk to the lodge. I hoped he hadn't gotten lost in the snow.

The window behind the couch faced the lodge. I sat up and peered out it. Nothing but a black snowy sky was visible. Maybe Carlos got distracted in the kitchen. He was used to working until the early morning hours on the ship. He probably decided to make a midnight snack.

I propped a pillow behind my head and tucked my feet back into the blanket. The flames in the woodstove flickered in a silent rhythm. I must have drifted off to sleep. The next thing I knew I woke to the sound of something pelting the metal roof.

Chapter Nine

What time is it? I thought, sitting up and rubbing my eyes. The digital clock on the kitchen stove read five o'clock. Where was Carlos? I never heard him come in.

Pain shot up the side of my neck as I stretched my arms over my head. Ouch. I rubbed it and sat up. Carlos must have snuck in. The fire had gone out, but the heat had kicked on.

I rolled my shoulders trying to loosen the knot in my neck and tiptoed into the kitchen. There was a prepackaged bag of ground coffee and paper filters sitting next to the coffeepot. Desperate times call for desperate measures, Jules. I ripped the bag open and filled the carafe with water.

So much for our discussion, I thought as I continued down the dark hallway to the bedroom. Sure enough, Carlos was sound asleep on the bed. He slept on his left side with his body facing away from me. He hadn't even bothered to crawl under the covers. I took the red and yellow woolen blanket at the bottom of the bed and carefully placed it over him. I must have really been out last night. I couldn't believe I didn't hear him come in.

Grabbing a pair of jeans and a sweater from my bag, I crept out of the room. I got dressed quickly and slugged down a cup of the uninspired coffee. Carlos had left the keys to the lodge on the counter. Thank goodness. I didn't need to wake him.

My coat was toasty warm from drying in front of the fire. I zipped it up and stepped out onto the porch. My snow boots were another story. They felt like ice as I squeezed my feet into them. I'd have to remember to bring them inside tonight.

The front steps were buried under a deep layer of snow. Icy pellets fell from the dusky early morning sky. That was the sound that had woken me. My feet sank into the powder. Another eight to ten inches of new snow had fallen overnight. A thin layer of ice was forming on the snow. It crunched beneath me as I made my way forward. The resort had been transformed into a winter wonderland overnight. And by the looks of the dark clouds above, there was even more snow on the way.

Brrr. A shudder erupted in my body. I trudged through the thick snow, trying to find the trail. The purplish sky was shrouded in clouds. I used the flashlight, looking for our footprints from last night. They had disappeared. I shined the light down toward the lodge. The rest of the cabins sat in a quiet early-morning slumber. I kicked up snow as I skidded down the hill. Ice hit my face. My nose started to run.

Wind battered the trees. Gavin was right. Mother Nature was putting on quite the show.

Once I made it to the lodge, I had a better sense of how much new snow had accumulated overnight. The front of the lodge door was covered in snow. Two snow shovels were propped next to the door. This must be a common problem. I grabbed one and dug out the bottom of the door.

After I had cleared a path in front of the door, I unlocked it and yanked it open. Inside the lodge, I could see my breath as I closed the door quickly behind me. My first order of business was to get this place heated up. I was surprised that Mercury hadn't run the heat overnight.

I flipped on the lights and found the thermostat. Heat—or lack of it—seemed to be the theme of this weekend for me. A stack of wood waiting to be burned was piled next to the fireplace. I considered lighting it, but I wanted to get a jump start on breakfast, especially since everything took longer to bake yesterday.

The kitchen windows were thick with ice. It reminded me of spun sugar. Everything was as I had left it last night with one exception. Two used glasses sat in the middle of the island. Odd.

Had Carlos had a drink with someone last night? Why did my head have to go there first? Maybe he ran into Mercury last night. Or got distracted.

I placed the glasses in the sink. Lance had asked for breakfast to be ready by nine. I had plenty of time—hopefully. My body is used to waking before dawn, and working in a quiet kitchen sounded like nirvana to me.

Breakfast would be a sampling of some of Torte's most popular pastries. In addition to pastries we would serve fruit salad with a yogurt dressing, and a baked potato and sausage casserole. I washed my hands and tied on my apron.

"Time to get baking," I said aloud to the empty room.

I started on the pastries first. When Sterling arrived, I would have him concentrate on the casserole. As I added warm water to yeast, a thought flashed in my head—sausage. I needed to thaw the sausages before I did anything else.

Where had Sterling put them? I thought as I removed packages of frozen corn and peas from the freezer. I scanned the shelves. Our sausages weren't here. Sterling must have taken them to the marina.

Shoot. I was going to have to trek down and get them.

I stirred the yeast. It could rise while I grabbed the sausages. Time to go back into the cold, Jules. I shivered at the thought as I zipped my coat and tugged the hood on tight.

The sky was a lighter shade of purple as I stepped into the biting wind. Snow swirled all around me. It was as if a wall of white had swept across the lake and was heading straight toward the lodge. The sound of the wind hissing through the sturdy evergreen trees felt ominous. It looked like the weather was getting worse by the minute.

It was hard to find the path to the marina. The lake was to my right. As long as I kept the lake to that side of me, I knew I would eventually run into the marina.

For a moment I thought I saw a flash of movement on the lake. I stopped and tried to get my bearings. Was someone out there? Or was it the whipping snow?

I crunched onward, trying to remember the last time I had been in a storm like this. Probably when I was a kid. It was incredible to watch the snow spit from the sky, but this wasn't a trek I would want to make again today. I'd have to be sure to grab as many supplies as I could carry.

After another hundred feet, the marina came into sight. Thank goodness. I let out a sigh of relief. I shielded my face with my hands as I turned into the wind toward the building.

It was hard to tell where the sky ended. Everything was a sea of white. I knew that there was a long dock attached to the marina, but it wasn't visible in the blinding white snow.

I felt my way along a short fence and up the marina's wooden ramp. It was slick with ice. I had to grab the wall to steady myself. I fumbled in my coat pocket for the key. Even through my insulated gloves the tips of my fingers felt numb. The gloves were too bulky. I'd have to take them off in order to use the key.

Pulling off one glove, I stuck the key in the lock and jiggled it. The lock didn't turn. I tried it again. Nothing.

What was going on?

I removed the key and examined the lock. It looked as if something had been forced into it.

Great. Now what?

I tried again. This time I gently twisted the key from side to side.

It wouldn't budge.

Time for a new plan, Jules. I blew into my hand to try and warm it. That's when I noticed a shaft of light from underneath the door. I kicked the door with my foot and to my surprise it swung open.

Maybe I should have tried that first.

Snow had blown under the door in drifts. The lights in the front of the marina were on and I could hear the sound of the heater humming. Puddles of melted snow pooled in front of wire shelves stocked with fishing bait and tackles.

Uh-oh. Someone must have left the door open last night, I thought as I stomped my boots and stepped inside. Melting snow dripped from the bottom of the marina's racks filled with chips, candy, and energy drinks. The entire store looked as if it had been blasted with snow.

What a mess.

I wasn't sure where to find the freezer. A long wooden counter ran the length of the back wall. A chalkboard displayed snow reports and fishing conditions as well as prices for rentals. I paused and studied the sign for a moment. The words FOR RENT and an arrow pointed toward a rack of hunting rifles hanging on the wall. You can rent a gun? No. I glanced at the rack, it was nearly full, with one empty slot. Then I looked more closely at the sign and realized the arrow was pointed at a row of fishing poles, not the guns. That made more sense.

There was no freezer in the front of the marina, so I headed toward the attached pizza shop. It must be in there, I thought.

The pizza shop was designed in the same knotty-pine style as the rest of the resort. It had a retro feel with old video-game consoles and a bookcase filled with a variety of board games, puzzles, and books. A genius distraction to keep hungry kids occupied while they waited for their pizzas. A large whiteboard with the pizza menu read: "Closed for the season. See you again in the spring."

I walked behind the counter into the pizza kitchen. The kitchen definitely hadn't been used in a few months. A layer of dust had formed on the countertops and the space smelled musty. The freezer was in the back. I opened to find it stocked with premade pizza crusts, cheese, and other supplies. But not our sausages.

Where else could they be?

I surveyed the shop again. A sign directed customers outside for ice. Could that be where Sterling had put them?

Pulling my gloves back on, I took a deep breath and prepared to head into the bitter wind again. Sure enough, there was a large chest freezer on the covered deck outside. Jackpot!

I brushed snow from the top of the freezer and pushed the lid open.

A shock assaulted my body as I lifted the lid. I threw my hand over my mouth and stepped away from the freezer.

Our supplies weren't inside the frozen cavern, but something else was. A body. A dead body.

Chapter Ten

My erratic heart rate when I saw Carlos yesterday was nothing compared to the crazy rhythm beating in my chest now. I let the freezer lid slam shut and jumped backward. This couldn't be happening.

I rested my hand on my heart, in hopes that it would calm to a normal rate. My head spun. The white sky became even more disorienting. Was I going to pass out? I grabbed the side of the marina wall to steady myself.

Okay, think, Jules. I inhaled arctic air through my nose.

There was a dead body in the chest freezer, and I recognized his bluish face. Tony. Someone had killed him and stuffed him into the freezer. Had lack of sleep caught up with me? Was I hallucinating?

I lifted the lid an inch and dropped it again.

Nope. That was Tony, and he was dead.

Now what, Jules? I rubbed my gloves together. Get back to the lodge, I heard my voice command in my head. Yes. I needed to move and get help *now*.

With one final glance at the chest freezer, I slid off the ramp to the marina and plowed forward through the snow. This time I didn't give any thought to the icy mixture pummeling my skin. I ran as fast as I could through the deep powder. My cheeks burned from the cold. My heart rate continued to soar.

Tony was dead.

I wasn't a fan of how lecherous he was, but I couldn't believe that someone had killed him. It had to be murder, right? Would someone kill himself in a chest freezer? No way.

Knock it off, Jules. Focus.

The wind howled. It felt like it was closing in on me. I lunged forward through the snow, but it didn't feel like I was making any progress. Was I going the wrong way? Between the weather and my heightened state of anxiety I could be walking on the frozen lake for all I knew.

I sucked in air. My nose dripped. Tony was dead. I couldn't stop the image of his blue face when I lifted the freezer lid from replaying in my head.

After a few more feet I caught a glimpse of the lodge. Thank goodness. I raced forward, nearly slipping. Windmilling my arms, I caught myself and ran up the front steps.

"Is anyone here?" I yelled as I flung open the lodge doors. I didn't even bother to stomp the caked snow from my boots or shake off my coat.

"Hello?" I called again.

To my surprise, someone responded. "Jules? Is that you?" Sterling stepped out of the kitchen into the dining room. He had his apron tied halfway around his waist.

A wave of relief washed over me. "Sterling, I've never been so glad to see you."

"What's wrong?"

"Tony." I swallowed and wiped my nose with my glove. It just made my face wetter. "He's dead."

"What?" Sterling came toward me.

I yanked my gloves off and wiped my nose again. "Tony's dead. I just found his body."

"You should sit down." Sterling grabbed a chair.

"No, it's okay." I drew in a long breath as if to prove that I was fine. I wasn't. "We have to get help."

"Really, Jules, you should sit down." Sterling pushed the chair closer.

My hands trembled. I wasn't sure if it was from the cold. "Have you seen Mercury yet this morning?"

Sterling's eyes were unyielding. "Jules, sit."

"Okay, I'm sitting." I sat in the chair. My right foot bounced on the floor. The nervous energy running through my body couldn't contain itself.

"You look like a Popsicle. I'm going to grab you a cup of coffee. Chill out for one second and I'll be right back."

I nodded. Tony was a Popsicle. A few minutes wasn't going to change anything, and sitting down made me realize just how cold I was. My foot continued to shake. My hands trembled and everything in my body felt out of synch.

Sterling returned quickly from the kitchen with a steaming mug of coffee. "Here." He started to hand it to me. His brow furrowed. "You're really shaky, Jules. Can you hold this?"

"Yeah. I think so." I took the mug. It quaked in my hands. A little coffee splashed out of the cup and landed on my jeans.

"Maybe you should just hold that to warm up for a sec. I'm not sure caffeine is the best idea for you right now."

"I'm okay." The hot cup stung my hands. I didn't care. I grasped it tighter.

"You keep saying that, but you don't look so great." Sterling winked. "No offense or anything."

I chuckled. That helped. Sterling was so calm. "No offense."

"What happened?" He pulled a chair away from the table and sat down next to me.

Between the comforting smell of the coffee and Sterling's grounding presence I started to feel calmer. Mom says that Sterling is an old soul. She's right. He exuded a relaxed, centering vibe as he waited for me to speak.

I took a sip of coffee. It exploded with flavor in my mouth. Who cares if the caffeine kicks your adrenaline higher, I told myself, taking another sip. This is exactly what I need.

Sterling crossed his legs. He wore a pair of black skinny jeans tucked into black combat boots. The look on anyone else might have been intimidating, but not on Sterling. His gentle spirit came through no matter what he wore.

"Thank you." I exhaled and wrapped both hands around the mug. "I needed this."

"No problem."

"Sorry, I'm a bit jumpy."

Sterling shook his head. "I think finding a body warrants a freak-out."

I tried to smile. "I guess so."

"So what happened, and what do you need me to do?"

I told him about going to the marina to look for the sausage and finding Tony's body in the chest freezer. I shuddered again as I recalled the sight of his blue face.

Sterling tugged at the strings on his black hoodie. "So the first step is calling the police, right?"

"Yeah, and we need to find Mercury. She needs to know." I took another sip of the coffee. It had cooled slightly. "And then Lance, of course."

He stood. "You call the police. I'll go track down Mercury."

"That sounds like a good plan." I rested the coffee on the table behind me. "Should I call 911?"

Sterling shrugged. "I don't know."

"I'll call Thomas," I said. "He'll know what to do."

Thomas was my high school boyfriend and Ashland's deputy detective-in-training. We'd rekindled our friendship and connected over a murder at Torte when I returned home last summer.

"Okay." Sterling nodded. He appraised me. "You're sure you're good before I go find Mercury?"

"Much better. Thank you."

Sterling cinched his hoodie over his head and started for the front door.

"Be careful out there," I called after him. "It's really bad."

After he left, I took a moment to calm my breathing and sip the coffee. Then I found the phone by the front desk. Like everything else in the resort, it was old school. The phone was attached to the wall and had a long black twisted cord. I picked up the receiver and started to place a finger in the rotary dial. I realized I didn't know Thomas's number. When I had returned home to Ashland and reconnected with Thomas he had added his number to my cell. That was one major pro of the digital age. No need to memorize anyone's number.

However, at the moment, it would have been helpful to have Thomas's number in my head. I should just call 911, right? Where were emergency services even located up this high? I remembered passing the fire station yesterday. Maybe they could send someone.

That was probably my best option. I dialed and waited for it to ring. The connection wasn't good. The line crackled as a woman's voice answered.

"911 operator, what's your emergency?"

"I'm at Lake of the Woods and there's a dead body here."

Static buzzed on the line.

"I didn't get that. You'll have to say it again."

I repeated what I'd just said, only louder.

"Lake of the Woods?"

"Yes!"

"You need an ambulance?"

"No. I think you need to send a detective. Someone has been murdered."

"Murder?" she yelled.

"Yes!"

The line went dead for a moment. I thought I'd lost her. Then she came back. "Our connection is bad. If I lose you, I'll call you back."

"Okay."

"This storm has been upgraded. We have blizzard conditions out there. I don't know how soon I can get help to you. Can you confirm this is *not* an emergency?"

Was murder an emergency? I guess not. Tony wasn't going anywhere. I explained the situation again, trying to speak as slowly and loudly as possible.

"I'm going to patch you in to Ashland police. As of about fifteen minutes ago we had trees down on OR 140. It's going to take crews a while to reopen that road. I don't think we can get a team from Medford to you."

She took my name and walked me through instructions, like reiterating that no one should touch the body or the crime scene. Right. There was no chance that I was going to touch Tony's body.

As I hung up, Sterling returned with Mercury. She looked like she'd just woken up. She wore a pair of flannel pajama bottoms, boots, and a fur-lined coat. Her hair was matted on one side like she'd slept on it.

"What happened?" She massaged her temples. "You found Tony? Are you sure he's not just passed out or something? He has a tendency to do that. I've found him all around the resort sleeping it off." She paced back and forth as she spoke.

"I'm sure," I replied. "He's dead. Someone stuffed his

body in the chest freezer." The words sounded like they were coming from outside of me.

Mercury ran her fingers through her hair and paused in front of the fireplace. "You're sure?" She gave me a quizzical look.

"Positive."

She started pacing again. "He can't be. I just saw him a couple hours ago."

"A couple hours?" I asked, glancing at Sterling.

"No, not hours. I mean last night. You know, we all did." She bent over and picked up a log. "I mean when he stormed out last night. That's when I last saw him. Wasn't that just a few hours ago?" She laughed uncomfortably and positioned the log in the fireplace.

"I guess so," I said.

A pile of old newspapers was stacked on the hearth. Mercury crumpled a handful of newsprint and tossed it into the fireplace. "What do we do now?"

"We wait." I tried to catch Sterling's eye, but he knelt in front of the fireplace and arranged the wadded-up balls of newspaper that Mercury was scrunching with force. "I called 911. They're going to try to send a team, but the roads are bad. The operator wasn't sure how soon she could get anyone up here."

Mercury stood on her tiptoes and reached for a box of matches on the mantel. She struck the side of the box and threw the lit match on top of the newspaper. With one poof the fire sprang to life. "This is terrible," she said, picking up an iron poker and stirring the flaming balls. "I checked the forecast last night. It's supposed to get really bad. In fact, I was planning to have Gavin help me make sure that all the cabins are stocked with candles and matches. If the wind continues to pick up, we might lose power."

Sterling stood and brushed newsprint from his hands. "Do you have a backup generator?"

Mercury nodded. "We do, but just for the lodge." She stabbed at the fire. "Every cabin has a woodstove, but I need to make sure they have enough wood. Usually guests like the ambiance of lighting a fire, but if we lose power that will be their only source of heat."

She sighed and returned the poker to the rack on the hearth. The fire crackled and popped. I hoped there was enough wood in my cabin. I hadn't bothered to check last night.

Mercury held her fingers on her temples as if willing her brain to work. "Okay, I have to focus. What do we do about Tony's body?"

"The operator said to leave him and the crime scene exactly as it is. She recommended finding a way to block access. We don't want Lance's guests going down there and disturbing the area."

"I can take care of it," Sterling said. He turned to Mercury. "Do you have any rope?"

She rubbed her eyes and rocked back and forth. "I'm sure I do in the storage room. I guess I should go with you. It is my lodge after all."

"Are you sure you want to do that?" I asked Sterling. Internally I was grateful that he volunteered. I had no desire to return to the marina.

"It'll be fine. All I'm going to do is rope off the marina."

Mercury clapped her hand over her mouth. "What about Gavin? I need to find Gavin. You didn't see him down there, did you?"

"No." I shook my head. "But it was early."

"Gavin's always the first one up." Mercury started to walk toward the back. "I'll find rope and then we better stop by his cabin on the way. Oh dear, I hope he's okay. I don't know what I'd do without him."

"I'm sure he's fine," I tried to reassure her. She didn't reply. She was already halfway to the storage room. "Wow, she's wound up," I said to Sterling.

"That's an understatement." He glanced at the fire. "I thought she was going to impale me with the poker."

"I'm going to call Thomas while you take care of the marina. If help isn't going to get here for a while, I want to see if there's anything else we should do."

"Good idea." Sterling tugged on his hoodie. "When did Tony leave last night?"

"I wasn't paying close attention to time—maybe around ten-thirty or eleven."

"And you found his body when?"

"A little after five."

"So there are about six hours between when he was last seen alive and when we know he was dead. That seems like a pretty tight window, don't you think?"

I grabbed the coffee that Sterling had given me earlier and took a sip. It had gone cold, but I didn't care. "I'll ask Thomas about that, too. Maybe we should write this down while it's fresh in our heads?"

"Isn't that why the police always question people right away while their memories are fresh?" He laughed. "Or is that just on TV?"

"No, I think that's true." I could hear Mercury's footsteps returning. "Keep an eye on her," I whispered. "I'm not sure I trust her."

"Why do you think I offered to go?" Sterling raised an eyebrow.

"Thanks," I mouthed as Mercury came toward us with a roll of twine tucked under her arm.

"Will this work?" She held up the bundle of string.

"We'll make it work," Sterling replied.

"I'm going to continue the breakfast prep," I said. "Murder or no murder, everyone needs to eat."

"I wish you wouldn't call it murder," Mercury said. "It sounds so terrible."

"It is terrible." I stared at the phone on the wall. Why wasn't the operator calling me back?

She tossed the twine at Sterling. "I know. I guess I never thought something like this would happen here."

Sterling started toward the front door. "Murder can happen anywhere."

He was right.

Chapter Eleven

I glanced at the clock on the wall. It was almost six-thirty. Where had the time gone? I had a ton of work to do before Lance and his guests descended on the dining hall. But first I had to check in with Thomas. Since I didn't know his number, I called Torte. Mom could track him down.

Andy answered on the first ring. "Torte, how can I help you?"

"Andy, it's Jules."

"Hey boss, how's the lodge? It's dumping snow down here. I can't imagine how much you must be getting up there."

"Yeah, it's coming down pretty hard. Is Mom around?"

"Sure, let me grab her. Hey, before I do, I wanted to ask—do I get a prize or something?"

"A prize?"

"Yeah, for making it snow?"

"What?"

"Remember how I told you that my snowflake latte was a gift to the snow gods? It worked! You mom is letting me take off early to go hit this fresh powder."

I laughed. "Good job. I'll be sure to bring you back something special." Yeah, like a dead body.

Mom's voice was full of energy. "Good morning, honey, I didn't expect to hear from you. How's everything going? It's a winter wonderland here. There's probably a good two inches on the ground and I'm watching fat flakes fall outside the window right now. I have a feeling the whole town is going to be out playing in it soon. I have Stephanie making extra cookies and muffins, and Andy has all of our extra carafes filled with his signature hot chocolate."

"That's great, Mom." I hated having to tell her my news and ruin her snow day. I paused and thought about how to frame it.

"Juliet, I'm sorry." She lowered her voice. "I know that you're probably upset."

How did she know?

"I am. I'm not sure what to do, so I was hoping maybe you could give me Thomas's number."

She sounded surprised. "Thomas? What does Thomas have to do with this?"

"He's a detective. He'll know what to do."

"Why do you need a detective? Are you planning to have Thomas run a background check on him?"

I wrinkled my brow. What was she talking about? Mom's hearing wasn't the best. Maybe she hadn't understood what I said.

"Mom, I don't think we're talking about the same thing. What do you mean, run a background check?"

"On Carlos."

"Carlos?"

"Isn't that why you're upset, honey? When Carlos showed up I didn't know what else to do. He said that he called to tell you that he was coming, so I sent him to you."

"Oh my gosh!" I laughed. "Carlos. Right. I'd forgotten all about Carlos."

"He's not there? He said he was heading to the lodge yesterday."

"No, he's here. He's definitely here, but that's not what I'm calling about."

She let out an audible sigh. "Whew. I was worried that you were going to be upset with me."

"Mom, no. Don't be silly. It's not your job to be in the middle of Carlos and me. I'm not mad at all. I mean, I was shocked to see him, a little heads-up might have been nice, but I'm not mad at you."

"I called you, but your phone went straight to voice mail."

"Right. There's no cell service up here."

Mom's voice was muffled for a moment as she answered a question in the background. "Sorry about that, Mrs. Ryder wanted to know if it was okay to park her cross-country skis next to the door. She skied in for a latte. Isn't that great?"

"Great."

"All right, so back to business, you're not upset about Carlos, but you need Thomas's number for his professional help? What's going on up there? Is someone hurt?"

"Worse."

"Worse! Juliet, is Sterling okay?"

Time to rip off the Band-Aid. "Sterling is fine. I'm fine. Lance is fine. Everyone you know is fine, but there's been a murder."

"A murder?"

"Yeah. The lodge's bartender has been murdered. I found him this morning."

"You found him!" she shouted into the phone.

"Don't freak out, Mom. I'm okay, but the roads are pretty bad. They're not sure if anyone is going to be able to get up here today, so I just want to touch base with

Thomas and see if there's anything else I should do. That's all."

"That's all? I'm not supposed to *freak out* when you casually mention that you found a dead body?"

"Mom, really, I'm fine."

"I need to call Doug right away. Hang on. I'll get Thomas's number for you. Then I'll call Doug, too."

Doug, aka the Professor, as everyone in town calls him, is Mom's boyfriend and Ashland's lead detective. He also serves as the town's authority on Shakespeare. If the Bard, as the Professor likes to call Shakespeare, were alive he'd probably have a hard time keeping up with the Professor's knowledge of his work. Once a month the Professor hosts a reading group where members dissect sonnets and translate passages. He's been known to dress in Old English attire and quote soliloquies on the bricks before performances in the summer season.

Talking to Mom helped me feel calmer. I knew that the second we hung up the phone, she would get in touch with the Professor. Between him and Thomas they'd know what—if anything—I should do.

Mom returned with Thomas's number. "I'll give the Professor the lodge's number and have him call you."

"That would be great. Thanks, Mom."

"Juliet, you take care of yourself. Carlos is there, right?"

"He's here."

"Good. I know he won't let anything happen to you."

I had to agree with her on that. Whatever the problems between us, Carlos would defend me with his life.

"Call me back when you can," Mom said.

We hung up and I dialed Thomas's number. He answered on the third ring. His voice sounded groggy. I had woken him. Thomas usually worked the late shift, and he wasn't a morning person.

"It's Jules," I said. "Did I wake you?"

"No, no," Thomas lied. "What's going on?" His words ran together in a mumbled just-woke-up kind of way.

"Sorry to bug you, but there's a bit of a situation up here."

"Situation?" Thomas sounded clearer.

"Well—uh—there's been a murder."

"A murder? Wait. Aren't you up at Lake of the Woods? When I stopped by Torte for my morning coffee yesterday your mom said you were catering an event for OSF."

"I am, and I found a body this morning."

"Whoa. Slow down, Jules. A murder? Why are you calling me? Hang up and call the police."

"You are the police, Thomas."

"Jules, you know what I mean. Lake of the Woods isn't my jurisdiction."

"I know. I called the local police, but they can't get here. The roads are blocked."

"What?"

"It's snowing like crazy."

"It is?"

"It's snowing in Ashland, too. Look out your window."

"Hold on." Thomas must have gotten up. I heard him whistle. "You're right, it is. Okay so walk me through this. What happened?"

I filled him in on everything that had happened from Tony's dramatic exit last night to finding the body and how Sterling was roping off the crime scene and the timeline we'd put together.

"Slow down, Jules. You're getting way ahead of yourself. Let me call dispatch and see what I can find out. Can I reach you at this number?"

"Yeah, I'm on the lodge's landline. Cell phones don't work up here."

"Okay. Sit tight. I'll call you back in a few."

The Professor and Thomas were on it. I had no doubt that not only would they get back to me, but that they would give me a clear direction on what to do next. Until then, I knew exactly what I needed to do: bake.

Chapter Twelve

I wanted to be able to hear the phone ring when the Professor and Thomas called back, so I propped the kitchen door open with a chair. In the blur of discovering Tony's body, breakfast had been put on hold. We'd have to scrap the sausage casserole. There was no way I was going to retrieve them from the chest freezer now. Unfortunately the sausage is what gives it a nice spicy kick. Without it the potatoes and eggs would be bland.

Sterling, I love you, I thought as I stepped into the warm kitchen. He had started a fire in the pizza oven, peeled and sliced potatoes, and had them resting in a water-and-vinegar bath so they didn't turn brown.

I dumped my cold coffee in the sink and washed my hands. The fire needed tending. After I added another log and stoked the flames, I checked my yeast. It had risen so high that it spilled over the sides of the glass measuring cup. If I could make it work, it would save me time.

Speaking of time, breakfast was due on the table in just over two hours. I needed a new plan. Instead of the sausage casserole we could toss the potatoes in olive oil, rosemary, and sea salt and wood-fire them. I knew we had peppers and sundried tomatoes. When Sterling returned, he could make an egg scramble with cotija cheese.

The question was what to do with the yeast? There wasn't time to make an assortment of pastries. We could do that tomorrow. I decided to make a simple sweet bread instead. We had plenty of oranges. I could pair them with cardamom. The sweet spice should balance nicely with a citrus glaze, and I could add chopped pecans and walnuts to a couple of the pans. I've learned over the years to make sure to have nut-free options for people with allergies and for the rare guest who just doesn't like nuts.

I sifted flour, salt, and sugar together, and began incorporating my monster yeast. Fingers crossed that it would rise again. Yeast can be fickle. If it failed, I didn't have time to make another round. Fortunately, this recipe was nearly foolproof.

The dough is extremely versatile. We use it every day at Torte. I like to experiment with flavor combinations. Customers come back for our standard cinnamon rolls that ooze cinnamon and are packed with walnuts and raisins. We serve them warm with a healthy dose of cream cheese frosting. Mom and I have perfected the dough recipe over the years. It always produces rolls that are slightly crisp on the outside and soft and gooey in the center. Swapping cinnamon for cardamom and orange should give Lance's guests the comfort of a warm roll with a unique zest.

I sprinkled flour on my hands and the island, and started kneading the dough. It stuck to my fingers. I shook more flour onto the counter. Working with sticky dough was like working on my relationship with Carlos. Too much flour and the dough would be tough and chewy. Not enough flour and the dough would be a clingy glutinous mess. Finding the point of harmony in kneading a dough that stretches and springs back together had taken me years of practice.

That should give me hope. I just need years of practice

in my relationships and eventually they'd turn out perfect.

Once the dough had been kneaded, I divided it into two equal portions and put them in bowls to rise. While they rose, I started on the filling. I rinsed my hands in the sink and gathered a pile of oranges on the island. Using the rind of citrus fruit is one of my favorite ways to add texture and a hint of bitterness to sweet dishes. I grated the oranges into a bowl. The fragrant rind was a beautiful color and added an aroma of spring to the kitchen.

I kept one ear toward the dining room, but there was no sound of the phone yet. I wondered if Thomas or the Professor had been able to find out if the local police were on their way. The overhead lights flickered as I squeezed the juice of the oranges into another bowl.

Uh-oh. That wasn't a good sign. Losing power was the last thing we needed.

My hands were wet with orange juice. I tasted my pinky. Delicious and so fresh. Lance was going to swoon over these rolls. I knew it.

I melted butter in the microwave and forked it together with some brown sugar and the orange juice. Then I opened a cardamom pod and scraped the aromatic black seeds into the mixture. A little goes a long way when it comes to the ancient spice. That's true of most spices, but especially with cardamom. It's always better to start slow, taste, and add as needed. I've tried to impart that advice to Stephanie, Sterling, and Andy. "Taste, taste, taste," that's our motto at Torte.

The fragrant blend of citrus and spice made my mouth water. I removed the towels covering the dough. It had risen nicely. Time to roll it. I sprinkled the countertop with flour and plopped a ball of the elastic dough in the middle. There's an art to rolling dough. One mistake that home bakers often make is applying too much pressure. This will make the dough too flat. I pressed lightly on the rolling pin and watched as the dough began to stretch.

Once I'd rolled it into a long oval shape, I brushed it with melted butter and then sprinkled the cardamom mixture across the top. I creased the edges and rolled it into a log. Grabbing my pastry cutter, I sliced half-inch portions, placed them in a greased baking pan, and then poured more melted butter over the rolls. I finished them off with a dash of grated orange rind.

They needed to rise for another fifteen minutes before I baked them, so I set them aside. Sterling returned as I washed my hands. The sound of his voice made me jump. I splashed soapy water in my eye.

"You startled me," I said, blinking. My eye began to tear. I wiped the corner of it with my pinky.

Sterling's face was flushed. "It's nuts out there. Two trees came down by the lake while we were at the marina. It sounded like an earthquake or something."

"You're okay?"

He stood by the brick oven and placed his hands in front of it. "Yeah. It freaked me out, you know. It was really loud."

I drained the potatoes. "Was everything okay at the marina?"

"It looked like you described it. I only saw one set of footprints, and even those had almost disappeared by the time Mercury and I roped the area off." He rubbed his hands together and stepped away from the stove. "Mercury is freaking out about the marina manager. He didn't answer when we knocked on his cabin. She's convinced there's some kind of serial killer up here and that he's dead, too."

"That's an unsettling thought." I spread the potatoes evenly on baking sheets.

"Come on, Jules, a serial killer—doubtful." Sterling shook his head and walked to the sink. "What do you want me to do?"

"Can you start on the eggs? I had to ditch the sausage casserole." A little shudder ran down my spine.

"Why?"

"The sausage is in the freezer with . . ." I swallowed. "Tony. We can't use it."

Sterling threw his head back and laughed.

"What?"

"Can you imagine? We could probably come up with a great name. Dead guy sausage has a nice ring to it. It's like that beer that Rogue makes—Dead Guy Ale. Maybe that's their secret ingredient."

"I don't think this is a good time to joke." I drizzled olive oil on the potatoes.

"Jules, you have to laugh, otherwise you're going to make yourself crazy." Sterling removed a carton of eggs from the refrigerator.

He was probably right. I have a tendency to take myself too seriously sometimes. It's something I've been trying to work on—to lighten up.

"Anyway," Sterling continued, cracking eggs into a mixing bowl. "The sausages aren't sleeping with Tony. It's so cold outside, I stuck our coolers on the back deck." He pointed toward the lake. "I figured it would be easier to walk outside and grab stuff versus having to trek down to the marina."

"I could kiss you, Sterling."

"Please don't." He made a face, then smiled. "That would be weird."

"Whatever." I laughed and rubbed the potatoes with sea salt. Sterling had broken my dark mood. "I called Thomas. He should be calling back soon." I glanced toward the dining room. It had been at least thirty minutes and still no call.

"I don't know if the phone lines are working." Sterling whisked the eggs. "Mercury is out looking at them now. One of the trees took down a line. She wasn't sure if it was the phone or cable."

Great.

Sterling turned on some music and we concentrated on our own tasks. The rolls had risen over the top of the baking pan. I slid them into the oven and finished the potatoes with a handful of chopped rosemary.

A little after eight, Carlos showed up. He looked like he could model for a ski magazine. He wore another turtleneck sweater. This time in a creamy cashmere that made his olive skin radiate. His jeans looked casually worn in, yet were tailored to his lean muscular build. There was only one thing holding back his modeling career, and that was the gnarly green and purplish bruise blemishing his otherwise perfect face.

He strolled toward me and kissed me on both cheeks. "Good morning, Julieta."

"Morning," I replied. "How's your cheek? It looks terrible. You better ice it again."

"It is nothing," he said, but he followed my advice and grabbed a package of frozen peas from the freezer.

Sterling waved his whisk in a greeting. Carlos inspected his silky mixture. "This is good work, no?" He looked to me for confirmation.

"Yeah. He's a quick study."

"*Sí.*" Carlos noticed the coffee carafe on the counter. "Is this still good?"

Carlos and I are both coffee snobs. I admit it. I'm not usually snobbish when it comes to good food. Of course, I prefer to use fresh and locally sourced ingredients in my baking and cooking, but I'm just as happy chowing down on a hearty bowl of homemade mac and cheese as I am noshing on a deconstructed five-course dinner. But when it comes to coffee, I am very particular.

"That's been sitting for at least an hour," I said to Carlos.

He frowned. "No. No good." He dumped the coffee in the sink. "I will make you a Spanish coffee, *sí*?"

"How do you make Spanish coffee?" Sterling asked.

Carlos put an arm around his shoulder. "Come watch."

"It's too early for that," I said, checking the rolls in the oven.

"No. It's fine. I'll show him how to brew." Carlos pulsed beans in the grinder. He winked at Sterling. "Later tonight I'll show you how to make a real Spanish coffee."

"I don't drink," Sterling said. I was impressed that he took responsibility for his past and was so open and honest about it.

Carlos understood his meaning. "That is okay. I make you one with no alcohol. Still very delicious. You will love it."

There are many varieties of Spanish coffee, but Carlos's version is a blend of dark brewed coffee with Kahlúa, Amaretto, and his own homemade coffee liqueur. He serves it flaming. It's a work of art and so strong that just one sip makes my head spin.

Sterling paid close attention to Carlos as he scooped beans into the coffeepot. I was glad that I wasn't the only one who got swept up in Carlos's easy charm.

Clunky footsteps thudded through the dining room. Were the board members already starting to gather? I glanced at the clock. We still had forty minutes before breakfast.

Mercury swung the kitchen door open. Her hair was

damp with snow. It looked fake, as if she were wearing a clumpy white wig. She hadn't changed. She was still in her pajama pants and snow boots. "The power's on in here?" Her words slurred a bit.

"Yeah." I motioned toward the overhead lights. "At least for the moment. They've flickered a couple times, but knock on wood, we're good." I knocked on the countertop.

She glanced at the lights. "We'll see. The phone lines are down, and I can't see anything past my arm out there. Gavin hasn't showed up here yet, has he?"

I shook my head.

"I can't believe he's not here. He usually has the fire going and the heat turned on in all the buildings before I'm even up." She rubbed her temples. Wet snow splatted on the floor. "You don't think he's dead, too?"

"Dead?" Carlos looked from me to Sterling.

I held up my index finger, signaling for him to wait.

Mercury tapped her forehead. She didn't appear to hear Carlos's question. "I don't know what to do. Do you think we have some kind of crazed killer here with us?"

"Killer?" Carlos asked again.

I shook my head at him.

Mercury paced in front of the brick oven. "I would send everyone home if I could. That seems like the safest solution, but no one can get out of here." She stopped and peered into the oven. "That smells amazing. What are you baking?"

"Orange cardamom rolls," I replied, stepping closer to her and resting my hand on her arm. "I know it's been an extremely stressful morning. Why don't you go sit down by the fire—we'll bring you a roll and coffee. You're right. No one can leave. Even if the roads were clear we'd still need to keep everyone here."

"We would?"

"Yes, this is a crime scene. The police are going to need to question everyone when they get here."

"Crime scene?" Carlos looked incredulous. I shot him a warning look. Mercury had stopped pacing and was staring out the window.

"Let me walk you to the fireplace," I said, leading her out of the kitchen.

Her erratic behavior wasn't good for her, and certainly wouldn't be good for the board members who were due to arrive for breakfast soon. I helped Mercury settle in front of the fire. You were worse than her a little while ago, I told myself.

"I'll have Sterling bring you a cup of coffee. Just relax for a minute. The police know what happened and they'll be here as soon as they can. Until then, we're just going to have to continue as best we can."

Mercury's dazed eyes focused on the flames. She nodded as I walked back to the kitchen. She seemed reassured by my words. I just wished that I believed them.

Chapter Thirteen

When I returned to the kitchen, Sterling was explaining what happened to Carlos.

Carlos sprinted toward me and grabbed my shoulders with his hands. "Julieta, why did you not tell me?" He studied my face. "You are okay, yes?"

"I'm fine." I placed my hands on top of his. A jolt erupted in my body. I'd forgotten how his touch affected me.

He released me. "And how was Tony killed?"

I shook my head. "I don't know. I didn't look at him close enough to see." I rubbed my arms.

Carlos wrapped his arm around me and kissed the top of my head. "Do not think of it, *mi querida*. I'm sorry I asked."

"It's okay." I leaned into him. He smelled like coffee beans and aftershave. "I guess I never even thought about how he might have been murdered. I was so focused on the fact that he was *murdered*."

"Murdered? Did someone say murdered?" Lance's voice sang behind me.

I flinched. Carlos strengthened his grasp around me.

Lance stood in the doorway. He tossed the teal scarf that hung around his neck to the side. "Darling, why so jumpy?" He strolled into the kitchen and let his eyes linger on the percolating coffee. "Too much caffeine, perhaps?"

I stepped away from Carlos. "Lance, we need to talk."

"Ooooh. So dramatic, Juliet. I love it. You're feeling the tension of this remote space, aren't you? Work it, darling. Work it."

"Lance, I'm not kidding. We need to talk." I bit my bottom lip.

"She's not kidding, is she?" he asked Carlos and Sterling.

They both looked at the floor.

"Well, now you're scaring me, darling." Lance rested his finger on his chin. "Out with it."

"There's no easy way to say this," I said, taking a deep breath. "Tony, the bartender, is dead."

Lance gasped. "What? You must be kidding. Although . . ." He paused and stared at the contusion on Carlos's face. "After damaging that chiseled profile, maybe he got what he deserved."

I shook my head. "No, I'm serious. I found his body this morning."

"That sounds ghastly. Surely you're not hinting at foul play?"

"It looks that way." I sighed.

Lance placed his hand over his heart. "Oh my goodness. This is too much. A board retreat in the middle of winter in the eerie Oregon forest and someone ends up dead. This has screenplay written all over it."

"Lance, this is no time to kid. Tony is dead."

He waved me off. "Death is the *only* time to kid, darling."

What did that mean?

"Any chance I can get a cup of that delicious-smelling brew?" Lance asked Sterling.

Sterling reached for a ceramic mug and poured Lance a cup.

Lance threw his hand to his forehead after taking a sip of coffee. "As always your coffee is pure perfection. What's the magic elixir?"

"I didn't make it. Carlos did."

Bowing to Carlos, Lance winked at me. "Ah, I see. Talent attracts talent." He cradled the mug in his hands. "Now on to this nasty murder business. I suppose I'm going to need to let my guests know about this development. Are the police here?"

"No." I explained the situation to Lance. When I finished, he held his mug out to Sterling. "Be a dear, and refill this, would you? This is playing out like an Agatha Christie production. Snowed in. Cut off from communication. And . . ." Lance paused and pointed to the overhead lights as they flickered again. "Soon we might be in the dark. This is too much. Absolutely too much. I need to go prepare a little speech. Ta-ta."

I was used to Lance's overly dramatic personality. Carlos, on the other hand, stood near the coffeepot, looking incredulous.

"It's all for show," I said. "He's always like that."

Carlos poured himself a cup of coffee. "I did notice that last night."

Hearing Carlos say the words "last night" triggered something in my brain. Carlos might have seen something last night. He was awake and here or outside when Tony had been killed. My eyes glanced to the sink where I placed the two wine glasses I found earlier. Had he been alone?

I wanted to ask him what—if anything—he'd seen, but was interrupted by the sound of voices gathering and boots tromping on the hardwood floors. The board members were arriving for breakfast.

Sterling sprang into action, stacking coffee cups, cream, sugar, honey, and our own blend of cinnamon, nutmeg, and allspice onto a tray. "I'll get everyone caffeinated."

"Great." I gave him a thumbs-up. The rolls and potatoes were done and warming in the front of the oven. We just needed to scramble the eggs and chop a quick fruit salad. I heated olive oil in a cast-iron skillet for the eggs.

Carlos slid behind me. "Julieta, I will make the eggs. I will give them a Spanish kick, *sí*?"

"Sure. Go for it." I handed him the skillet and walked to the fridge. I grabbed a cantaloupe and honeydew melon. I'd slice those and add blueberries, strawberries, grapes, and bananas. Then I would dress the fruit salad with yogurt vinaigrette made with Greek honey yogurt and lemon juice.

Sterling returned and began stacking plates and silverware. "Lance is in his element out there."

"Not a surprise." I sliced the honeydew. "Has he gotten to the murder yet?"

"Are you kidding?" Sterling balanced the plates on his arms. "He's going to stretch this story out for as long as possible."

While I diced the fruit, I watched Carlos work. The muscles in his back tightened as he shook the skillet over the open flame with one arm, and reached for a handful of chopped peppers with the other. He sprinkled the peppers and incorporated them into the eggs with two quick flicks of his wrist. On the ship there were always foodie groupies, as we affectionately called them, five or six young women, mainly waitresses, who would gather to watch Carlos orchestrate dinner service. They would gasp and sigh as he massaged pork loins with sea salt and artfully drizzled a blood orange sauce on the rim of a plate. When Carlos cooked, he cooked with love. It came through in everything he touched, and how he moved his body.

I found myself forgetting to breathe as I watched him fry the eggs. Focus, Juliet.

"Lance wants me to report that the guests are getting restless," Sterling said, as he swung the kitchen door open. He checked behind him to make sure it shut. "Honestly, I think he wants us to serve breakfast so he can keep them on the edge of their seats with his 'important and stunning news' as he put it."

"We're ready." I nodded to the oven. "The rolls can go first. You can just serve them in their baking dishes. Be sure to tell everyone that the pans are hot, though."

Sterling pulled on oven gloves and removed the first tray of golden brown rolls. The orange rind glaze had oozed and melted between them. I had a feeling they were going to disappear fast.

"After you take those out, come back for the potatoes. They need to go onto a serving platter. I'll finish up the salad and bring it out." I poured the lemon dressing over the fruit and tossed it with salad tongs. The confetti-colored creamy salad would be a nice cool pairing with the other hot breakfast items.

I rinsed my hands in the sink. Carlos caught my arm and held out a spoon of eggs for me to taste. "Try these."

I opened my mouth. A burst of flavor hit my palate. The eggs were soft without being mushy. They were light and rich at same time. The richness came from the spice of the peppers and the blend of garlic and onions that Carlos had added. He topped them with crumbled cotija cheese, giving them a velvety finish. "Yum." I closed my eyes and savored the taste for a minute.

When I opened my eyes Carlos was waiting expectantly for my response. "You like them, *sí*?"

"I love them."

Saying those words to him with our bodies only six inches apart might not have been my best idea. I could feel the space between us closing in.

Carlos's voice was low and husky. "You love them?" It sounded like his words were inside my ear.

My head felt heavy. It was like an imaginary cord was pulling me into him.

His voice was thick with want. "Julieta."

"Carlos, I . . ."

He placed his finger on my lips. "Do not speak."

I resisted the urge to kiss his finger. It burned on my lips.

The room was thick with desire and the scent of eggs starting to burn.

Burn!

"Carlos! The eggs." I jumped back.

He twisted around, oven mitt in hand, grabbed the skillet and moved the eggs to an unlit burner.

"Are they scorched?" I felt my cheeks. They were on fire.

"No. I can save them," Carlos said. He reached out and touched my arm. "We continue where we left off later, *sí*?"

"I have to take this out to the table." I ignored his question and picked up the fruit salad. Adjusting my apron, I hurried out to the dining hall. Hopefully my blazing cheeks wouldn't give me away. I really needed to pull it together. Carlos had me acting like a schoolgirl. Normally, I'm more composed than this. No one else could rattle me the way Carlos could. I wasn't sure what that meant, but I knew I had to tap into the professional chef inside. I had a full day of meals to cater and a murder to worry about.

Lance stood at the head of the table with a grave look on his face. The board members sat around the long table, clutching their coffee mugs, completely captivated by what Lance was saying.

I murmured an apology and reached over one of the board members to place the fruit salad in the center of the table.

"Ah, Juliet, you're just in time for the big reveal." Lance's eyes twinkled. "And I think our guests will want to hear what you have to say."

"Hang on." I held up my finger, trying to buy time. The last thing I wanted was to be part of Lance's drama. "We're just putting the finishing touches on breakfast. The rest of the food will be right out." I scooted away.

Carlos had plated the eggs and garnished them with diced red chili peppers, cheese, and a few sprigs of cilantro. They looked gorgeous. I took them from him and waved Sterling into the dining room with the trays of potatoes.

The guests let out an audible sigh as we delivered the food.

Lance raised one palm in the air and clapped his fingers into it. "Divine. Absolutely divine. Isn't this the most delectable meal you've ever seen?"

Board members clapped in agreement. I could feel my cheeks heating again.

"Dish up while it's hot." Lance swept his hands across the table.

I started toward the kitchen. He grabbed my sleeve. "Do wait, darling." Sterling and I stepped backward and stood against the far wall.

The board members passed around the steaming platters of food. It was fun to watch their faces light up as they bit into the warm sweet rolls and savored Carlos's spicy eggs. "I think it's a hit," Sterling whispered.

Lance cleared his throat, and brought his hands together in a prayer position in front of his chest. "If I could have your attention while you eat, I want to get on with the ghastly news that I need to share."

Forks clinked on plates as Lance continued. "I'm afraid I must report that not only are we snowed in and cut off from outside communication, but that our dear chef Juliet made a tragic discovery this morning." Lance closed his eyes, placed one hand on his heart, and inhaled through his nose.

The room went silent. Lance opened his eyes. "I'm afraid, my friends, that there's been a murder."

There were gasps and murmurs from the crowd. "Murder?" someone asked.

Dean Barnes, who wore his signature checkered cap, choked on a potato. He dropped his fork on his plate and clutched his throat. The woman sitting next to him pounded on his back. He coughed and heaved. I was just about to run over and perform the Heimlich maneuver on him, but one giant whack to his back sent the potato flying onto his plate.

His face had a bluish tint. He removed his hands from his throat and breathed deeply. "Did you say murder?"

Lance, who'd also looked ready to leap into action when Dean had been choking, returned to his solemn stance. "Yes. Murder."

"Who?" the woman sitting next to Dean asked. She darted her head around the table nodding at each board member, as if trying to get a head count.

"Not one of us." Lance gave her a reassuring look. "Tony—the bartender who made . . . well, as you know, made a bit of a scene last night—was discovered dead this morning."

Another round of gasps sounded from the board members. People started to chatter among themselves. Lance picked up his knife and tapped it on his water glass. "I know you likely have many questions. I do as well, but due to the fact that we're stranded here together for who knows how long." He paused and looked out the window. Snow lashed against it. The wind howled in perfectly timed response. "Anyway, Juliet has spoken with the authorities." He curled his index finger. "Come, come, Juliet."

I walked over and stood beside him.

"What did the authorities recommend we do while we await their arrival?"

Where was Mercury? I craned my neck toward the fireplace. She wasn't there. Shouldn't she be giving the board directions? It was her lodge after all. Not to mention the fact that one of her staff members was dead.

Lance nudged my waist. "Juliet?"

"Oh, right." I returned my focus to the table. "They're working to get help up here as fast as they can. In the meantime, they said to proceed as normal. They said no one can leave, but it's not like that's an option anyway." I tried to laugh. It sounded forced.

Dean raised his hand. "Where's the body?"

Lance looked to me for approval. We hadn't discussed whether or not to tell everyone where the crime scene was. They could figure it out on their own if they walked around the resort, but given the blizzard conditions outside, I doubted anyone would.

I shrugged.

Lance pursed his lips. "The scene has been secured."

"But where is it?" Dean asked.

Why was he so insistent?

"I can assure you that it's nowhere near the lodge. None of you are in danger of stumbling over a body on your way back to your cabins tonight." Lance chuckled. The group did, too. "The bigger concern for the moment is our power situation." Lance scanned the room and looked toward the bar. "Mercury, are you in there?"

No one answered.

"Whitney, go track down Mercury." Lanced snapped his bony fingers. "We need a power plan. Ha! Get it? Power plan."

Whitney didn't even bother to swallow the piece of cantaloupe in her mouth. She pushed back her chair and spilled her coffee in the process. Dean helped her mop the coffee with a forest-green napkin that had a silhouette of a deer stitched in the middle. Whitney gave him a look of thanks. "I'll find her right away," she said to Lance. If possible, she looked even more frazzled than she had yesterday. Her wiry hair and twitchy eyes matched her skittish attitude. At least she was dressed for the elements today in a bulky sweater and another pair of skinny jeans. Instead of pumps without socks she wore a pair of Uggs.

She left her tablet on the table and darted toward the front door. Dean watched her leave. For a minute I thought he might go after her, but instead he picked up her tablet and stored it by his feet. Of all the board members he was best outfitted to follow her into the inclement weather. He wore a thick hunting jacket, chaps, Wellington boots, and a cap. Was that all that he packed? He looked exactly the same as he had yesterday, and like he could step onto the set of Mom's latest television obsession—*Downton Abbey*.

"Anything else we need to know from the authorities?" Lance asked me.

I shook my head.

Lance clapped his hands together. "Excellent. It's back to business for us, then."

I pulled Sterling into the kitchen before Lance could rope me into anything else.

"He enjoyed that way too much," Sterling said.

Carlos was rinsing dishes in the sink. In all the years

that I'd known him, I'd never seen him wash a dish. We had an entire dishwashing staff for that on the ship. Chefs don't wash dishes. I couldn't believe my eyes.

"What are you doing?" I asked.

"I'm helping you. I'm washing the dishes." He held up a soapy plate to prove his point. "Am I doing it wrong?"

"No." I shook my head. "I just can't believe you're washing dishes. You never wash dishes."

"I do for you," he said with a seductive smile.

Sterling laughed. "I've heard that's the way to a woman's heart. Do the dishes, and the laundry."

"Stop, you two." I fanned my face. "You're going to make me faint with all this romantic talk."

We all laughed. Sterling took over dish duty. I sent Carlos out with a fresh pot of coffee. I figured he was the least likely of the three of us to get wrapped up in Lance's theatrics.

"Okay, one meal done. Two to go. Plus snacks." I flipped open my notebook. "Now it's on to lunch. I'm thinking we do a hearty stew and toasted open-faced sandwiches in the brick oven. Does that sound good?"

"Is there anything you're not going to bake in that thing?" Sterling asked.

"Not if I can help it. Don't you think we need one at Torte?"

"It's pretty sweet." Sterling scrubbed a skillet with a Brio brush.

For the next hour Sterling, Carlos, and I worked in an easy cadence. Sterling cleared breakfast dishes and finished loading the dishwasher. Carlos started on a homemade beef stock for the stew base, while I assembled the ingredients I needed for my cookie dough. I planned to bake them right before lunch. That way we could serve them warm.

Mercury burst into the kitchen a little after ten with

Gavin Allen, the marina manager who had been missing, trailing behind her. "Good news, everyone. Gavin is fine."

Gavin's Lake of the Woods sweatshirt was tattered. One of the sleeves was ripped and the logo was nearly worn off. It stretched over his belly. "I don't know what all the fuss is about. I was asleep."

Mercury laced her fingers together and cracked her knuckles. Deep bags had formed under her eyes. "I know, but like I told you, after we learned that Tony was dead I was worried about you. We couldn't find you."

Gavin rolled his eyes. "The one time I sleep in."

"What if we have a serial killer or something up here?" Mercury rubbed her temples.

"I know every square inch of this place. Trust me, there's no serial killer hiding out up here." Gavin hoisted up his tool belt. "I checked every building. No one could survive out in this weather for long."

His words seemed to relax Mercury, at least for a moment. She glanced at the cookie dough on the island. "It looks like you have everything under control in here."

"So far so good," I said.

"That's one piece of good news at least." She sighed. "I was telling Gavin that he's going to have to become a bartender today. I don't have anyone else to work the bar, and the storm is getting worse. I think we might lose power."

"We're going to lose power, you can take that to the bank." Gavin sounded sure of that. "I've been up here since 1981. This is one of the worst storms we've had in a while. Snow's blowing off the lake. Trees are coming down. Phone lines are already down. It's going to happen."

Mercury ran her hands through her hair. She still hadn't changed out of her pajama bottoms. "I don't know what we're going to do. I need you at the bar, but I also need someone to help me get wood and extra supplies to all the cabins. I can't do it myself. Oh, I wish my husband was here." She sounded like she was going to cry.

Carlos stepped toward her. "I have a suggestion."

"Yes?"

"I could tend bar for you."

"You could?"

"Yes, I'm a chef. I know how to mix drinks." He looked at Gavin. "If that's okay with you."

Gavin gave him a thumbs-up. "Fine by me. It's all yours. My idea of bartending is cracking open a can of beer."

Mercury threw her arms around Carlos. "Oh, thank you! Thank you. I'll pay you, of course."

"No, no. I do this for you." Carlos smiled at me.

"We'll discuss it, but can you come with me now? I'll show you where everything is, and then Gavin and I can start delivering supplies to the cabins."

"Of course. It will be my pleasure." Carlos took off his apron and folded it on the counter. "I'll be back soon," he said to Sterling and me as he left with Mercury.

Having Carlos man the bar was a win for me, too. As much as I enjoyed having him in the kitchen, he was also a distraction.

"The guy is doing back flips for you, Jules."

"He is, isn't he?"

"And the tension in here is off the charts. I feel like I'm on the set of a Spanish soap opera or something." Sterling started the dishwasher.

"Whatever." I laughed and shook my head.

"I'm serious, Jules. Carlos is crazy about you, and you're as cool as this cucumber." He pointed to a basket of vegetables on the island.

"Am I? I feel like I'm acting like a total idiot."

"What?"

"Yeah. I haven't been able to focus on anything this morning."

"You fooled me. Lance must be right about your acting skills."

I couldn't believe that Sterling wasn't picking up on how nervous I was. I agreed with him that the tension in the kitchen was thicker than any stew and that Carlos was doing everything he could to prove his commitment to me. I just wasn't sure if it was because he really cared or if it was because he felt guilty.

Chapter Fourteen

"Let's talk about something else, like lunch." I changed the subject.

Sterling came over to the island. "What do you want me to do next?"

We checked off tasks. Sterling would assemble the sandwiches while I made stew. My focus returned as I strained the broth that Carlos had started. We make all of our stocks by hand. It takes longer than using commercial beef or chicken broth, but it's well worth it in terms or flavor. It was chock-full of onions, carrots, garlic, and celery. It reminded me of winter evenings as a child. My dad would make a pot of stew, Mom would bring a loaf of bread home from Torte, and we'd snuggle together on the couch and watch a movie.

Carlos says that food is love. I say it's memory.

"Since we're on the subject of love, what about you?" I asked Sterling. "How are you feeling about Stephanie?"

He stoked the flames in the oven, and pushed up the sleeves of his hoodie. "Hey, that's not fair. I thought you said we were dropping the subject."

"You don't have to talk about it. I'm the last person who will push you on that. Now, Mom might not let you off so easy when we get back."

"She has a way of getting people to talk."

"Yeah. You know what her secret is?" I stirred the flavorful stock.

"She's a good listener?"

"That and pastry."

Sterling laughed. "Torte's pastries do have a certain effect on people." He ran his finger over the tattoo of a hummingbird on his forearm. I knew that the tattoo was a permanent reminder of his mother.

"Does talking about my mom bring up memories of your mom?"

His eyes misted. "It does, but in a good way. It makes me feel closer to her, you know?"

I did. Losing a parent young had left a lasting mark on both of us.

"Having Helen in my life helps ease the sting a little." Sterling smiled, but there was pain behind his eyes.

"I feel the same way about the Professor. It's weird because I didn't even realize how much I missed having a father figure in my life."

Sterling reached for a loaf of sourdough bread. "So, really, we're both messed up and broken."

"Looks that way, doesn't it?" I grinned and gave him a loopy smile. "Is that why we're both unlucky in love?"

"Probably." Sterling sliced the loaf with a serrated bread knife. "My mom used to blame it on my birth date. I was born on Valentine's Day. She said I was born a lover not a fighter."

"I didn't know you were a Valentine baby. We'll have to throw you a bash next month."

"Don't. I've come to hate the holiday." Sterling grabbed another loaf and stabbed it with the knife.

I wondered if he meant because of Stephanie or because Valentine's Day reminded him of his mom. Either way I didn't push him. We were so alike. I knew he needed space and quiet to work through whatever was going on.

As we prepped lunch, I couldn't stop circling through who could have killed Tony. It was probably to avoid having to think about Carlos.

"Who do you think did it?" I asked Sterling as I diced more fresh onions for the beef stew.

"No idea." Sterling spread butter on the sliced loaves. "Mercury was pretty jumpy this morning."

"I thought so, too."

"But then again, her bartender was murdered so I guess it would also be weird if she wasn't jumpy."

"Good point." I wiped the corner of my eye with my sleeve. The onions were making my eyes tear. "Given what happened last night, she had a motive. She was pretty upset with Tony. I got the impression she would have fired him on the spot if they were alone and if she wasn't in desperate need of a bartender for the weekend."

"Me, too."

I scraped the onions into a sauté pan and began chopping celery and carrots. My beef stew recipe had been passed down from my grandmother. She used to make it on Sundays, letting it simmer on the stove for hours. We didn't have that much time. But thanks to technology, I did have a modern gadget that would make the beef so tender in minutes that it would fall apart on the fork. A pressure cooker.

Thirty minutes in the pressure cooker and the beef would taste like we'd slow-cooked it for hours. I usually prefer to cook the old-fashioned way—low and slow. That's how we make our stews at Torte. We start in the early morning hours while most of Ashland is still in a silent slumber. By the time customers roll in for lunch, our stews are thick with flavor. But in situations like this where we were crunched for time and responsible for presenting meals and snacks every few hours, I was thrilled to use the pressure cooker.

"What about Whitney?" Sterling asked. He had finished buttering the bread and walked to the fridge. He removed blocks of white cheddar and Swiss cheese. We decided on two open-faced sandwiches for lunch. Sticking with the comfort theme, we were going traditional with a grilled ham and Swiss with honey Dijon mustard, and a roast beef and sharp cheddar with our own version of yellow mustard.

"What about her?" I added the carrots and celery to the onions, which had turned translucent.

"She had a motive, right? Tony messed up the alcohol order, made it sound like it was her fault and then he hit on her."

"He was hitting on every woman here." I stuck out my tongue. "I guess that makes me a suspect, too."

"Come to think of it, I was going to ask you where you were last night." Sterling winked. "It's pretty convenient that you just happen to stumble upon his body, if you ask me."

"Stumble—right." I shuddered. "Actually that raises a good point. I don't think there's any way a woman could have done it?"

"Are you going all sisterhood—female power—on me?"

"No. That's it. Power. How could a woman have physically lifted Tony's body into the freezer?"

Sterling stopped slicing cheese and held up the knife. "Well played, Jules. Tony was a big guy. Forget ruling out just the women. Not many men could lift him, either."

"Could you?" I wrinkled my brow.

"Doubtful." Sterling shook his head. "I was wondering about Dean Barnes. He and Tony got into it last night, but the guy's in his sixties. Tony must have weighed at least two-twenty. It would take a really strong guy to lift that much weight."

"Tony said Dean was following him around. I wonder what he meant by that? He cut Dean off at the bar yesterday, broke his wine glass, and soaked him with wine. But that's a stretch—killing someone for spilling on you? Yikes."

"I'd be in deep trouble. I spilled a woman's coffee last week at Torte." He gave me a sheepish grin. "I comped her drink of course."

"Of course." I smiled. "What if whoever killed him had an accomplice? Two people could have lifted him, don't you think?"

Sterling nodded and returned to slicing the cheddar cheese. "Probably. Yeah, I think so."

I tried to imagine what it would be like to lift a dead body. I had enough trouble lifting a ten-pound sack of potatoes. I couldn't imagine the strength it would take to not only move Tony, but lift his dead weight into the freezer. The killer had to be a man. I ran through the men at the lodge—there were two hefty board members whom I hadn't met, but who had both consumed multiple helpings of our buttered mashed potatoes last night. Lance, like me, was thin and lanky—no way did he have the strength. Gavin certainly did, as did Carlos, but that was ridiculous. Carlos was no killer.

After I finished sautéing the vegetables for the stew, I dredged the beef in flour, salt, and pepper, poured olive oil into the pressure cooker and turned it on high. I added the beef and let it brown. Once it had seared on all sides, I added the beef stock and secured the lid. Now all I had to do was sit back and let the pressure cooker work its magic.

When it started to sizzle, I would lower the heat. In

the meantime, I needed to peel and boil potatoes. While I scrubbed the potatoes with a vegetable brush I replayed everything that happened last night. There wasn't a single person he hadn't offended. That made everyone a suspect. I wished that the phone lines weren't down. Thomas would know what to do.

Lunch prep was seamless with Sterling's help. He layered thinly sliced meat and cheese on the buttered bread. We'd toast the sandwiches right before lunch was served. They would only take a few minutes in the hot oven. While I finished peeling potatoes, he assembled a tray of condiments, spicy mustards, mayo, three kinds of lettuce, tomatoes, red onions, and our famous Torte pickles that Mom canned this summer.

The kitchen smelled of hearty beef and vegetables as the storm raged outside. I was thankful for the warmth of the wood fire. Snow and wind battered the windows. The lights continually flickered, but—knock on wood—they came back on. I decided it was time to get moving on the cookies, not only because lunch would be served in twenty minutes, but because I wanted them to bake before the power went out. I'd never baked cookies in a wood-fired oven and I didn't want to try today.

The recipe I was using for double-chocolate cookies was extremely versatile. I started with butter, eggs, sugar, vanilla, and then sifted Dutch cocoa, flour, and baking soda. I incorporated the ingredients together until the dough was creamy. At Torte, we add a variety of chocolate chunks and nuts to the cookie batter. For Lance's guests, I added both dark and milk chocolate chips. Once the cookies had cooled, I would spread on cream cheese frosting and dust them with more cocoa.

I scooped round balls of the dough onto cookie trays. As I slid the first tray into the oven, there was a soft knock on the kitchen door. "Come on in," I called. It was probably Lance coming to check on how close we were to being ready to serve his hungry guests. They had been meeting in the dining room all morning. Sterling and I couldn't help but overhear their lively debate about the lineup of plays and Lance's new plan for raising more "funds and friends" as he said. I was surprised he was knocking. That wasn't his style.

I nearly dropped the second tray of cookies on the floor as the door to the kitchen swung open. Thomas stood in the doorway. "Jules, I thought we'd find you in here."

Chapter Fifteen

"Thomas!" I shoved the tray into the oven and ran over to hug him. His navy Ashland City Police jacket was soaked with snow. I didn't care. I threw my arms around him, and then released him. "Wait." I looked at him with disbelief. "What are you doing here?"

He chuckled and brushed wet snow from his shoulders. "Um. I heard there was a murder."

I punched him in the arm. His jacket was cold to the touch. "Ha ha, very funny. I mean how did you get up here? I thought all the roads were closed."

"I have my ways." He shook snow from his sandy hair.

"Seriously, Thomas."

His face turned serious. "The Professor and I left as soon as you called. The roads from Medford are closed, but we came up Dead Indian Road."

"You drove Dead Indian Road in this?" I pointed to the window.

Sterling whistled. "Impressive. That was a crazy drive with no snow."

Thomas took off his coat and stepped closer to the brick oven. "Tell me about it. We took the Range Rover and even with four-wheel drive it took us this long to get here."

"When did you leave?"

"Right after you called."

"But that was hours ago."

"I know." Thomas held his hands in front of the hot bricks. "We didn't go much more than ten miles an hour."

"Where's the Professor?"

"He's assessing the crime scene. I promised him a warm coffee." Thomas glanced to the coffeepot. "Any chance we can get a thermos of your brew?"

"Of course." I took his coat and hung it on a hook near the door. "Let me make you a fresh pot."

"As long as it's quick. I told the Professor I'd be right back to help him survey and bag the crime scene, but honestly I'm kind of glad to get a minute to catch my breath. My heart rate spiked just walking from the marina up here. This altitude is a killer." He placed his hand over his heart and breathed slowly. "Sorry, bad choice of words."

I rolled my eyes and dumped beans into the grinder. "Coffee will just take a minute. Sterling, will you pop a couple sandwiches in for them, too? Roast beef and cheddar or ham and Swiss?" I asked Thomas.

"Don't go to any trouble," Thomas said.

"It's no trouble. I promise. You have no idea how happy I am to see you."

Thomas pretended to be embarrassed. "Aw, Jules, you say that to all the men in your life, don't you? But in that case, I'll take a ham and Swiss if you're offering."

Sterling placed one of the sandwiches into the ovens. I checked the cupboards to see if there were any thermoses.

"So you want to give me the quick rundown?" Thomas pulled a stool to the island and turned on his iPad. He and the Professor were a unique combination. The Professor took all his notes by hand in a Moleskin notebook.

Thomas is a product of the digital age, and uses his iPad and phone for everything.

I held up a finger as I pulsed the beans in the grinder. "Hang on one sec," I called over the sound of grinding beans.

With the coffee going, I joined Thomas at the island. "I still can't believe you made it."

"Jules, come on, I would drive anywhere for you." He held my gaze.

Uh-oh. My stomach sank. I was thrilled to see Thomas, but I hadn't considered one minor glitch. Carlos. Thomas and Carlos had never met. I wasn't sure how either of them were going to react. Thomas and I were old friends. At least that's what I thought we were. I'd been confused about my feelings since I returned home, and even a bit jealous when Thomas showed interest in a fellow chef who was in town for a baking competition. It had been easy to fall back into old habits with Thomas. His slightly goofy attitude always made me smile. He knew how to lighten my mood.

We picked up where we left off a decade ago—as friends. He had hinted that he had regrets about our breakup after high school, but nothing more. Mom thought he was still in love with me, but I think it's more that he's happy to have a familiar friend back in town.

"And for a murder investigation, right?" I punched him in the shoulder again.

"Ouch." He rubbed his shoulder then grinned. "Right. You got me. Okay, on to business. What time did you discover the body?"

I told Thomas everything about finding Tony, the time-line Sterling and I had worked out, and gave him a brief rundown of the guests. He listened attentively and took notes on his iPad while I spoke. A couple times he stopped me and asked for clarification, like whether or not there were footprints near the marina. I didn't remember seeing footprints, but then again I wasn't paying attention on my way down to the marina and I wanted to get out of there as fast as I could after I found Tony.

The coffeepot beeped.

"That's my cue." Thomas clicked the iPad off and stood.

Someone cleared their throat behind me. I turned to see Gavin Allen standing in the doorway. He wore a heavy parka with the Lake of the Woods logo embroidered on the front pocket. "Everything okay in here?" he asked, stepping into the kitchen.

"We're fine," I replied. "Would you like some coffee?"

Gavin shook his head. "No time." He patted his tool belt. "Too much to do out there, but Mercury asked me to check on you."

"We're good." I pointed to Thomas. "In fact, we're really good now that the police are here."

"I heard." Gavin tipped his fishing cap to Thomas. "It's back to the cold for me. Holler if you need anything." He backed out the door.

Sterling removed the toasted ham and Swiss from the oven while I filled a thermos with coffee. Thomas put his coat back on, and stored his iPad in the inside pocket to shelter it from the storm.

"Is it safe to walk down to the marina?" I asked, handing him the stainless steel thermos.

Thomas shrugged. "I guess so. I'll watch for falling trees."

"That's not funny." I wrinkled my brow. "It's dangerous out there."

"I know, Jules. I'll be fine. It's like a couple hundred feet away."

Sterling wrapped two large pieces of sandwich into tinfoil and gave it to Thomas.

"Thanks," Thomas said, holding up the sandwich and thermos. "The Professor and I will need to take your official statements later, so don't go anywhere." Thomas grinned.

For the first time since I'd found Tony I felt a sense of relief. Thomas and the Professor were on the case. They could handle it from here. All I needed to do was bake, and deal with Carlos.

"Things could get interesting around here." Sterling gave me a knowing look as if he was reading my mind.

I played dumb. "What do you mean?"

Sterling nodded at the door. "I think you know exactly what I mean."

"Do you think it's that bad?" I winced.

"I think you have two guys who have it bad for you."

"Thomas and I are just friends." I could hear the hesitation in my voice.

"Sure you are." Sterling nodded, mocking approval. "I look at all of my friends like that."

I sighed. Was he right? Was Mom right? Could Thomas still be in love with me? No way. If anything he was in love with the idea of me. The old me. The high school me. I wasn't the same Juliet that I'd been in high school. So much had changed since then. I'd changed. I didn't want to go back.

"Thomas and I are just friends," I said again to Sterling. "*Friends*."

Sterling caught my eye and shook his head, giving me a look like he was trying to warn me about something.

"What? You don't believe me?"

"Believe what?" Carlos's thick Spanish accent sounded behind me.

I jumped.

Carlos stepped into the kitchen. "Who is your friend?"

"No, no, it's nothing." I turned to face him. "We were

just talking about my friend from high school, Thomas. I think I told you about him. He's a detective."

"I do not know that name," Carlos said.

"It doesn't matter." I waved him off. "He and the Professor made it up here. They're going to investigate Tony's murder. I was just telling Sterling that I'm so relieved to have them here."

Carlos nodded, but I noticed that he locked his eyes on Sterling, looking for some kind of reaction. Sterling busied himself with the sandwiches. "You want these in the oven, right, Jules?"

"Yep. Everything else should be ready to go." I smiled at him in thanks and walked to the stove to check on the stew. The pressure cooker beeped. I needed to wait a few minutes before taking off the lid, otherwise a blast of potentially dangerous steam would be released.

While I waited for the beef, I stacked bowls for the stew. Even though it would take a little longer, I wanted to serve the stew in individual bowls versus family style. It would ensure that everyone got a hot bowl of stew, and eliminate the risk of Lance's board members sloshing hot stew on each other.

"Can I help?" Carlos asked.

"You want to ladle the stew? If Sterling and I both serve it will go faster."

Carlos was already washing his hands. "Julieta, for you I will always ladle the stew." He blew me a kiss.

I knew that he was joking, but I had a sinking feeling that Carlos and Thomas meeting wasn't going to be a joking matter. The sooner Thomas and the Professor figured out what happened to Tony and could return to Ashland, the better.

Chapter Sixteen

Lunch was met with rave reviews by the board members. They polished off every last morsel of the toasted sandwiches and I literally had to scrape the bottom of the pot to dish up seconds of the stew. Apparently being snowed in with a dead body made people hungry.

I couldn't blame anyone. It was impossible to get Tony out of my head. Each time I came from the kitchen to restock the platter of cookies or fill water glasses, I caught sight of the Professor and Thomas interviewing each guest.

They had taken up residence by the fireplace. The Professor sat on a patched leather chair with one leg casually resting on his knee. He wore his signature tweed coat and jeans. With his reading glasses pressed against the bridge of his nose and pencil in his hand, he looked more like he was auditioning cast members versus interviewing potential murder suspects.

Thomas had pulled up a dining chair and took notes on his iPad while the Professor asked the questions. His style was completely different than the way most detectives were portrayed in movies and television. He was quiet, thoughtful, and sincere. He didn't pound the coffee table or invade anyone's personal space, but I knew from experience that his method worked. People felt at ease around him, and because of that, he was able to get them to open up.

When they finished with one of Lance's board members, I took the opportunity to bring them a plate of cookies and fresh mugs of coffee.

"Thank you, Juliet. This is exactly what we needed. A bit of sustenance." The Professor held up a cookie and gave me a nod of thanks. "Might we bother you for a moment of your time?"

"Sure." I sat on the couch. "How's it going?"

The Professor rubbed his beard. "Murder. It's a messy business. There's no way around it. Do you know what the Bard said about death?"

I shook my head. The Professor was notorious for his ability to quote Shakespeare.

" 'He that dies pays all debts.' "

"Meaning?"

"Meaning our job—" he nodded at Thomas—"is to figure out what debts Tony had to pay." He took a bite of the cookie. "Of course, unfortunately he paid the highest debt of them all—murder."

"Right." I grabbed a cookie, too. I'd been so busy cooking and baking that I hadn't taken time to eat myself. It's a bad habit, and one that Mom had been hounding me on. I'd dropped a few pounds since returning to Ashland. A few pounds that I didn't need to lose. Mom was worried that I was too thin. She'd been shoving extra pastries and cakes in front of me at every opportunity. Remember to eat lunch, I told myself as I bit into the double-chocolate cookie with cream cheese frosting. The rich chocolate dough had a tang from the sour cream and the cream cheese frosting gave the cookies a hint of sweetness.

"I know that Thomas has already spoken with you, but

alas, we're going to need you to go over every detail again. As you know when it comes to murder no stone can be left unturned."

I wiped cream cheese from my lip. "No problem."

"Let's start from the beginning then, shall we?" The Professor leaned back toward the fire. I replayed last night's events, and then explained how I discovered Tony's body this morning. Had it really just been this morning? This day felt endless and it wasn't anywhere near over.

When I finished the Professor rested his notebook on the coffee table. "I see."

What did he see? Nothing made sense to me.

Thomas cleared his throat. "I have a few things I need to follow up on, is this a good time?"

The Professor nodded.

Scrolling through his iPad, Thomas found the page he was looking for. "We interviewed Carlos." His voice sounded forced when he said "Carlos." "He said that he was with you in your cabin all night, is that correct?" Thomas stared at the iPad.

All night? Had Carlos lied to Thomas and the Professor? Why?

"Uh, he was with me most of the night," I replied.

Thomas perked up and gave the Professor a look I couldn't decipher. "I'm going to need you to elaborate. When exactly was Carlos with you last night?"

"Basically the whole night. He left to come grab a bottle of wine." I could feel heat rise in my cheeks. Why was I embarrassed to tell Thomas that my husband came down to get us a bottle of wine?

"And when was that?"

"I'm not sure. Sometime after midnight probably."

Thomas typed rapidly. "And when did he return to the cabin?"

"Well, I'm not exactly sure on that, either. I fell asleep."

"So for all you know, Carlos never returned to your cabin last night?" Thomas looked triumphant.

"No." I sat up on the couch. "That's not what I'm saying. I just don't know the exact time he came home because I fell asleep. He was there this morning."

"Hmm." Thomas tapped the screen. "So you're telling us that there are four or five hours where your husband's whereabouts are unknown?"

I wanted to punch him in the arm, and not for fun this time. "Thomas, what are you trying to say? Are you trying to imply that you think Carlos, my husband, who met Tony for the first time last night, killed him? Seriously?"

"Jules, this is a murder investigation. We have to follow through with every lead and establish alibis for everyone who was here when Tony was killed. That includes your ex-husband and you."

The fact that Thomas referred to Carlos as my "ex" wasn't lost on me. I thought about correcting him, but I had a feeling that would make things worse.

"You have to admit it is a little strange that your ex-husband showed up here and someone gets murdered a few hours later. He claims to have been with you, yet you've just informed us that he had plenty of time to kill Tony, and we have a witness who placed him here at the lodge last night."

"You have to be joking." My knee bounced on the floor. "What possible motive would Carlos have for killing Tony? He didn't even know him."

Thomas gave me a challenging look. "We have a number of witnesses who reported that the two of them had an altercation last night."

"It wasn't an altercation. Carlos stepped in and helped Lance. Tony was belligerent with everyone. Ask Lance or Mercury."

"We will." Thomas nodded. "However, we also heard that Tony was hitting on you and that Carlos threatened him if he continued."

I rolled my eyes. "Hardly. He told Tony to knock it off. That was it."

Thomas didn't look convinced. He typed something on his iPad.

I turned to the Professor. "This is crazy. There's no way Carlos had anything to do with Tony's death. No way."

The Professor gave me an apologetic stare. "I'm sure you're right, Juliet. I found Carlos to be . . ." He paused and searched for the right words. "Absolutely charming, but Thomas is right, we have to follow every lead at this early stage."

"Understood, but you're not going to find much by focusing on Carlos." I glanced behind me. Sterling had finished clearing the lunch dishes. The board members were regrouping for their afternoon session. "Did you need anything else from me? I should probably get back to work."

The Professor waited for Thomas. Thomas scrolled through his notes. "No. I think that's it for now, but Jules, be careful."

"Thanks." I couldn't keep the sarcasm from my voice. I stood and walked back to the kitchen without another word. How could Thomas think that Carlos had anything to do with this? I was fuming.

If I was being honest with myself one of the reasons I was so angry with Thomas was because he had rattled me. Where *was* Carlos last night? What did the two wine glasses I found on the island have to do with him? I wasn't lying to myself. Carlos was no killer. But he and I were working on rebuilding trust, and I didn't trust that he had told me the whole truth. He was lying to me about something. The question was what?

Chapter Seventeen

"How did it go out there?" Sterling asked. In the short time that I'd been gone he had managed to rinse and load the dishes, scrub the stockpot, and wipe down the counters.

"Don't ask."

"That bad?"

"Worse," I sighed.

Sterling walked to the oven and opened it. He removed two ceramic bowls with oven mitts and slid one in front of me.

"What's this?"

"Stew. I saved a bowl for each of us. You should eat something."

"You're worse than Mom, but thanks! Smart move. They were like vultures. We're going to have to make some extra snacks this afternoon."

"Your mom made me promise that I'd remind you to eat. Just doing my job." Sterling handed me a spoon.

The stew was rich in flavor, but I would have liked it to be a bit thicker. "It's kind of thin, isn't it?"

Sterling shrugged. "Tastes great to me."

"I guess I'm just a perfectionist when it comes to food, but the altitude is throwing everything off."

"What happened out there?" Sterling stirred his stew.

"Thomas grilled me about Carlos. He thinks *Carlos* is a suspect."

"What?"

"I'm serious. That was at least half of our conversation."

"No way."

"That's what I said." I wondered if I should tell Sterling about the fact that Carlos had left the cabin last night. As irritated as I was with Thomas he did have a reason to be suspicious. I decided against saying anything. We had enough to do, and I wanted to talk to Carlos on my own.

"They'll figure it out, Jules." Sterling sprinkled a pinch of salt on his stew. "Thomas is probably kind of freaked out that Carlos is here."

"Yep. You nailed it." I grinned. "On to other topics. Let's think about some hearty afternoon snacks. I was thinking of making an almond pastry. Do you want to make an antipasto tray? We can marinate veggies and then put out salami and cheeses."

"Sure. Just tell me what to do."

I emptied my bowl. Having food in my stomach helped me feel more settled. "Then we need to start on dinner prep. Everything is taking longer at high altitude so I want to make sure we have plenty of time."

Sterling added our bowls to the dishwasher and clicked it on. I walked him through the marinade recipe. With that under control, I creamed butter and sugar in the mixer for my almond bars. The bars bake in sheet pans and rise about an inch. Once they had cooled I would top them with a layer of almond frosting and chocolate glaze.

The scent of almond extract lifted my spirits as I whipped it and eggs into the batter. This weekend was turning into a disaster. Thomas might be jealous of Carlos, but I had to figure out what Carlos had been doing last night. I was worried that I wasn't going to like whatever I found out. He must have been sharing a late-night glass of wine with someone. But who? Why would he come all this way just to sneak around with someone else?

I sifted flour, baking soda, and a pinch of salt into the mixture and blended it together. Then I greased two large sheet pans and pressed the dough into them. The almond crust should only take about thirty minutes to bake. That would give me plenty of time to let it cool while I worked on the frosting. I wanted to serve snacks around three o'clock to give everyone time to get hungry for dinner again. Lance's entire agenda revolved around food.

The guests were probably going to be sick of seeing us by the time the weekend was over.

"Hey, can you taste this?" Sterling asked after I placed the sheet pans into the convection oven.

"It's what I do," I teased. The marinade he had whisked together consisted of white wine vinegar, olive oil, and a blend of spices. I dipped my pinky in. "It's good," I said, letting the taste circulate in my mouth. "Maybe just a touch more vinegar. I want the veggies to have a bite."

Sterling shook in two glugs. "Like that?"

I tasted it again, and handed him the bowl. "You try it. What do you think?"

One of the things I wanted to help Sterling with was developing his palate. He had a natural ability, but I knew that he didn't trust it yet.

He followed my example and stuck his pinky into the marinade. I waited while he closed his eyes and savored the taste. "Yeah, that's much better. It's zesty."

"Exactly!" I tasted it again. "Good job. Now you can add carrot sticks, celery, peppers—toss them completely and then stick them in the fridge. They can marinate for a couple hours."

"I'm on it."

With the almond bars baking and marinade finished, I turned my focus to dinner. Tonight I planned to go with a rustic Italian theme. For a starter, we would serve wood-fired garlic-butter breadsticks. Guests would have two options for their main course, a traditional lasagna with a red meat sauce and a vegetarian lasagna with a cream sauce. Dessert would be individual dark chocolate tarts garnished with fresh berries, and cream.

For a unique side dish, I wanted to teach Sterling how to braise green beans. Usually braising is reserved for rough cuts of meat, but I love using the slow-cooking method with vegetables.

I would make the pasta by hand. It's more time-consuming, but there's no comparison in terms of taste. Fresh pasta elevates a basic dish. It would give me a chance to use my pasta roller, and hopefully give my head a break from thinking about Tony's murder.

Pasta can be intimidating, but it shouldn't be. There's nothing simpler when it comes to the ingredients required—flour and water. Maybe a pinch of salt and a few eggs for Italian-style noodles, but otherwise it's as easy as combining flour and water. The difficulty comes in creating the right density for the dough. I call it finding the perfect hydration level. If a dough is too wet or dry, it's impossible to work with. I've spent years experimenting with different ratios of water to flour.

Then there's the issue of rolling out the noodles. If the noodles are too thin, they'll break. If they're too thick, they'll become a gummy gooey mess. It takes a little patience and finesse, but it's totally worth the effort.

To start, I measured flour and piled it onto the island. Then I made a hole in the center with my fingers, sweeping flour to the sides to create a volcano with a soft crater in the middle. Since we were going with an Italian theme I cracked eggs into the crater, and added two extra yolks. I've found that the addition of yolks gives the noodles a lovely satin texture.

Using a fork I began pushing the flour into the pool of eggs. There's debate among chefs about adding salt to the noodles versus adding it to the water. I like a hint of kosher salt in my pasta. The only caution is to avoid sea salt; it will ruin the silky-smooth texture of the dough. A sticky ball began to form as I forked the eggs and flour together.

At this stage in pasta making it becomes more of an art than a science. I determined how much more flour to add based on the feeling of the dough. Once it held together, I began using my bench knife to fold in more flour.

"That's quite the process," Sterling said, watching as I ditched the knife and started kneading the dough by hand. This is my favorite part of pasta making. I know some people dread the kneading process, but it's nearly impossible to overknead the dough.

"You want to give it a try?" I asked, rotating the dough and pressing my hands into it.

"I think I'll just watch this time."

"It's super easy. I'll keep working this for about ten minutes or so. I don't want to dry the dough out, especially with the thin air up here."

"How can you tell when it's done?" Sterling studied the dough.

"You want it to have nice elasticity." I pressed into the ball of dough with my finger. "It should be springy."

"What do you do with it when it's done? Stick it in the fridge?"

"No. Not unless you want gray noodles."

"Really?"

"Yeah, if you refrigerate the dough it will turn a grayish color. It doesn't affect the flavor, but, yuck!" I stuck out my tongue. "No one wants to eat gray noodles."

Sterling laughed. "Can you imagine serving Lance gray noodles?"

"He would flip." I dusted more flour onto the counter. "Once I finish kneading this, I'll wrap it in plastic and let it rest for a few hours. Then I'll teach you how to roll it, and get you started on the beans."

"Sounds like a plan," Sterling replied. The oven dinged, signaling that the almond bars were ready. He walked over to remove them from the oven. "Uh, Jules. We have a problem."

"What kind of problem?" I replied with my back to him.

"You better come look at this."

I brushed flour onto my apron and went to see what was wrong. My jaw dropped as I stared at the oven. The almond bars had risen to the size of a basketball. They were wedged between the oven racks.

"How did that happen?" I threw my hand over my mouth. "I've never seen anything like that before."

Sterling bent his head toward the oven. "How are we going to get that out of there?"

"That is crazy. It has to be the altitude." My mouth hung open as I gaped at the sight. I felt like we were in an episode of *I Love Lucy.* Mom used to love watching reruns of Lucy's antics in the kitchen when I was a kid. "What if you hold the bottom of the pan and I'll try to remove the oven rack?"

Sterling handed me two oven mitts. "Go for it."

It was impossible not to laugh as we tugged and twisted the humongous almond cookie bars from the oven. What a rookie mistake. I should have accounted for the altitude and adjusted my recipe. Thank goodness Carlos wasn't here. He would never let me live this down. Once we finally got it out, Sterling placed it on the counter. We both stood back and stared. Then we collapsed in another fit of laughter.

"That's insane. I should take a picture," Sterling said.

"I know." I laughed and shook my head. "The question is, can we salvage it?"

Sterling looked doubtful.

I racked my brain, trying to remember everything I could about high-altitude baking. "What if we stick it outside in the snow? The cold air might deflate it a bit."

"Where do you want me to put it?" Sterling asked.

"Um, somewhere where it won't get wet." I glanced out the window. "That might be hard. We can cover it in foil and you can stick it under the overhang. It's worth a shot, right? Otherwise we can make a new batch. This time I'll cut way down on the baking soda."

Sterling covered the monstrous mound with tinfoil. "I sort of hate to let it deflate. This is pretty awesome."

I shook my head as he walked away. I couldn't believe how much the altitude was impacting everything. For the remainder of the weekend, I needed to carefully review and adjust each recipe.

At that moment a loud explosion shook the kitchen. For a second I wondered what I'd done this time. Had I forgotten to turn off the pressure cooker? The lights flared and then cut out. Everything went dark.

Chapter Eighteen

The power was out. Excellent. As if cooking at high altitude wasn't enough of a challenge, now I was going to have to do it without electricity. What else could go wrong this weekend?

Everyone in the dining hall gasped. I heard Lance trying to calm them down. "Not to worry, it's just a tree, darlings. Just a big nasty tree."

Mercury had mentioned that the lodge had a generator. Hopefully she'd be able to get power restored to the lodge soon. In the meantime I needed to implement a backup plan. Since the stove was gas, we could manually light the burners and use them for our pasta sauce, the beans, and boiling the noodles. The pizza oven would have to be our primary source for baking.

I dug through the top drawer to find matches and lit the candles on the windowsill. Mercury had left us Mason jars with giant votive candles. I lit those as well and placed them strategically around the kitchen. Our biggest obstacle was going to be seeing in the dim kitchen.

The flaming candles and light from the brick oven gave the kitchen a romantic glow. I positioned one of the votives in front of me and reviewed the menu. It was doable. Except that using any of our kitchen equipment was out—mixing would have to be done by hand. And hopefully Mercury had a French press. We could boil water and make coffee in the French press. Otherwise guests were going to have to go without.

Sterling returned. "Uh, so the power's out."

"Yep." I held up the Mason jar. "Looks like we're going really old school this afternoon. How is it out there?"

"It's nuts. I've never seen that much snow."

"What's the vibe in the dining room?"

"Lance has it under control. He's playing up the drama factor, of course. But they've got tons of candles and the fire is going. They'll be fine. Mercury is running around outside with Gavin trying to get the generator working."

"Fingers crossed," I said.

"Well, if nothing else we'll have some really puffed-up cold almond pastry to give everyone."

"I like your attitude. That's something all good chefs need—a positive attitude and an ability to improvise."

I went into organization mode. It's a skill I perfected on the ship. Running an efficient kitchen requires quick thinking and delegation. "Keeping everything at temperature won't be an issue," I said. "We need to limit how often we open the fridge and freezer until we see if Mercury can get the generator working. Everything in there should be fine for a couple hours. We can always take stuff outside as needed, so I guess our focus is dinner." I handed him a list of ingredients for the pasta sauce. "You start prepping everything for the red sauce and I'll make the frosting for the almond bars—or hunks—or whatever we're going to call them."

Sterling and I navigated dinner prep in the candlelight. I melted chocolate on the stove and removed cream cheese and butter from the fridge. Getting it to room temperature, or even slightly warm, was going to be essential. Usually we whip it on high speed to give our frostings a light and creamy texture. My forearms were about to get a workout.

Mercury came in to check our progress. If I thought I was having a hard day, her day had to be a thousand times worse. Her pajama bottoms were damp with snow. Her hair was plastered to her forehead, and her cheeks looked windblown. "I'm not here with good news." She sounded dejected. "Gavin can't get the generator going. He's trying one more thing, but if it doesn't work it looks like we're going to be without power until a crew can get through."

"That's okay," I tried to reassure her. "We've got a plan. Guests might have to huddle together, but at least they'll be fed."

She gave me a half-smile. "That's good, but I'm worried about the cold. The fireplace is our only source of heat."

"We'll boil water for tea and hot chocolate. I saw that you have a stash of instant tea and packages of hot chocolate. We'll keep that supplied." Usually I'm not a fan of watery hot chocolate, but desperate times called for desperate measures. We didn't have enough burners or time to make our signature milky hot chocolate.

Mercury looked relieved. "That's a good idea. I'll ask Carlos to bring out a couple bottles of peppermint schnapps and Kahlúa. That should raise everyone's spirits."

"Definitely." I checked the clock on the wall. It must be battery operated because its second hand clicked in a steady rhythm. "It'll be happy hour soon. Crack open some bottles of wine, we'll have warm drinks, warm food, and a cheery fire. It'll be fine."

"I appreciate the pep talk." Mercury actually smiled.

"Do you have a French press? If you do, we'll get coffee steeping, too."

Mercury walked to the far wall of cupboards and bent down on her knees. She removed a toaster and stuck her head into the cupboard. "That's weird," she said, holding up an empty bottle of wine. "How did that get in here?"

"No idea." I shook my head.

She looked puzzled. "Why would someone put an empty bottle in here?"

I didn't respond. The first thought that flashed in my mind was that someone who had a drinking problem probably stashed it in there. I knew Mercury's husband usually ran the kitchen. Could he have an addiction?

Mercury reached back into the cupboard and found the French press. She pushed to her feet and handed it to me. "This isn't yours, is it?" She held the empty wine bottle in her other hand.

"Nope." I caught Sterling's eye. He grimaced.

Sterling had been in recovery for a couple of years after spending time on the streets in Northern California. I knew there was no way it was his, either. Once he turned his life around, he said he never looked back. He told me he didn't even like the taste of alcohol anymore. I could tell by his expression that he was thinking the same thing that I was—whoever stashed the empty wine bottle probably had a reason they were hiding it.

Mercury studied the label. "This is one of our most expensive bottles. It's a private reserve. This is a hundred-and-fifty-dollar bottle of wine."

She tucked the empty bottle under her arm, and sighed. "Okay, I have to go check on whether or not Gavin has made any progress with the generator. Let me know if there's anything else you need." She started toward the door, paused, and looked back at both of us. "Thank you for being so professional and calm. I really do appreciate it."

"This place gets weirder and weirder." Sterling raised one eyebrow after Mercury left. "Who do you think is drinking in secret?"

"I don't know. Maybe Mercury's husband? He's usually the one running the show back here, but who knows. It seems like there's been a steady stream of people in and out of the kitchen since we've been here."

As I spoke I thought about finding the two used wine glasses on the island this morning. Could whoever had been here last night shared that bottle of wine? Did Carlos have anything to do with the empty bottle of expensive wine? He was definitely a wine connoisseur and appreciated a good bottle, but he would never drink someone else's reserve wine without permission. Would he?

I had to stop second-guessing Carlos, and more importantly myself.

Sterling had diced onions, garlic, and fresh basil for the tomato sauce. He placed them in ramekins next to the stove. "These are ready to go. You want me to start on something else, or should I get coffee going?"

"Why don't you do coffee and water for tea and hot chocolate. I'll start the sauce as soon as I finish the frosting." I returned to the stove and added cubes of butter into a saucepan. Could the wine bottle and glasses have anything to do with Tony's murder? I hadn't mentioned them to Thomas and the Professor, but I probably should. It might be a stretch, but what if whoever killed him plotted how to do it first? What if two people were responsible for his murder? Maybe they had a drink before they trekked down to the marina. Or, maybe they had a celebratory drink after they finished the deed. I shuddered at the thought.

"Are you getting cold?" Sterling asked. He lit the burner next to mine and placed a tea kettle on it.

"Yeah, it's starting to cool off in here, isn't it?" That wasn't a lie. The temperature had dropped since we lost power. I didn't want to tell Sterling that my mind was running wild scenarios about Tony's death.

"Do you want my coat?" Sterling asked.

"No. I'll be fine. I just need to keep moving." I danced back and forth on my feet to prove my point.

"Should I go check on the almond bars?"

I stirred the molten chocolate then lifted the spoon a few inches above the saucepan. The glossy liquid poured in a thin stream. I stuck my pinky in for a taste. The buttery chocolate melted in my mouth. "That would be great. This is ready. Let's see if we can get creative and salvage something."

Sterling didn't bother to put on a coat. He pulled up his hoodie and left to brave the elements once again.

"Hello?" a timid voice called.

"Come on in."

"Sorry to bother you," Whitney said. She wore a fur-lined parka and matching gloves. "Oh, it's much warmer in here. You're lucky."

"Is it cold in the dining room?" I set the spoon on the stove, and removed the chocolate glaze from the heat.

"Lance had us all get our coats," she said, glancing around the room as if she were looking for something.

"Well, we're going to bring out hot chocolate and tea. Hopefully that will help keep everyone's spirits up and keep your hands toasty."

Whitney didn't make eye contact. "Good," she said, not paying any attention to me. "Lance wanted me to check."

"Did you need something else?"

"Huh?" She seemed to register that I was in the room. "No. Not really. I misplaced something and wondered if

I left it in here." Her eyes lingered on the cupboard where
Mercury found the empty bottle of wine.

"Your tablet?" I asked. This was the first time all
weekend I'd seen Whitney without her tablet clutched
under her arm.

"What? Oh, my tablet. No, it finally died. Not that it
mattered. I couldn't connect to the Internet anyway. I
even walked down to the lake early this morning to see
if I could get a signal down there. Mercury said sometimes that works."

"You were at the lake this morning?" I remembered
seeing a flash of movement on my way to the marina. Had
I seen Whitney?

She scrunched her curls. "Uh, just for a couple minutes. I couldn't get a signal so I gave up. It was too cold."

"Feel free to look around if you want." I walked to the
island and unwrapped blocks of cream cheese.

She started to back out of the kitchen, her eyes still
glued to the cupboard.

"Really, I don't mind. You're welcome to check anywhere you need." I was hoping she'd take me up on my
offer. I wanted to watch her. Was she really so desperate
for cell service that she had braved blizzard conditions,
or was her trip to the lake connected to Tony's murder?

"Uh, well, as long as I won't be in your way." She
trailed off as she shuffled toward the cupboards in her
Uggs.

"Nope. Not at all. Go for it." I began creaming the
cheese and butter together. I didn't want Whitney to think
that I was watching her, so I kept my eyes focused on the
bowl.

She checked a few cupboards. I got the sense that she
wasn't being thorough because she barely opened them
and then quickly shut each one. After checking three or
four of the cupboards near the brick oven, she headed for

the cupboard that had held the wine bottle. She sank to her knees and removed the toaster. Aha! My instincts were right.

I added confectioners' sugar and a dash of almond extract to the butter and cream cheese. My arm needed a break from stirring.

"You didn't happen to move anything from this cupboard by chance?" Whitney asked from her knees. Her face was neutral, but her eyes gave away her distress. They darted from side to side.

"What are you looking for?" I deliberately didn't answer her question.

Before she could respond, Sterling came back into the kitchen with a deflated tray of almond bars. "It worked!"

Whitney scrambled to her feet.

"Hey." Sterling gave her a look of surprise. "I didn't see you down there."

"Sorry. I better get back out there." Whitney scooted past Sterling without another word.

Drat. I was hoping that she would tell me what she had been doing in here last night with an expensive bottle of wine and two glasses. Whitney had to have been the one who hid the bottle, but why? Could she have arranged a secret meeting with Tony? Over a glass of wine, Jules? I asked myself. I wasn't sure what Whitney's connection was to Tony's murder, but I knew I had to find out who she met last night and what she was doing on the lake.

Chapter Nineteen

The almond bars were ice-cold and had deflated to an acceptable four inches. I cut out a corner from the tray and popped it into my mouth. The texture wasn't exactly as I wanted it, but it had a decent crunch. I figured with a generous layer of almond cream cheese frosting and the chocolate glaze, they would be fine.

Sterling arranged packets of tea and hot chocolate in a basket.

"Any word on the generator?" I asked, giving the frosting one more good whip.

"No, but you'll be happy to know that Thomas is in the bar grilling Carlos."

"Perfect." I grabbed a stainless steel pastry spatula and began spreading the frosting on the almond bars. It was hard to silence the perfectionist in me. For mixing by hand, the frosting was perfectly acceptable. I was pretty sure that Lance and his guests wouldn't know the difference. It had a lovely subtle almond flavor and I had managed to whip out any lumps. The industrial mixer would have given it an airier texture.

Let it go, Jules, I told myself as I whisked the chocolate glaze and drizzled it over the top. You're baking at high altitude and without power.

Sterling delivered steaming carafes of water and the basket of teas to the dining room and then came back for the tray of antipasto. I sliced the bars into squares and fanned them onto a glass platter. They actually looked decent enough to serve.

Thomas came in just as I was about to hand the platter to Sterling. "Hold up, let me get my hands on one of these," Thomas said, giving me a sheepish grin as he snagged a bar.

"They're not my best. Don't hold it against me. We're working under very unusual circumstances."

He held the bar in front of a candle. "Looks pretty good to me." He took a giant bite, swallowing half of the bar. "Mmm-hmm," Thomas mumbled. "Yep. These are pretty terrible. I should probably have another." He grabbed another bar.

"Take those to the guests before Mr. No Palate here eats them all," I said to Sterling.

Thomas pretended to be hurt. "No palate?" he said with a mouth full of almond bar. "That's not fair."

"Who has no palate?" Carlos entered the kitchen.

"I was teasing Thomas," I replied, nodding to the tray in Sterling's arms. "Those aren't my best effort. The altitude is throwing everything off."

Carlos picked a bar from the tray. He carefully broke a piece off it. "These rose too high, yes?"

"Yep."

He tasted the almond bar. Watching him savor the tiny morsel was like a sensory experience. He closed his eyes and inhaled through his nose while he chewed. No one would accuse Carlos of not having a developed palate.

Thomas rolled his eyes and started on his second bar. "If you ask me, Jules, I think these are great."

Carlos finally swallowed his tasting bite. "The flavor is good, yes, but I think too much baking soda, no?"

"Exactly. Thank you," I replied.

Sterling cleared his throat. "Should I take these out now?" He stood waiting by the door.

"Yeah, yeah. Go." I motioned him forward.

Thomas shook his head. "I don't know what you're talking about with baking soda. I think these are awesome. Everything you make is awesome, Jules." His voice caught a little.

This was it—Thomas and Carlos in the same room. The contrast between them was staggering. Thomas with his boyish face, light eyes, and blond hair looked like an all-American football star. Carlos oozed sexiness with his olive skin, dark hair, and piercing eyes.

"Ha! I wish." I laughed, trying to break the tension. "I've had my fair share of disasters over the years, but this one takes the cake."

Carlos moved to be closer to me. Thomas frowned and inched closer to the island to make room for him. "This is what it means to be a chef." He held up the almond bar. "Sometimes things do not go our way, but we must improvise." His eyes twinkled. "You improvised well, Julieta. I like the frosting and glaze."

I noticed Thomas flinch when Carlos called me Julieta. No disaster in the kitchen compared to being sandwiched between these two.

"Did either of you need something?"

Thomas arched his shoulders back. "No, I wanted to check on you. See how you were holding up."

"Me, too." Carlos slipped his arm around my waist.

"Actually." Thomas reached for his iPad. "I have a few details regarding the case that I'd like to go over with you."

"Okay." I waited.

Thomas stared at Carlos. "In private."

"Ah yes, police business." Carlos pursed his lips. "I

will leave you for now, but I will be back soon?" He kissed the top of my head before he left.

"What's going on?" I asked Thomas. "Do you care if I work while we talk? Everything is taking so much longer than I expected."

"No, do whatever you need to do. Can I help?"

I walked to the sink and tossed him a soapy sponge. "Sure, you can wipe down the island while I get the pasta maker prepped."

Thomas caught the sponge and grinned. "At your service, chef."

"So what's the scoop?" I asked.

Thomas glanced behind him to make sure we were alone. We were. I could hear Lance talking to Sterling out in the dining hall. Thomas lowered his voice anyway. "I thought you might want to know that we think that we've determined cause of death."

"Really?" I tried to keep my voice nonchalant as I lugged the pasta maker onto the island.

"Yep. Gunshot."

"Tony was shot?"

Thomas nodded and scrubbed chocolate from the far side of the island top. "From the looks of the site of entry, the Professor thinks it was probably a hunting rifle of some kind."

"Where was he shot?" Granted I hadn't stayed around to get a better look, but I didn't remember seeing a bullet wound or even any blood.

"He was shot from behind."

That made sense. I'd seen his face, but not the rest of his body.

"So someone shot him and then put him in the freezer?"

"As far as we can tell, yeah." Thomas walked to the sink. "We'll need confirmation from the coroner of course, but he was already dead when he was placed in the freezer."

I was surprised that Thomas was sharing so much information with me. After I'd helped him when a customer was murdered at Torte, he had backed off from wanting me involved in any police investigations.

"Whoever killed him had to be a man, right?" I reached into the flour canister and sprinkled flour onto the crank. The pasta maker does best when liberally floured. I have a strict routine that I follow: flour, crank, roll, repeat.

"The Professor doesn't want to rule anyone out at this point, but yeah—lifting the body would take some serious strength, that's for sure. Although, like the Professor says, people can do amazing things when under stress. Your fight-or-flight automatic response kicks in, and who knows."

I twisted the crank with my hand to make sure it was nice and smooth. There are automatic pasta machines these days, but I prefer the old method of using the hand crank.

"Do you have any suspects in mind?" I asked. I considered telling him about the hidden wine bottle and Whitney.

"Carlos is pretty strong, isn't he?" Thomas folded his arms across his chest.

"We're not going to do this again, are we? Carlos is not a killer."

"Jules, you have to look at it from my perspective. I have to check and double-check everyone's alibi. Carlos is a stranger. Think about it, he shows up and someone is dead. Conveniently, Carlos has taken over Tony's job here. I'd say that gives him motive."

"You have to be kidding me!" I couldn't stop myself from shouting.

Thomas raised his hands in the air. "Calm down. Just hear me out. I know you haven't wanted to talk about whatever happened between you and Carlos since you returned home. Everyone in town is cool about that. No one cares, but Jules, I have to ask you, do you really know Carlos?"

I cut him off. "Of course I know Carlos! He's my husband."

"Estranged husband." Thomas twisted his head to the side and wrinkled his mouth.

"Thomas, that's not fair. What happened between Carlos and me is just that—between us. It has nothing to do with anyone here, and I know for a fact that there is no possible way that Carlos killed Tony."

Thomas scrunched his brow. "Maybe, but you understand why we can't rule him out, don't you?"

"No!" I exhaled. "Carlos is a professionally trained chef. He's one of the best chefs in the cruise industry. He's highly sought after. Ask him about all the offers he's received to work for different cruise lines." I tried to steady my breathing. "You're telling me that a head chef for one of the biggest cruise lines in the world would come up to Lake of the Woods in the middle of the Oregon forest and kill a bartender for his job? That's ludicrous. That is seriously the most ridiculous thing I've ever heard you say."

I knew immediately I'd gone too far. Thomas swallowed and looked at his feet.

"Look, I'm sorry," I said. "I didn't mean to be rude, it's just that I know Carlos, and I know he's not a killer."

Thomas shrugged. "I hope you're right. You probably are, but I want you to be careful."

I wanted to tell him that the only danger I was in around Carlos was the danger of losing my heart.

"The Professor asked if you would be willing to come

down to the crime scene and answer a few questions for him. He said that if it's too upsetting for you, you don't have to, but if you're up for it he'd like to walk through exactly where you went this morning."

"Okay." I wiped my hands on a dishtowel. "I can do that."

"What about your dinner prep?"

"The noodles can wait. Let me check in with Sterling and get him started on a couple things, then I'll head down there."

Thomas agreed. "I'll wait out by the fireplace. The Professor asked me to escort you." He turned and left the kitchen.

I took a moment to gather my thoughts and regulate my breathing before going to get Sterling. How could Thomas possibly consider Carlos a suspect? Was he acting this way because he was jealous? It wasn't like Thomas to have such an outlandish theory. I knew one thing for sure; I had to get to the bottom of the empty wine bottle and glasses. I just had a feeling it would point me in the right direction. As soon as I finished with the Professor, I had to find Carlos and figure out what he knew.

Chapter Twenty

The arctic air took my breath away as I followed Thomas to the marina. After a few minutes of being lashed by the wind, I was nostalgic for the chilly kitchen. Thomas kept a tight hold on my arm as we trudged through the wet snow. I couldn't believe how much snow had fallen since this morning. The resort was completely enveloped in the storm. Snow blew in every direction, making it nearly impossible to tell where the ground ended and the sky began.

"Do you know where you're going?" I shouted to Thomas.

I couldn't hear his response over the howling wind, but he yanked me onward.

Everything seemed to slow, as we finally made it to the marina. He led me onto the porch and past the chest freezer. I knew that Tony's body was still inside. I turned my head and stared out into the blinding white snow as we walked past.

"Are you sure you're okay to do this, Jules?" Thomas sounded concerned. "Like I said, the Professor said it wasn't necessary, only if you were up for it."

"I'm fine. I'm up for it. Let's get it over with." I hurried inside the marina. The power was out here, too. It made the space feel even creepier. Maybe I wasn't up for this. What was I thinking?

"Ah, Juliet," the Professor greeted me from the fishing counter. He stood next to Gavin Allen. They both held LED lanterns in their hands. "Thank you for coming down. I hope it's not too much trouble?"

"Not at all," I lied.

The Professor nodded. "That will be all for the moment, Mr. Allen. I do thank you for your time."

Gavin gave him a two-fingered salute and tromped past Thomas and me. I caught a whiff of WD-40. "I'm going to give that damn generator one more shot," he grumbled. "Everything around this place is fallin' apart."

The resort seemed well maintained to me. It certainly wasn't as luxurious as a cruise ship, but people came to Lake of the Woods seeking a retreat from the modern world. That's why Lance chose this place.

"Juliet." The Professor raised his lantern. It cast a halo on the wall behind him where dozens of hunting rifles and fishing poles hung on a wooden pegboard. "Did Thomas explain what I'd like you to do?"

I nodded. "You want to go back over the crime scene, right?"

"Indeed. It would be most helpful." He eyed me carefully. "As long as it's not too distressing for you."

"It's not high on my list of things that I want to do, but if it will help the investigation, I'm fine."

The Professor addressed Thomas. "If you will be so kind as to hold this." He pressed the lantern into Thomas's hands. "Hopefully this experiment will shed some light onto our investigation. If you'll pardon my pun."

Thomas led the way outside. The Professor had me show him which direction I'd come from and the exact path that I'd taken this morning.

"You're quite sure that you didn't see or hear anything when you arrived on the scene?" he asked.

I paused and retraced my steps. My sole focus had been finding the sausages. I wasn't expecting to discover a body. "I don't think so," I replied.

"That's fine. Quite fine, actually. And once you came inside, could you be so kind as to show us exactly where you went?" The Professor motioned to the marina. "Take your time."

I led them back inside. We re-created my path from earlier. I explained how I had searched for the freezer. I took them to the pizza shop and the closed-up kitchen.

"Do you notice anything different?" the Professor asked, while Thomas positioned the lantern to illuminate the room. "Anything that's been moved or out of place?"

Was there anything missing? I racked my brain. Why hadn't I paid closer attention this morning?

I felt like there was something I was missing. I just couldn't place what it was.

"Take your time," the Professor said in a reassuring voice.

It was difficult to see in the dusky light, even with Thomas moving the lantern across the wall. The pizza kitchen looked like I remembered it—still untouched. "Can we go back to the shop for a minute?" I asked.

"Of course." The Professor stepped to the side to let me take the lead.

He and Thomas waited silently while I scanned the shelves. There were rows of chips, gummy candies, fishing tackles, and bait. I asked Thomas to shine the light behind the counter. Everything seemed to be as I remembered it—the chalkboard with the ice-fishing report and rental rates for gear.

My eyes lingered on the gun rack. That was it! There

was a gun in each row. This morning one of the guns was missing. Could that be the murder weapon? Had someone shot Tony and then come back and replaced the gun?

"The guns—I think the guns are different," I said to the Professor, pointing at the rack. "I'm not positive, but I think one of them was missing this morning. I'm pretty sure the top space was empty."

Something smacked the side of the building. We all jumped.

"That was a big branch," Thomas said, craning his neck toward where the sound came from. "Doesn't look like it came through the roof at least."

" 'Blow, winds, and crack your cheeks! Rage. blow!' " The Professor smiled. *"King Lear."*

"Did King Lear enjoy the blowing wind and cracking cheeks?" I asked.

He chuckled. "Ah, now that would be an entertaining debate, wouldn't it?"

I wasn't sure. I had asked the question in earnest. I had had enough of blowing, raging wind to last another ten years.

"You have been most helpful and perceptive, Juliet," he continued. "Yes, quite perceptive, indeed." He moved behind the counter. "Shall we have a closer look?"

Thomas held the lantern above his head.

The Professor pointed to the top of the rack with his pencil. "You believe this gun wasn't here this morning, correct?"

I grimaced. "I think so, but I'm not positive. I remember noticing the guns this morning because of that sign." I pointed to the chalkboard. "It looks like the words 'for rent' are pointing at the guns. It made me pause when I saw it, I don't think you can rent guns for hunting, can you?"

"No. You are quite correct on that."

"That's what I figured, and when I looked closely at the sign I realized the rental was referring to fishing poles not guns. But then I wondered why there were so many guns hanging up there, and if they're real."

"Oh, they're real," Thomas interjected.

"Can you bring the light this way, please?" The Professor motioned Thomas closer. "Is there anything else different or out of place?" he asked me.

I felt like I was taking a quiz and not doing well. "No," I said, shaking my head.

He tucked his pencil behind his ear. "Thomas, you know what to do. I'll escort Juliet back to the lodge."

What did he mean by that?

"Shall we?" He offered me his hand.

I wasn't looking forward to going back into the blowing snow, but if it meant leaving the marina, it was worth it. The Professor guided me outside. Right away we discovered the cause of the crash we'd heard inside. A ten-foot-long tree limb had fallen onto the side of the marina.

"It's crazy out here," I said to the Professor.

"Yes, this is one of the worst storms to blow in for a while." He stepped over another fallen branch.

"Can I ask you something?" I had to shout a little over the wind.

"Of course." He paused.

I wanted to keep moving. Branches littered the ground. I didn't want another one to snap over our heads. "It's about Thomas."

The Professor gave me half a nod.

"He seems to think that Carlos had something to do with Tony's death." I waited to see how the Professor would respond.

His face was passive.

"There's no way that Carlos had anything to do with Tony's death," I continued. "You know that, right?"

"Thomas is a thorough investigator. He takes to heart what I believe Euripides said: 'Leave no stone unturned.' "

"I know that he's doing his job, but I wonder if . . ." I trailed off.

The Professor met my eyes. "You wonder if?"

"Nothing. Forget it." I didn't want to tell him that I thought Thomas was jealous.

"Juliet, as the Bard always says, 'Truth will come to light.' That's our job." He looked to the sky. "Shall we continue?"

I trudged behind him, stepping over debris from the storm and trying to shield my face from the snow.

"So do you think Tony was killed with one of the hunting rifles?" I asked. Maybe I would have better luck asking the Professor general questions about the investigation.

"Perhaps."

"Who do you think could have lifted him?"

"That is the question, isn't it?"

The Professor was tight-lipped. I wasn't going to get anything out of him. We continued toward the lodge. When we arrived on the porch, he stopped. "Before we go inside, there's something else I want to speak with you about." His face turned serious.

"Okay." I ducked under the overhang, out of the direct wind.

"It's about your mother."

"What about Mom?"

"Have you spoken with her recently?"

"I speak to her every day."

He cleared his throat. "Of course. I mean about us."

I wasn't sure how to respond. Mom and I had talked about her relationship with the Professor. I knew that she was happy to have found companionship, and had been enjoying their time together.

"What about you?"

He shuffled his feet, brushing snow into a circle. "Well, I wondered if she had mentioned anything." I'd never seen the Professor act nervous before. He was usually so composed.

"Mentioned anything about . . . ?"

"Us."

I had to hold back a smile. The Professor was smitten with Mom. "I know that she's really enjoying spending time with you."

He looked slightly relieved, but I could tell he was waiting for me to say more.

"She had a great time on the wine-tasting trip you took a while ago."

Wooden slats came into view under his feet, from where he'd been kicking snow. "Did she say anything else?"

I wanted to joke and ask him whether he wanted me to pass her a note when we got home. "Nothing specific, why?"

"I've been considering asking her an important question and I'm not sure how she will respond."

A serious question. Was he talking about proposing?

"Are you thinking of asking her to get married?" I couldn't keep the shock from my voice. The Professor and Mom had only been dating—at least officially— since I'd been home. Marriage already?

He coughed. "I would like to ask your mother for her hand." He looked at me, as if to gauge my reaction. "Eventually, of course."

"Does she know?"

"No. We haven't discussed anything as of yet. I'd appreciate it if you would be discreet."

"Of course." I couldn't believe he was telling me this.

"Well, in that case, shall we go inside? Your lips are turning blue."

They probably were blue from the shock of the Professor's words. He wanted to marry Mom. I wasn't expecting that news. How would she react? They hadn't discussed it. I wondered if I should find a way to hint around the subject, or if it was better not to say anything at all. After Dad died, Mom had been on her own for so many years, especially after I left for culinary school. I was thrilled that she had found happiness again. But marriage—I wasn't sure. Did she even want to get married again? I was going to have to tread carefully.

Chapter Twenty-one

I returned to the kitchen shivering and in a daze. The Professor and Mom getting married. On one hand I couldn't imagine Mom marrying anyone new, and on the other hand visions of creating a custom wedding cake flashed through my head.

"Is everything okay, Jules?" Sterling asked. "You look kind of out of it."

Focus, Jules, I told myself. Worrying about Mom and the Professor could wait. "I'm fine," I said, heading for the sink. "Seeing the crime scene again rattled me a little, that's all. How are things going in here?"

Sterling lifted a pot of water. "It's taking about three hundred years to get this to boil."

"It's the altitude." I dried my hands on a towel and reached for my apron. How long had I been gone? The clock read four o'clock. About thirty minutes. "How long have you had it going?"

"The entire time you were at the marina. On high and it's barely starting to boil." He shot his thumb toward the dining hall. "They went through everything I took out there. I keep telling Lance that more water is on the way, but it's taking forever. I don't know how we're going to get the noodles done and restock the tea."

"We can't catch a break this weekend, can we?" I looked at the slow rolling boil Sterling had going. "That's fine for drinks. Why don't you fill the kettles with this one, and I'll get more going right away for the noodles. We're just going to have to do the best we can."

All of a sudden the lights flashed and the sound of electricity hummed. A cheer erupted in the dining room. Gavin must have fixed the generator. The power was back on.

Sterling raised his hand in a high five.

I hit his hand. "All right. I spoke too soon. Maybe we can catch a break after all. New plan. Nuke water for drinks in the microwave, and let's keep this going for noodles."

"You got it."

Speaking of noodles, I needed to start rolling the dough. I had a new appreciation for overhead lights as I dusted my hands in flour. Thank goodness Gavin had fixed the generator. Daylight was fading fast. His timing couldn't have been better. The oven beeped, signaling it had power again.

We still had the altitude to deal with, but at least we had a fully operational kitchen. "Can you turn the oven up to four hundred and twenty-five?" I asked Sterling, my hands coated in flour. "Let's try cranking the temperature up. I remember from culinary school that high-altitude ovens run twenty-five to fifty degrees hotter."

He stuck a pitcher of water in the microwave and turned on the oven. "What's next?"

"I'll roll out the lasagna noodles first, then we can start layering the pans." I unwrapped one ball of dough and checked the consistency. It was drier than I had hoped. While I cranked a piece of it through the pasta maker, I couldn't stop thinking about Mom and the

Professor. It was a welcome distraction from the matters at hand. We could host the wedding at Torte. I imagined stringing twinkle lights and hanging paper lanterns from the ceiling. We could drape the front counter with flower garlands, and decorate each table with beautiful arrangements.

I loved weddings. Carlos and I got married on a whim. We were docked in France for a few days. One evening in a hidden alley café, we lingered over a bottle of wine. We were the only couple left in the charming old-world restaurant. I'll never forget the smell of musty old bricks, when Carlos reached across the table and massaged my hand.

"Julieta, will you marry me?" He locked his eyes on mine.

The intensity of his gaze took my breath away. I laughed it off at first. "Stop teasing."

"I do not tease, *querida*. You are so beautiful tonight. The candlelight shimmers like gold in your hair."

I remember his gentle caresses and the look of longing in his eyes. "You're serious?"

A huge smile spread across his face. "Tomorrow you will marry me, yes?"

"Tomorrow?"

"*Sí,* tomorrow." He waited for my response with bright eager eyes.

"I will," I replied without even thinking. "Yes! I will."

He stood and pulled my face to his across the table. The waiter and chef applauded as we kissed. A celebratory bottle of champagne was delivered to the table. We shared a toast with the staff. The combination of wine and bubbly champagne went to my head. Carlos had to steady me as we stumbled back to the ship.

The next morning when I woke, I had a pulsing

headache from the champagne. Carlos was gone. A note sat propped on my bedside table with a single red rose in a vase.

"Today is the first day of the rest of our lives together, Julieta. You are so beautiful when you sleep. I will return soon. Love, Carlos." He'd arranged coffee and breakfast to be delivered to our room.

We both had a stretch of three days off together. I felt like a queen, sipping coffee in our tiny bedroom. As promised, Carlos returned late in the morning with an armful of packages.

"Good morning, how did you sleep?" He kissed my forehead. His eyes twinkled with delight as he placed the packages on the foot of the bed. "I have some surprises for you."

"What have you been up to?" I said, sitting up.

"It is your wedding day. I must make it special for my bride." He riffled through one of the bags until he found what he was looking for. I knew immediately from the size of the jewelry box what must be inside.

Was this really happening? I wanted to pinch myself to make sure I wasn't dreaming, but I was worried that if I did I might wake up.

Carlos came to the side of the bed, and dropped to his knee. He extended the small gold box. "Julieta, will you marry me?"

I gulped back tears, as I opened the box. Inside was the most breathtaking ring that I'd ever seen. A cushion-cut brilliant diamond was framed in a delicate halo of dainty diamonds on a vintage band.

"Carlos—how did you?" I couldn't form words.

He smiled broadly. "I have been saving up for this moment. Do you like it?"

I removed it from the box and held it in front of me. "It's the most beautiful ring I've ever seen. I love it."

Placing his hand over mine, he turned the ring so that it reflected the light. "I had it engraved, look."

Inside the band it read, "J and C. Love at Sea."

I couldn't contain my joy. Tears spilled from my eyes, as Carlos slipped the ring onto my finger. It fit perfectly.

He held my hand in his as he kissed my tears of joy away. "It is perfect on you, yes?"

"Yes." I grinned.

Leaning in, he kissed me soft and slow. I could taste my salty tears mixed in. This was the happiest day of my life. After a moment, he released me and jumped to his feet. He clapped his hands together. "Wait, I have more surprises for you."

I wondered how long I'd slept in. Carlos must have perused every shop in Marseilles. He lavished me with gifts. There were a pair of strappy satin sandals, shimmering brushed-gold earrings and a matching necklace, and a knee-length ivory halter dress.

"How did you do all this?"

"Do you like it?" He looked unsure. "I think the dress will look perfect with your skin and hair."

"I love it. I love all of it." I kissed him again. "I just can't believe you did all this so fast."

"No, not so fast. I have been planning for a while, you see."

Carlos was a romantic at heart. He often surprised me with a chocolate on my pillow or a special meal that he'd bring to our room after all the guests on the ship were fast asleep, but nothing compared to our wedding day. He had worked out every detail. We were married in the afternoon by the ship's captain. Our friends gathered on the deck to watch us exchange vows.

The ceremony was simple and sweet. I held a bouquet of ivory roses. Carlos wore a matching suit. I remember looking out onto the vibrant blue Mediterranean sea and thinking how his eyes reflected the color. The city of Marseilles with its white sand beaches and red rooftops sat in the background. Our friends joined us at a hillside café for dinner and dancing. It was a magical, surreal evening. I'd never felt more beautiful or alive. The only thing missing was Mom.

Everything happened so quickly, I didn't even have a chance to call her to tell her the news until the next day. She sounded slightly nostalgic when I said, "Can you believe it, Mom? I'm married!"

"I'm so happy for you, darling," she said, an ocean away. I knew that she was, but I couldn't tell if she was holding back tears. I was so consumed with my own happiness. We didn't have a chance to talk very long. Carlos had planned a quick honeymoon. The ship was due to depart in two days. He rented a cottage on the cliffside overlooking the sea. I promised Mom I would call her when we set sail again.

Carlos and I spent two blissful days listening to the sound of waves crashing on shore and watching fishing boats bob along the sea. The world looked completely different and so much more beautiful in his arms. He pampered me for two languid days. I sipped strong espresso under the French sun while he ran to the patisserie for chocolate croissants. We swam in the salty surf and blended in with tourists in the busy open-air markets. After filling canvas bags with bread, wine, cheese, fish, and handpicked farm vegetables, we would walk back to our cottage wrapped in each other's arms.

I never wanted to leave. We daydreamed about buying a rundown shop in the village and turning it into our own restaurant. Carlos could cook, I would bake, and we'd spend our free time with our feet in the Mediterranean Sea. Alas, our real lives beckoned. Our ship was setting sail, so we waved au revoir to our little cottage on the cliff and promised we'd find our way back someday soon.

"Jules, did you hear me?" Sterling's voice shook me from the happy memory.

"What's that? Sorry." I realized my hand was still turning the crank. The pasta machine was empty.

"I asked what you want me to do next," he said, staring at me. "Are you okay, Jules?"

"Yeah. This day is getting to me, that's all. I'm ready to be done."

"Tell me what you need me to do, I've got this. If you need to go take a break, it's cool."

I smiled. How had Mom and I gotten so lucky with our staff at Torte? "I appreciate it. I really do, but we're almost done. I can hang in a little longer." Time for me to get into chef mode. "How's the sauce coming?"

"Pretty good. You should taste it, though." Sterling opened a drawer and took out a spoon. He scooped sauce on the spoon and walked it over to me. The acidic tomatoes had a nice bite. We had added a trio of meats—beef, lamb, and Italian sausage. I like the density of using more than one meat. The combination gave the sauce a rich, hearty flavor. "It's good," I said to Sterling. "Hit it with a pinch more basil and then go ahead and spread a thin layer on the bottom of the pans."

He added chopped basil and gave the sauce one final stir. Then he brought the pans to the island. While I rolled out noodles he gently layered them in the pans, alternating with the meat sauce, a blend of eggs, ricotta and mozzarella cheeses. I showed him how to grate Parmesan and mozzarella over the top.

When we were finished we had two gorgeous pans of lasagna that could grace the cover of any gourmet magazine.

"Should I stick them in?" Sterling asked.

"Go ahead, and say a prayer to the cooking gods while you're at it. We need these beauties to bake."

The sound of heavy footsteps thudded toward us. Gavin Allen pushed open the kitchen door. "You got power?"

I clasped my hands together. "We do. Thank you."

His grease-coated hand went to the hammer looped on his tool belt. "One good smack finally did the trick." He shook his head. "Everything in this damn place needs fixin'."

"Can we get you some coffee, something to eat?"

He stared at the coffeepot. "Can you make it to go? I've got work to do at the marina. The place is a mess, thanks to Tony."

I found a paper cup in the cupboard and poured Gavin a coffee. "Cream and sugar?"

"Black." He took off his fishing cap.

"How about a sandwich or a cookie?" I asked.

He brushed snow off his cap and then put it back on his head. "Nah. Coffee is good."

I handed him the cup. "How's the investigation going at the marina?"

"No idea. I've been banging away on that stupid run-down generator. I told Mercury she needed a new one, but she didn't listen." He gave Sterling and me a nod. "Thanks for the coffee. I'll be on my way."

After he was out of earshot Sterling whispered, "He's cranky."

"Can you blame him? I wouldn't want to be working outside right now, either." I picked up a bottle of olive oil and walked to the stove. "Let's get started on the veggie option." I added a healthy glug of oil to a nonstick sauté pan. Sautéing the vegetables would preserve their moisture and crispness.

Sterling watched as I cranked the burner on high and began to brown the veggies. "Can you babysit these?" I asked, handing him the pan. "Don't turn your back—these will burn like a wildfire if you don't watch them."

"I'll guard them with my life," Sterling teased.

"Make sure you grip the pan firmly and use your elbow to jerk it over the heat," I directed. The smell of leeks, onions, and mushrooms sizzled in the hot pan. "That's it. Nice work." I returned to the island and rolled out another round of noodles for the lasagna. Then I whisked a white cheese sauce and began layering the delicate noodles with Sterling's sautéed veggies, fresh herbs, and a blend of Italian cheeses.

"These are good to go." I slid a pan into the wood-fired oven. "Now we wait!"

"Knock, knock," Lance sang, as he stepped into the kitchen. A gold paper crown adorned the top of his head. "What are we waiting for? Dinner? I'm assuming things are progressing now that your kitchen is illuminated."

"What's with the crown?" I asked.

Lance reached to his head and touched the paper crown. "Oh, this silly thing? It was from a bonding exercise we were doing earlier. They named me king. I'd forgotten I still had it on."

He didn't take it off. I had a feeling that Lance enjoyed being king of this cold castle.

"Do tell," he whispered, coming closer. "What's the word on this *murder* business?" He emphasized the word by clutching his throat and sticking out his tongue.

"How would I know?" I brushed flour from my hands. My pores felt like they were clogged with flour, oil, and soot from the fire. I wondered if I looked as disheveled as I felt.

"Juliet, don't play coy with me. We've been friends for far too long."

Actually Lance and I had met this summer when I returned to Ashland. Six months wasn't "far too long" in my opinion.

"If anyone is in the know, it's you," he continued. "And since this is my party, darling, I want in on the action. Murder is good for business in the theater."

"Lance, stop. Murder is not good for business in real life and you know that as well as anyone else." I knew that Lance was simply playing his part. It was his style and, I had come to realize, his way to deal with stress.

"Kidding, darling." He raised his hands in a fake protest then he pulled up a bar stool. "Do tell, though. What do you know?" His eyes gleamed with excitement.

I twisted my ponytail tighter. "Lance, you hired us to cook. If you want dinner served at a reasonable hour tonight, then you better let us work."

"She's no fun when she gets like this, is she?" Lance said to Sterling.

Sterling laughed. "Nope. She's all business. She likes to run a tight kitchen."

Lance shook his head. "Tsk-tsk. It's probably from all that time on the ship."

"It's called being a professional," I bantered back.

"Speaking of ships, let's chat about some of the sailors on board. I bet they were tight, if you catch my drift?" Lance winked.

I rolled my eyes.

"Better yet, let's discuss that delicious Spaniard of yours." Lance clapped twice. "The ladies are certainly enjoying having a Latin lover behind the bar. Such an improvement from backwoods Tony."

"Lance, I'm serious. We have to work. Things are taking so much longer at this high elevation. I swear I don't know anything about the case. Ask Thomas. He seems convinced that my Latin lover had something to do with it."

Lance gasped and threw his hand over his mouth. "What? Now this is a juicy development. Carlos a suspect? Please, darling, that man could charm his way into the heart of a mass murderer, but a killer himself? I think not."

"That's exactly what I told Thomas, but he doesn't believe me. If you want to help, go find Thomas and back me up."

"Juliet, I always have your back, darling." Lance tapped his fingers on the butcher block. "I suspect we have a love triangle in the works here, don't we?"

"I don't know what Thomas's problem is. All I know is that Carlos is high on his list, and he won't listen to me—at all."

Lance winked at Sterling. "Darling, I think we all know what's going on here. Old flame meets new flame. Watch out—it's about to get hot in here." He stood up and blew air kisses at me. He turned and pranced out of the room. I knew that Lance would eat up the idea of a love triangle, but I also hoped he would follow through on my advice and talk to Thomas. If Thomas wouldn't listen to me, maybe he'd listen to another voice of reason. *Jules, you are in way over your head if you think Lance is a voice of reason,* I thought as I watched Lance make his exit.

Chapter Twenty-two

Both Carlos and Thomas checked in on me multiple times while Sterling and I finished dinner prep.

"Wow, I don't envy you, Jules. No wonder you're kind of spacey," Sterling said after Thomas left for the second time. "He knows that you're married, right?"

"I think he's trying to be sweet," I said. "He really sounded like he was worried about me. Like he thought Carlos could be dangerous."

Sterling rinsed green beans. "Look, I like the guy, but I have to be honest with you, Jules. I think he's stepping over a line here."

"What do you mean?" I chopped thick slices of center-cut bacon into tiny squares. We would render the bacon fat and smash in garlic for the beans. Adding the diced bacon to a cast-iron skillet, I started it sizzling.

"I mean, everyone knows that you and Carlos have had some issues, but he's your husband. Thomas is crossing a line. If I was in his place, I'd back off. Way off. You don't treat a married woman like that, especially with her husband here."

"Treat me like what?"

"Jules, come on." Sterling shook the beans in a colander and started to snap them in half. "I've seen the way

Thomas looks at you. He's into you. No judgment there, but even with Stephanie, when she pulled away I backed off. That's what you're supposed to do as a guy. Not step up the pressure. Isn't that what Carlos has done? Given you space?"

I dropped three bulbs of garlic into the bacon and smashed it. The garlic would do its job of infusing the bacon fat with flavor, then I'd remove it. "Sterling, I think you should consider a career in counseling."

"That would be something. Former junkie turned counselor. Would I put that on my business card?" He snapped a bean in half.

"It's called life experience. People can relate to that, and I'm serious, you always seem to understand what's going on. I never thought about it like that with Thomas. It's weird because I thought we were friends, but you might be right. It feels like he wants something more than I do." The bacon smelled so good, I had to resist swiping a taste.

"Because he does, Jules. Trust me." Sterling raised his brow.

"But what you just said about Carlos—that's why you backed away from Stephanie?"

He shrugged. "It's the right thing to do. My mom used to say that if you hold on too tight you squeeze life away. It's better to loosen your grip, let it breathe, you know?"

"I don't know anything, except that once again, you've proven that you are one of the wisest people I know." The bacon had fried perfectly. I drained some of the fat and removed the garlic.

"Does that come with a raise?" He crunched on a bean.

"It should. Maybe we can start a side business at Torte where you and Mom counsel customers. We can reserve one of the booths. Make a sign that reads THE BAKER IS IN.

Sterling brought the beans to the stove. "I don't know about that, but I am hoping that like Carlos said, giving her some space will bring Stephanie back to me."

"You and Carlos talked about Stephanie? When?" I motioned to the beans. "Go ahead and dump those in." He did. The green beans crackled in the fat. I sprinkled them with sea salt and then covered them with homemade chicken stock. After they came to a boil, we would cover them and let them cook on low for thirty to forty minutes. The process of braising the beans would result in soft beans with a wallop of flavor.

Sterling watched as I tossed the beans over the heat. "Earlier today. He's a great guy, Jules."

I handed the skillet to Sterling and returned to the island where my shortbread dough was resting. Like everything else at this elevation, it was drying out fast. I quickly pressed the dough into the tins with fluted edges, and stuck them in the oven. If there was a love triangle, Sterling had made it clear whose side he was on. I was surprised that he had opened up to Carlos about Stephanie. We didn't have time to dissect either of our relationships more, as we prepared to deliver dinner to Lance's guests.

While Sterling covered the beans with a lid, I checked on the lasagna and bread. The bread was rising nicely and the cheese on the top of the lasagna pans was starting to bubble. We were close to being ready for dinner service. I sent Sterling to deliver plates and silverware, and make sure that Carlos had opened the wine to give it time to breathe.

Everything came together. I removed the lasagna to let it rest while I sliced the bread. Thank goodness it had risen to a normal size and baked with a golden-brown crust. The inside was light and airy, as I sawed through it. Sterling removed the beans from the heat. They smelled so rich and delicious, I knew they would be a hit.

I noted the crown was still on Lance's head as I sliced through the top layer of gooey cheese on the lasagna. The board members had removed their coats, gloves, and hats when the heat came back on. Their winter gear was piled on the couch. The windows sweated with condensation, and the fire burned low.

Whitney and Dean Barnes sat next to each other. They were in a deep discussion about something when I refilled their water glasses. Neither looked up. I heard Dean say something like, "We'll deal with that back in Ashland."

I wondered what they were talking about.

Lance may have been king, but Carlos was the star of the show. He had set up a temporary bar on a serving tray next to the table. There were five bottles of uncorked wine waiting in a neat row.

"This first wine is from the southern hemisphere," Carlos said as I finished filling water glasses and placed the pitcher on the table. No wonder Lance was thrilled that he had volunteered to run the bar. He was taking Lance's board members on a tasting tour. Carlos used to do this for staff members on the ship. He wanted his staff to be well versed in the ship's vast collection of wine. Since we had travelers from every corner of the globe, he also wanted staff to be knowledgeable about different growing regions and the kinds of wine that they produced.

He held the bottle with the label positioned so that everyone at the table could read it. "This is a beautiful Malbec from Argentina. It comes from a deep, plumlike grape. It is also very popular now in French wine." The bruise on his cheek had darkened into a blackish purple, the same color as the wine.

I watched Lance's guests as they sat captivated by Carlos. He circled the table, pouring everyone a taste of the wine. "We will only be tasting red wines this evening, to pair with Julieta's Italian meal." He shot me a dazzling smile.

My heart skipped.

Carlos swirled a glass above the table in one fluid motion. He breathed in the wine, closing his eyes and swaying slightly.

One of the female board members audibly sighed.

I couldn't blame her. Without even trying, he exuded a casual confidence. It was one of the many reasons I fell for him—hard.

"The grapes in this wine are from Mendoza. They grow in small tight clusters," Carlos said. "A French vintner first introduced plantings of these grapes in the late eighteen hundreds. No one thought they would thrive in the high altitude of the Mendoza region, but now they are Argentina's most popular wine."

I had heard this speech before. Carlos felt it was his responsibility as a chef to help his guests discover new wines. I waved and ducked back into the kitchen.

Sterling was cleaning saucepans and the cast-iron skillet. My tart crusts had baked nicely. I melted dark chocolate, butter, and heavy cream on the stove and poured the luscious liquid into the tins. It would harden in the freezer and then I'd top each tart with whipped cream and berries.

"Home stretch," I said to Sterling as I slid a tray of tarts into the freezer.

"Why don't you take off, Jules? I've got this. You've had a rough day. You should try to get some sleep."

"It's not even seven. I'm not that bad, am I?" I laughed.

"I didn't want to say anything about the bags under your eyes, but . . ." Sterling winked.

"Ouch." I put my hands under my eyes. "That's what little sleep and a lot of coffee does to you."

"I'm serious, though, Jules. If you want to take off early, I'm happy to clean up."

"Let me at least finish dessert, and then I just might take you up on that."

"You should."

While I waited for the chocolate tarts to firm up in the deep freeze, I whisked heavy cream, sugar, and vanilla together. Each tart would get a dainty dollop of whipped cream. Then I would garnish them with a blackberry and a sprig of mint.

Sterling checked on dinner. "Carlos is killing it out there."

"Bad choice of words."

"Sorry. He knows his wine. They're eating up his every word."

"I'm not surprised." The cream had formed into soft peaks of white. It reminded me of the snow outside. "How's dinner looking?"

"Good. They're almost done."

"Perfect. I'll put the finishing touches on the tarts, and then we can start clearing plates."

"Plates, yes, but don't touch anyone's wine glass. Lance told me he wants Carlos to do a dessert pairing, too. They're on their last taste of the dinner wines. Carlos is going to see if the bar has any sweet wines in stock."

I checked the tarts in the freezer. The chocolate had firmed with a satin-smooth finish. I took a spoon and began scooping puffs of whipped cream onto each tart. Then I placed a berry in the center of the cream. The contrast of color was striking. I garnished each one with a final sprig of fresh mint. Sterling cleared the dinner dishes, and brought dessert plates to the tables.

"Should I wait on coffee, if they're still drinking wine?" he asked.

"Wait. Carlos will have them entertained for hours." Maybe I would take him up on his offer. With a captive wine-loving audience, Carlos would be in his element until long after midnight. I needed to sleep.

Sterling and I delivered tarts to the table. Lance gushed about my artistic design. It couldn't have been easier to make the tarts. When I said as much, he waved me off. "You know what I always say about simple elegance. Too many people try way too hard, darling. You, on the other hand, have perfected the art of simplicity."

I'm sure I blushed. Carlos returned from the bar with a tray of sweet white and red wines and three kinds of port. Yep, I was right. The already tipsy guests weren't going back to their cabins anytime soon. By the looks of Carlos's tasting tray, they might all be camping out in the lodge tonight. This was my chance to sneak out.

I helped Sterling finish clearing the dinner plates, and made sure he was really okay with sticking around.

"Jules, you know you're going to be back here before dawn anyway. I'd rather sleep in the morning. You look beat. Go. I've got this."

I didn't even hesitate. He was right. I'd been up since five, and had started my morning off by discovering a dead body. If that wasn't cause enough for ditching out on the dinner dishes, I didn't know what was.

I pulled on my coat and tied the hood tight over my head. Hopefully, Carlos would be so wrapped up in his lecture that he wouldn't notice me sneaking out.

He was pouring tastes of moscato, as I ducked past the table. "This is an Italian sweet wine from the Rhone Valley," he said, pouring the gorgeous rose-pink wine into a glass.

The sweet wine has a little effervescence and a dry fruit finish. It pairs perfectly with desserts.

Lance held his glass up for Carlos to fill. "Yes, I believe they call it a *muscat blanc à petits grains,* is that right?"

"Well done. You know grapes." Carlos clapped him on the shoulder. "But this is a *muscat rouge*—see the beautiful color?"

Glad that they hadn't noticed me, I hurried past the bar and toward the front door. The Professor, Thomas, and Mercury sat at a high bar table. They appeared to be having a serious conversation. I had to admit that I was curious, but I didn't want to risk hanging around and getting sucked into the wine tasting.

I pushed open the front door and stepped out into the cold night air. The snow had died down. It fluttered in light tiny flakes. The wind had ceased as well. Hopefully that meant the roads were being cleared and we could all leave tomorrow, on schedule.

In the distance I heard the sound of a howl. I picked up my pace as I trudged through the powder to my cabin. The only light was from the flashlight I'd brought along. I'd forgotten that none of the cabins had generators. The rest of the resort was plunged in darkness.

Maybe I should have stayed in the toasty lodge and indulged in some wine tasting after all. I illuminated my feet. The cabin was straight up the hill, but I found myself winded after only a few feet. Breathing was a struggle in the thin air.

Once I made it to my cabin, I shook snow from my boots and stomped on the welcome mat. Without even thinking, I reached for the light switch. Nothing happened.

No power, remember, Jules? I scolded myself and

shone the flashlight into the kitchen. Where were the matches?

I tripped over Carlos's slippers. Just like old times. He used to leave his slippers in front of my side of the bed on the ship. It used to drive me crazy. Tonight it made me smile.

I found a box of matches above the stove, and lit two candles on the kitchen counter. Then I fumbled through the cupboards to see if there were any more candles. I couldn't find any, but I did find a lantern like the ones Thomas and the Professor had at the marina, in the hallway cupboard. I turned that on, too, and placed it on the coffee table in the living room.

Despite the flickering candles and glowing light from the lantern, the cabin still felt like a freezer. I knew I needed to start a fire.

Mercury and Gavin had supplied the cabins with extra firewood, blankets, and flashlights earlier in the day, but for some reason it looked like they'd forgotten to stock mine. There were two pieces of firewood stacked next to the fireplace. I moved the lantern to the top of the woodstove in order to allow for better light.

I crumpled up newspaper and tucked it into the stove, then I placed the two pieces of wood like an X above the newspaper and threw in a match. The newspaper caught fire immediately. Hot flames warmed my face and danced across the wood-beamed ceiling. However, they quickly died out as the newsprint disintegrated into tiny ashes.

Crud. That didn't work.

Better try again, Jules.

Building a fire wasn't a skill of mine. There was never a need on the ship, not to mention that none of the staterooms or staff quarters had wood-burning fireplaces.

I took more newsprint and wadded it into tight balls. This time I placed six balls under and around the logs.

Then I struck the match against the box and carefully lit each ball. The newsprint flamed to life.

There was no kindling in the cabin, so I kept balling up paper and adding it to the fire. After a few minutes the logs finally caught. I knew they weren't going to last for long. I was going to have to trudge back to the lodge for more firewood. There was no way two logs would keep the cabin warm for the night.

I added the rest of the newsprint, and shut the door to the woodstove. As much as I wanted to curl up on the couch with a hot mug of tea, waiting was just going to make things worse. I tugged on my coat and gloves, and stepped into my ice-cold boots.

Had Mercury simply forgotten my cabin, or were all the cabins like this? If so, it was going to be a long, cold, miserable night. The lodge was the only bright spot in the otherwise black forest. It looked like something out of a postcard with its snow-covered roof, smoke circling from the chimney, and golden light radiating from the windows.

I followed my boot prints back from where I'd just come. At least the lodge looked welcoming. I shined the flashlight on the snow, and stepped carefully.

All of a sudden I heard a bang behind me. I jumped and dropped the flashlight.

What was that?

A tree limb falling?

Maybe it was a giant clump of snow sliding off the roof.

I reached for the flashlight. Another bang reverberated against the evergreen trees.

Was that a gunshot?

Every muscle in my body tensed.

I froze.

Bang! Another shot sounded.

That was definitely a gun. Who was shooting?

I picked up the flashlight and shone it in the direction of the gunshots. It created a spotlight on the trunk of an evergreen tree, but I couldn't see anything. My heart thumped in my chest as I directed the light from tree to tree. There was nothing out there. At least not that I could see.

Time to get moving, Jules, I told myself. I started toward the lodge. That's when I heard the sound of footsteps crunching in the snow behind me.

Chapter Twenty-three

Run! I commanded my legs to move.

Was whoever had been shooting coming after me?

I hurled my body forward.

The footsteps came faster.

Why was someone chasing me?

My breath caught in my chest. Pain seared my lungs. From the combination of the cold and the thin atmosphere, I couldn't fully catch my breath.

"Hey!" someone shouted behind me.

I didn't stop.

The lodge was about forty feet away. I could smell smoke from the chimney. I was so close to safety.

My assailant shouted again. "Stop!"

I ran faster, nearly falling on the slippery uneven snow.

I scrambled up the lodge's porch. My feet slid from underneath me. I landed on my butt.

The next thing I knew someone pulled me up from my shoulder. I let out a scream.

"Are you okay?" Dean Barnes held my coat by the shoulder. A hunting rifle hung over his arm.

"Were you shooting out there?" I tried to pull away from his grasp.

He kept a firm grip on my coat. "Following my favorite

country pursuit—target practice. I saw your light flash. I thought something was wrong."

"Something *was* wrong! You scared me to death. Why are you shooting in the dark?" My legs felt shaky.

"It's a hobby." He released me. Snow covered his knee-high British hunting boots and was spattered on his trousers. He must have been deep in it.

"A hobby? Shooting randomly in the woods is a hobby?"

Dean shifted the rifle on his arm. "It is in the English countryside where I come from. We have shooting parties on Sundays. I'm a skilled hunter. You were in no danger. Although the winter fox that happened by . . . he's another story."

My mind couldn't keep pace with the questions forming in it. Dean was skilled with a rifle. He was older, but he was in good shape. Could he have killed Tony? Thomas said Tony was shot with a hunting rifle. Why was he outside shooting in the dark, when all the other board members were bonding with Carlos over delicious wines?

"Why aren't you inside?" I asked.

"I'm nursing a bit of a headache today. I decided it might be better if I didn't indulge this evening."

"So you're shooting in a snowstorm in the dark?"

"You make that sound so uncivilized. Practicing hunting targets, that's all, my dear." He tapped a pair of binoculars hanging around his neck.

"You were target shooting at night, in a storm?" I repeated the question. Dean's story was highly unlikely.

"Yes," he said with a nod. "Shooting at night adds a certain challenge."

"But anyone could have walked by. You could have shot one of the board members on their way back to their cabins."

"Nonsense. I was out of range of the cabins." He

pointed behind us. "I was shooting targets when I spotted a sly fox disappearing into the forest."

"How did you get to me so fast, then?"

"Don't let these old knees fool you. I can keep up with the young chaps when we're on the scent of a fox. I saw your light. It was the only light in the darkness so it wasn't hard to find you."

Dean sounded sincere, but I wasn't sure if I believed him. Target shooting in the dark didn't make any sense to me. I'd have to ask Thomas if that was a thing.

"I do apologize if I scared you. To be frank, I have a bit of cabin fever. I needed a break from the lodge."

I couldn't shake the feeling that Dean had been chasing me. If I hadn't made it to the lodge, what might have happened?

The front door swung open at that moment. Thomas looked surprised to see us standing there. "Hey, what's going on? I didn't know the party had moved outside." He looked from me to Dean. I noticed his eyes linger on the rifle. Thomas kept his tone playful. "Are you bringing new meaning to serving fresh food? Going out to shoot breakfast?"

"I wouldn't put that past some chefs." I laughed. "Especially up in Portland. I can imagine that concept really taking off."

Thomas smiled then he returned his gaze to Dean. "What's going on with the rifle?"

Dean told Thomas the same story he had told me. When he finished, Thomas frowned. "Target shooting is illegal on this property. You can't use that here."

"I didn't know that," Dean replied, putting his other hand over the gun.

"And you have a license for that, right?"

Dean nodded. "Yes, of course I have a license."

"I'm going to need to see your license and ask you to

secure the weapon in your cabin." Thomas turned to me, "Sorry, Jules, I'm afraid that means no fresh meat for breakfast tomorrow."

"I guess I'll just have to make do with pastry."

"Let me walk you back to your cabin," Thomas said to Dean. "We'll take a look at your license and then we can call it a night, what do you say?"

Dean agreed. He apologized again for scaring me, and left in the darkness with Thomas. I could tell that Thomas was equally suspicious, and I had a feeling he was planning to check more than Dean's hunting license.

The board was tasting an after-dinner port when I walked past the dining room. Carlos gave me a suggestive smile and held up the bottle. Lance grabbed my arm as I tried to sneak past him into the kitchen. "Darling, your husband is absolutely the most charming man on the planet." His words slurred as he spoke. Obviously he'd been enjoying every stop on Carlos's world tour of wines. "You two could do this. This could be your thing. Carlos talks wine and you delight everyone with pastry. It's a brilliant idea. Absolutely brilliant. In fact." He paused and swayed slightly. He braced his hands on his chair to steady himself. "We should do this as a fund-raiser at the theater one night. I can see it now, 'OSF and Ashland take you on a world tasting tour.'"

"That could be fun," I replied. I wondered if Lance would even remember his brilliant idea in the morning. His paper crown was tilted on the top of his head, and his cheeks were flushed with color.

He clapped his hands together. "Everyone, I've just had the most brilliant idea. What if we re-create this magical evening back in Ashland? Carlos, what do you say, would you be up for a wine-tasting tour at OSF?"

Carlos looked at me. "If Julieta would like that, yes of course."

"Julieta would *love* that." Lance blew me an air kiss. "Right, Julieta?"

"We'll have to talk about it," I said.

"Talk! Who needs to talk?" Lance said to the board. "Let's vote right now. Who wants to do a wine-tasting night like this in Ashland?"

Everyone raised their glasses and shouted yes, in unison.

Lance gave me a smug look. "There you have it, darling. We'll figure out all the details in the morning. Ta-ta!"

I gave him a thumbs-up and headed to the kitchen.

Sterling was stacking clean plates in the cupboard. "What are you doing here? You've been gone for what, twenty minutes? Couldn't handle being away that long?"

"No, not at all. I was looking forward to curling up on the couch in my sweats with a hot cup of tea, but there's a small problem. My cabin doesn't have any firewood." I didn't tell him about Dean. There was no need to worry him.

"I thought Gavin and Mercury restocked all the cabins earlier?"

"Me, too. But they missed mine. That's why I'm here. You haven't seen her by chance, have you? I checked the bar. She's not there and I didn't see her in the dining room, either."

Sterling shook his head. "No. She hasn't been in the kitchen all night. Maybe you can take some of the firewood out by the main fireplace. I think they're on their last taste of port. Once they're done tasting wine, everyone should head back to their own cabins, right?"

"Right. That's a good idea. I don't know where else Mercury would keep the wood, and I don't really want to have to search around in the dark to try and find it."

"Do it, and go get into your sweats," Sterling commanded.

"Okay, okay, I'm going." I backed out of the kitchen.

Carlos was pouring the last of the port, and Lance was trying to rein in the raucous board members. I didn't make eye contact with either of them while I loaded as much firewood and kindling as I could carry and headed for the door. I practically sprinted back to my cabin. I knew that Thomas had accompanied Dean, but I didn't want to take any chances with another run-in.

My pathetic two-log fire had burned out. I dropped the kindling and firewood on the floor and started from scratch. This time I layered newspaper, kindling, and three smaller logs. It caught with the first strike of the match, and within a few minutes the fire was crackling and actually pumping heat into the cabin.

To celebrate my success, I filled the teakettle with water and set it on top of the woodstove. In addition to the terrible coffee I'd made this morning, the cabin also had a selection of teas and packets of hot chocolate, just like the variety we'd made for Lance's guests this afternoon.

I opted for an herbal mint tea. While I waited for the water to boil, I made my way down the dark hallway and dug through my suitcase for a pair of sweats and a sweatshirt. I opted for a Southern Oregon hoodie that Mom had given me. Too bad Sterling wasn't here. He would appreciate that I owned a hoodie.

The cozy warm sweats felt soft on my skin. I padded back down the hall and curled up on the couch. It was mesmerizing to watch the flames on the candles and fireplace flicker against the reflection of the shadowy windows.

My encounter with Dean ran through my head. Why would he bring a hunting rifle to a retreat with theater people? And why would he be shooting it in the middle of the night? Could he have killed Tony? It was certainly a possibility, but there were two things that bothered me.

First, did he have the physical strength, and second, what possible motive could he have?

The teakettle let out a low whistle. I pushed to my feet and removed it from the stove. With a steeping mug of mint tea in my hand, I curled back up under the blanket. There was one thing I was happy about, and that was the possibility that Thomas might shift some of his focus away from Carlos and onto Dean.

A knock sounded on the sliding glass door. I held the lantern up. Thomas stood with an armful of firewood. I set the tea on the coffee table and opened the door for him.

"What's all this?"

"I heard that you needed more wood," he said. "Where do you want this?"

"That's so nice of you. You didn't need to do that."

"Already done." He pretended to drop the wood. "Unless you want me to ditch it in the snow."

"No, no, come in. You can put it by the fire. Thank you."

Thomas stomped his boots. "Should I take these off?"

"No, it's fine. Just come in. That looks heavy."

"Please." Thomas did a half curl-up with the stack of wood. "I used to be all-state in football, remember? This is nothing." He stacked the wood next to the fireplace and flexed his muscles. Thomas and Carlos couldn't be more opposite in appearance. Thomas, unlike some of his friends, had maintained his football physique. With his broad shoulders and sandy hair, he could blend in with Andy and his teammates at Southern Oregon University. Carlos, on the other hand, had a slender sculpted frame and a casual European sexiness that American men just didn't have.

Why was I comparing them? What was wrong with me? "You want some tea?" I asked Thomas. "I just made myself a cup."

"Sure. I won't turn down an offer for a warm drink. It's freezing out there."

"What's your pleasure?" I asked, showing him an assortment of teas.

"How about passion fruit. I'm a fan of passion."

"Good to know." I poured hot water into a mug and added Thomas's tea bag. Was Sterling right? Was Thomas crossing a line?

"What did you find out from Dean?" I asked, bringing Thomas his tea. He stood in front of the woodstove warming his hands. I returned to my blanket on the couch.

"Not much. He did have a permit for the gun at least."

"Have you ever heard of someone target shooting at night? I mean, is that even possible?"

"Anything is possible, Jules." Thomas took a sip of tea. "This is nice, thanks."

I laughed. "That required the least amount of effort of anything I made today. You're very welcome."

"Hey, it's a hot cup of tea. I'm not complaining."

"Or you're just way too easy to please."

Thomas poked at the fire with a piece of kindling. "In answer to your question, though, yes, hunters have night vision devices, special headlamps—there's all kinds of equipment on the market that allow people to hunt at night. The bigger issue for me is why was Dean shooting here in the resort? It's illegal. Dean knows that. I could have given him a ticket. If someone wandered by, yikes." Thomas frowned. "Any experienced gun user knows that."

"Did you search the area where he was shooting? No one else is missing, are they?"

"Yes, and no. Everyone is accounted for, and I checked the area. There's nothing there other than a few bullet holes in a couple trees."

"Dean told me that he used to have shooting parties on his family land in the English countryside. That means he has to be very familiar with a gun."

"Uh-huh, and?"

"Well, don't you think that makes him even more of a suspect? Who else knows how to use a gun?"

"Probably quite a few people. We're in the heart of hunting and fishing territory." Thomas tossed the stick of kindling into the fire.

He had a point.

"Jules, everyone is a suspect. Everyone. We're combing through every detail. The Professor is being extra cautious with this crime scene since we're it right now. I just bagged bullets I found near the trees where Dean was shooting. I promise, we're doing everything by the book."

"I'm sure you are." I sipped my tea. It had gone cold.

"Listen, I know this is a touchy subject for you."

"Thomas, stop. I know what you're going to say, and we're not going to get anywhere on the subject. Maybe it would be better to table it." I folded my arms across my chest.

"Jules." He studied my face. "I'm doing my job. We both want the same thing. We want to figure out who killed Tony, right?"

"Right," I said through a clenched jaw.

"Don't do that."

"Do what?"

"Close up on me."

"I'm not closing up on you, Thomas. I'm frustrated."

"Jules, I'm just doing my job." His voice was pleading.

I sighed. "I guess I'm confused. Maybe I'm reading things wrong, but I get the vibe that you don't like Carlos, and not because you think he's a suspect. I get the sense you don't like him because of me." I let the words linger.

Thomas didn't respond for a moment. He added another log to the fire.

I'd spent too much time hiding from my problems. I decided I might as well just say what I was thinking aloud.

"Thomas, I'm not trying to make things weird between us, but that's the thing. They are weird between us. There's been this underlying tension since you showed up. I don't like it, so I'm saying so out loud. You're a good friend, and I don't want to ruin that."

He closed the woodstove and turned to me. "I feel the same way, Jules, and as your friend I'm probably acting weird because I feel protective of you."

I started to protest, but he cut me off. "Not like that. I know you can hold your own with just about anyone." He laughed then met my eyes. "It's Carlos. I don't trust him."

"Thomas, come on. We've been around and around about this. Carlos is not a killer."

"I didn't say he was. I don't trust him because of you."

"Me?" I took a sip of my tea.

He nodded. "Jules, it doesn't matter what happened between you and Carlos. It's none of my business." Placing his tea on the woodstove, he sighed. "Here's the thing, when you first came home to Ashland you were really sad. You're not anymore. You've taken over at Torte and everyone in town knows that. Seeing you with Carlos, I don't know, you're different . . ."

Before he could continue there was a rap on the sliding glass door. Carlos smiled broadly and held a wine bottle in his hand.

Chapter Twenty-four

I waved Carlos in. He flinched when he saw Thomas, but quickly recovered and walked to the couch. He leaned down and kissed my cheek. His lips were cold. "Julieta, tonight I remembered the wine."

"I'm surprised you're upright. It looked like the board was enjoying the wine tasting—really enjoying it."

"*Sí, sí.*" Carlos grinned. "But you know that I take a small, small taste to describe the flavor." He placed the bottle of wine on the coffee table. "This we drink tonight, unless you have other plans." He stared at Thomas.

Thomas cleared his throat. "I need to be on my way." He ignored Carlos and directed his attention to me. "The Professor and I have the cabin next door. If you need anything tonight—anything—I'm within earshot."

"What did he mean by that?" Carlos asked after Thomas left.

I shrugged. "I don't know. For some reason he has you pegged as a suspect in Tony's murder, and dangerous."

Carlos walked to the kitchen and began opening drawers. "For some reason? I think we know the reason. He is in love with you."

"What?"

"He is in love with you, Julieta. It is obvious." Digging

through a drawer, he reached into the back and pulled out a corkscrew. "Ah. We will have wine tonight."

"Thomas isn't in love with me," I protested.

Carlos poured wine into two stemless glasses. "Julieta, please do not pretend you don't see it. The question is, do you return his feelings?"

"What?"

He handed me a glass and sat next to me on the couch. Our knees touched. I felt a jolt of energy run down my leg.

"Do you love him?"

"No! Of course not. Why would you even ask that?"

Carlos swirled his glass. The flames from the candlelight flickered on its smooth edges. They reminded me of dancing fireflies. "Love is complicated, no?"

"I'm not in love with Thomas." I held my glass firmly, and met his eyes. "And honestly, I don't think he's really in love with me."

Carlos tilted his head to the side and laughed. "Julieta, it is obvious. You can see it, no? He is desperately in love with you. I understand his feelings."

"He's not. We're old friends. That's all."

"Hmmm." Carlos held his glass to the light, and took a slow sip.

"If Thomas is in love with me, that's his problem. Not mine. He's a good friend. That's all." I took a sip of the wine. It slid down my throat like velvet.

Carlos considered my words. He set his wine down and positioned his body so that his arm wrapped around my shoulder but he was facing me. "It is easy to fall in love with you."

I held my breath.

He spoke in a throaty whisper. "Julieta, I have missed you."

"I've missed you, too."

One of the logs in the stove fell, sending sparks onto the hearth. We both started at the popping sound. I felt like sparks were flying between us.

I reached for my wine. "Carlos, I need to understand why you didn't tell me about your son."

Carlos watched me as I drank. The wine warmed my cheeks. It was a French Merlot. I could almost taste the sandy clay-limestone earth in the finish.

"You never gave me a chance to explain, *querida*."

"We're here now. I'm listening." I leaned back against the couch and waited. My heart pumped. The wine gurgled in my stomach.

He removed his arm and sat so our eyes were level. "I never meant to lie to you. I should have told you when we first met. I don't know why I didn't. Then it never was the right time. We fell in love so fast. I couldn't find the words to tell you. I knew you would be angry, not because of my son, but because I didn't tell you."

I massaged my temples. "So you decided to keep lying to me? I don't understand."

"It is complicated, Julieta."

"It's not that complicated."

"I mean, I do not know where to start."

Taking another sip of wine, I inhaled an oaky scent. "I'd say, how about if you start from the beginning. We were married for three years. Three years, Carlos, and in that time you failed to mention that you have a son. Tell me what I'm supposed to do with that information? How would you react if it was me?"

Carlos reached for my hand. I wanted to pull away, but his soft touch had a calming effect on me. "I did not know at first. Sophia, she did not tell me."

Sophia was Carlos's girlfriend before me. Carlos is ten years older than me, and I knew when we met that he'd had a number of lovers. It didn't bother me. I had dated

Thomas for years, and had a few minor flings on the ship. When Carlos and I met, though, it was different. The chemistry between us was undeniable. Everyone around us felt it. It was like our bodies were magnetized to each other. He and Sophia broke up when he took the job as head chef. She stayed behind in Spain. Maybe I was blinded by new love, but I believed him when he told me that she was nothing more than a distant memory.

She used to call every once in a while. I figured she still held a torch for him. It was understandable. His dark eyes drew in women at every port. I would chuckle when they batted their lashes and giggled when he walked past. Our connection was so intense that I never worried about him straying. I took it in stride. I used to tease him about being a Casanova.

He would kiss my forehead. "Julieta, you are the only love in my life."

I felt like the only love in his life. Carlos was a consummate romantic. It wasn't just our wedding day. He constantly tucked love notes under my pillow and sang me to sleep. We had something special. Something unique. Something that most people spend their entire lives searching for.

And then it ended.

I'll never forget collapsing to my knees and feeling like someone had kicked me in the stomach the day I found the letters from Carlos's son tucked into his sock drawer.

How could he have kept something so important from me? I didn't breathe as I shoved my clothes into a bag. I had to get off the ship. Right then. Carlos was my world. His lie crushed me.

The rest of that day is etched in my memory. I remember Carlos returning to our cabin. His smile was bright as he danced into our room. It quickly faded when he saw the stack of letters flung on our bed.

"Julieta, I can explain."

"Explain what? That you've been lying to me for years?" My eyes welled with tears. I pushed past him and walked out without another word. Mom knew something was wrong the moment she answered the phone, and I sobbed, "Is it okay if I come home?"

"Honey, that's not even a question. You know you can always come home."

"I mean for a while."

"Okay," she replied, waiting for more.

"I can't talk about it right now. I'm catching the next flight."

"Okay." Mom repeated the word like she was trying to make sense of what I was saying. "I'll be here. We'll figure out whatever's going on together. I love you, Juliet."

"Thanks, Mom," I gulped back tears. "I love you, too."

I don't remember the flight or even disembarking the ship. I just remember that the moment my feet hit the welcoming sidewalks of Ashland, I knew I'd made the right decision. The past six months had made me stronger, more confident. I felt whole again.

Now Carlos was so close that I could smell the musky scent on his skin and the faint sweetness of the evening's wine. I'd been dreaming about and dreading this moment since I'd returned home. Suddenly, I wasn't sure I wanted to hear what Carlos had to tell me.

Chapter Twenty-five

"Did you read my letters?" Carlos asked.

I shook my head. Carlos's first letter arrived with a bouquet of roses. I'd tucked it away at home. I couldn't bring myself to read his words. There was something about seeing it in print that seemed too hard to digest. After that, the letters kept coming. One every other week. They all sat unread in my sock drawer. The irony wasn't lost on me.

"I thought maybe you had not." Carlos looked at me. "Are you hungry, Julieta? I brought something special for you."

"Not really."

He jumped to his feet anyway. I wondered if he was stalling. He strolled to the door and reached into his coat pocket. Returning to me, he offered a small package wrapped in brown craft paper and tied with twine. "You remember that chocolatier in Florence?"

I unwrapped the package. When we'd been docked in the small coastal town of Livorno, we rented a car and drove to Florence for the afternoon. It's one of my favorite Italian cities, bursting with color, tourists, and art. We wandered into a chocolate boutique squeezed between two museums. I'd never tasted such exquisitely lush chocolate. We spent an hour sampling unique flavor combinations like dark chocolate with cherries and chilies and chocolate and ginger.

"When we docked last week, I went back and bought this for you."

The chocolates had a gorgeous satin sheen. I chose a milk chocolate truffle.

"Yes, that should be good with the wine." Carlos encouraged me to try it.

I bit into the silky chocolate. With one taste, I was back in the crowded streets of Florence, under the Tuscan sun. My mouth remembered the young musician busking in front of a gelato stand and the artistic ceilings in Florence's many ancient churches.

That's what I love about baking. It's more than art or science. It's memory.

The sweet memory vanished as I swallowed the chocolate and met Carlos's eager stare.

"It is still, good, yes?"

"It's amazing. Just like I remember it." I washed the chocolate down with wine. "Maybe even better."

"Like us, yes?"

"Carlos." I sighed. "You broke my trust. You shattered everything I thought we had together."

"We still have each other, no?" He placed his hand on my knee. "I still love you, Julieta, but you did run away, and you never read my letters, either? I tried to explain."

"I wasn't ready."

"Are you ready now?"

"Honestly, I'm not sure. You broke my heart, Carlos."

"Ah, *querida,* I am so sorry." He caressed my cheek. His eyes were searching, pleading with me to believe him. "I did not know how to tell you. I did not want you to leave. I never wanted to hurt you, or break the heart that I love the most."

I untied my ponytail and let my hair fall to my shoulders.

Carlos smoothed it down. "Julieta, you are so much more beautiful than you were in my dreams these months apart."

If anyone else spoke to me like this, I would laugh, but when Carlos said that he'd been dreaming of me in his thick Spanish accent, my pulse thumped in my neck despite my best effort not to get swept up in his charm.

"But if you had just been honest with me from the beginning I wouldn't have left."

"I know." He stroked my hair. "You see, Sophia did not tell me I had a son until long after he was born. Her family did not approve. She asked me not to speak of him to anyone. I had to beg her to let me write to him, to tell him that he had a father. A father who would love him and stand up for him."

"What do you mean, her family didn't approve?"

"Sophia's family is devoutly religious. She was raised by her grandmother. Having a child without being married brought shame to her family."

"Shame to her family? You realize we're in the twenty-first century, right?"

Carlos laughed. "*Sí,* I do. Those are not my words. Those are the words of Sophia's family. We were lovers, yes, but I would not have abandoned her if I knew that she was pregnant. She didn't tell me. She didn't tell anyone."

I thought about how different our worlds were. I couldn't imagine an unmarried adult woman bringing shame upon her family in Ashland.

"Sophia went away to have the baby. She planned to give him away, but after he was born she could not do it. He was—he is—so beautiful."

A tear spilled from Carlos's eye.

"When she returned home, she refused to tell her grandmother who the father was. I had already set sail. She wanted to raise her child on her own. She did, until he began to speak and then she realized her mistake. A boy needs a father. She called me to tell me that I had a son. It was before you and I met, you see. At first I couldn't believe that he was my son, but then I went home and I met him. I knew right away. Like with you, it was love at first sight."

Hearing Carlos gush about his son made my heart swell. He obviously loved his son.

"You want to see a picture of him, of Ramiro?"

"Ramiro. That's your son's name?"

"Sí." Carlos nodded. "It means wise. He is already so wise. It's a good name." He removed his phone from his back pocket and scrolled to a picture of Ramiro. They were sitting on the beach, wearing matching blue and white striped swim trunks and licking dripping ice-cream cones. Ramiro had Carlos's dark eyes and casual posture. I could see the resemblance right away. Ramiro was a mini Carlos.

"The schoolgirls must swoon around him." I expanded the picture to get a closer look of Ramiro's face.

Carlos laughed. "He has no eye for girls. Yet."

"I have a feeling that's going to change."

"No, no. Don't say that. Ramiro is such a sweet, gentle boy. I am not ready for him to grow up yet."

"Fair enough." I handed him back his phone. When I clicked it shut a photo of us on our wedding day filled the screen.

"That was a beautiful day, no?"

"It was. I just wish I understood why you kept it from me for so long. I get that Sophia wanted to keep it a secret, but then it came out, right? Everyone back in Spain knows that Ramiro is your son?"

"Yes."

"So why not tell me?"

Carlos looked dejected. "I don't know. I've asked my-self that a thousand times. I thought it would push you away."

"It did."

"I never lied to you about anything else."

"But you lied to me about having a child. That's pretty major. A child. I almost wish you had cheated on me."

"You cannot say that. I have not cheated on you. I never would. Ramiro is eight years old. You and I have only known each other for four years."

"I get that, but I'm saying that hiding the fact that you have a son is worse for me. Much worse."

Chapter Twenty-six

"Julieta, I will find a way to make you understand. I will find a way to earn your trust. You will watch and see." He leaned in and kissed my forehead.

I closed my eyes. His lips brushed one cheek, then the next. I inhaled. My heart pounded. I was desperate for his kiss. He kissed my earlobe, whispering, "Julieta, my love."

The next thing I knew our lips met. His kiss was gentle at first. Then searching. Our bodies arched toward each other. His hands were in my hair and down my back. It was like the past six months of emotion were wrapped up in one single kiss.

When we finally came up for air, Carlos planted a kiss on my forehead and said, "See, maybe I will show you this way." He leaned back. "This is good with us, yes?"

"Carlos, I never said I didn't love you. Yes, this is good, but I don't know where we go from here."

"I will show you. I promise."

"But there's more to it than that." My throat tightened. "I don't want to go back to the ship. I've missed you, but I haven't missed that life. I love being home in Ashland. I love Torte, the customers, the town, everything. I'm really happy."

Carlos waved his hand in a flippant motion. "That is okay. I will follow you anywhere. If you love Ashland, then I will love Ashland, too."

"I'm not sure that you will, though. It's small. It's really small." I couldn't imagine Carlos blending in, in the quaint artistic town. Nor could I imagine him enjoying being tethered to one place. Carlos was a free spirit—he was better suited for life at sea.

"This is okay. We do not need to decide this tonight. You look tired. Curl up in my arms. I will keep you warm while you sleep."

Carlos was right. We had so many more things to discuss. We weren't going to solve everything tonight. My eyelids felt heavy. I craved the comfort of Carlos's arms. I'd been sleeping alone in a twin bed in Ashland for too long.

He held out the blanket and shifted so that both of our legs stretched out side by side on the couch. "Close your eyes, Julieta." He massaged my shoulder as my eyes fell shut.

Was I dreaming? Carlos's arms were exactly where I wanted to be, yet I knew that it wasn't going to be that simple. How could we make this work? How could I trust him again?

I must have dozed off. I woke warm and relaxed. Carlos propped a pillow under my neck.

"What happened?" I asked, blinking my eyes.

"You fell asleep." Carlos held another wool blanket in his arms. "The fire started to die. I tried not to disturb you." He tucked in my feet. "Are you warm enough? It is cool in here, no?"

I hadn't been cold with Carlos's body next to mine. Now I shivered a bit. "What time is it?"

"It's late." Carlos stoked the fire.

"How long have I been asleep?"

"Maybe a few hours."

"Did you sleep?'

"No. I did not sleep."

Carlos thrived with little to no sleep. He rarely slept through the night on the ship. He couldn't. Most chefs are used to sleeping off hours. Carlos just didn't sleep. After he finished dinner service, he would cook for his staff and me. We'd often eat paella and drink Spanish wine at midnight. I would sneak off to bed, knowing that I had to be up early to check on breakfast service.

Usually, I didn't hear Carlos come into our room at night. He had perfected the art of being stealthy. When I'd wake up in the morning, his arms and legs would be wrapped around mine. Sometimes he slept for an hour or two after I left. Sometimes he would indulge in an afternoon siesta. But with three or four hours of sleep and a couple shots of espresso he was good to go.

Not me. I don't need eight or ten hours of sleep, but I'm not very functional unless I get at least five or six.

"I am sorry to wake you," Carlos said, shutting the doors on the woodstove. Sooty smoke puffed into the room.

"It's okay." I sat up.

Carlos pointed to the teakettle. "Do you want me to brew you a cup? It might help you sleep again."

"And thaw my fingers." I wiggled my hands. The tips of my fingers were numb.

"It is not this cold on the ship. I find myself missing the sun." Carlos filled the teakettle. I was surprised that water still flowed from the tap.

In the distance a lone wolf's howl echoed. I rubbed my shoulders and pulled the blanket up higher.

"Do not worry, Julieta. We are safe here." Carlos placed the kettle on the woodstove.

"I know." The friction from rubbing my shoulders was

warming my hands. "I think the reality of the situation is hitting me for the first time. It's been such a bizarre and busy couple of days. I still can't believe that Tony's dead. Did that really happen?"

Carlos checked the fire. Smoke billowed into the room when he twisted the crank to open the iron door. He coughed and waved smoke from his face. The smell reminded me of my childhood, when Dad would build a fire in our basement and we would curl up on the couch to watch movies together.

"I think it is better to keep this shut, no?" Carlos closed the door and returned to the couch. He scooted next to me. I offered him part of the blanket which he willingly accepted. "It is terrible that you had to see a body, Julieta. Who could have done something so terrible?"

"Thomas thinks you did it." A second later I wished I had kept quiet. Carlos shrank back on the couch.

"Me? Why would he think this? I did not kill Tony."

"I know that, but Thomas and the Professor have to follow up with every clue." I felt myself needing to defend Thomas.

"But what clue do I have?"

"You fought with Tony."

Carlos shook his head. "That was nothing. Nothing. You know that. I did nothing more than help get him outside and tell him that was no way to treat a woman. Any woman."

"I know," I agreed. "But people witnessed you argue with Tony."

"This does not make sense." Carlos cracked his knuckles.

"Carlos, there is something else that Thomas and the Professor asked me about. They must have asked you, too. Where were you when Tony was killed?"

"I was here. With you."

"Not the whole night. You left to get wine and then you never came back. I didn't see you again until the morning."

"Julieta, I came back maybe ten minutes after I left you. You were sleeping so soundly I did not want to wake you."

"But what about the wine?"

"What wine?"

"I found two wine glasses and an empty bottle of wine in the kitchen this morning. I'm pretty sure they have some connection to Tony's murder. I don't know what the connection is, but it can't be a coincidence."

Carlos waited for me to say more.

"Did you meet someone for a drink in the kitchen last night?" I held my breath, saying a silent prayer that he wouldn't say yes.

"No, no. I did not meet anyone." Carlos looked out the window into the black night sky.

"Did you see anyone in the kitchen?"

He laced his fingers together and stretched. "I did see someone, but she asked me not to say anything. I did not think about it being connected to the murder, as you say."

"Who did you see?" I felt the familiar hum of anxiety.

"Whitney."

"Lance's assistant, Whitney?"

"*Sí.*" Carlos nodded. "She was drinking wine and crying when I went back last night."

"Crying?"

"*Sí*, she was sad about something with the wine. She said that Lance would be firing her for sure."

"What about the wine?"

"I do not know. She didn't say."

"Did you have a drink with her?"

"No. I did not. I tried to comfort her, but she did not

listen. She was very distraught. She pleaded with me not to say anything to Lance. I agreed. It does not matter to me. These things they happen. It is a mistake. Lance seems to me to be reasonable. He would understand this mistake, I think, but she would not listen. She ran away."

"Ran away?"

"*Sí.* She left."

"And what about the wine?"

"What wine?"

"The wine she was drinking. I think it's important. Do you remember if there were two glasses?"

Carlos closed his eyes. "I think, yes. There were two glasses."

"So Whitney must have been having a drink with someone before you came in." My head was clear. I was fully awake now. "You have to think hard—did you see anyone? Did you hear anyone?"

"No." Carlos shook his head again. "I don't remember hearing or seeing anyone."

"But you're sure there were two wine glasses?"

"*Sí.*"

"What about the wine? Was the wine bottle full?"

"Uh, I do not remember seeing a bottle of wine."

I crossed my legs on the couch. "Okay, let's think about this. There were two wine glasses, but no bottle of wine and Whitney was alone. When you came into the kitchen you startled her. She was worried that Lance was going to fire her and then she left. Is that right?"

"*Sí.* I do not understand why this is so important, Julieta. Isn't this the job of the police?"

"Yes, but Thomas is convinced that you had something to do with Tony's murder. We have to tell him about this. This makes Whitney a top suspect."

"I do not think that Whitney could have killed Tony. You think this?" Carlos frowned.

The teakettle whistled. We both jumped. Carlos stood. "You sit. I will get the tea. What would you like?"

"Anything is fine. Something calming, though. No caffeine."

"No caffeine?"

Carlos and I had a running joke about my ability to drink coffee at pretty much any hour. At our midnight dinners on the ship, I'd often pass on wine and opt for an espresso or latte instead. "No one else can drink coffee like this and sleep." Carlos would tease me in front of his staff. "My wife is a, how do you say? Anomaly? I do not recommend this for you." I would toss a dishtowel at him and slug my coffee in one gulp. Everyone would laugh. I missed those days, and yet I didn't want to go back.

Bringing me a lemon herbal tea, Carlos sat again. "You believe that Whitney killed Tony? I do not understand."

"Me, neither." I grasped the mug. It warmed my hands. The heat was welcome. "I'm not sure if she physically could have done it, but maybe she had help."

"Why would she do this, though?" Carlos dunked his tea bag in his steaming mug.

"I don't know. That's the problem. What's her motive? Could she have been so worried about Lance firing her, that she would kill to keep her job?"

"That does not seem right."

I sighed. "No. It's a stretch. But I know that the wine had something to do with Tony's murder. I just have to figure out what. When I figure that out, I think we'll know who killed him."

"This is not for you to figure out." Carlos looked concerned. "This is for the police."

"I know, but if I can help Thomas solve the case then he'll stop focusing on you, and I'll feel better."

Carlos plunged his tea bag farther into the mug. Hot water sloshed from the sides, spilling on the blanket. "Is this the only reason you want to help Thomas with the case?"

"What do you mean?"

"Julieta." Carlos wiped his hands on the blanket. "Is it because you enjoy working on this case with Thomas?"

I drank the sharp lemon tea, trying to buy myself time to respond. Carlos's words cut through me. I'd been telling myself that the reason I was involved was to protect Carlos. But that wasn't entirely true. He was right. I enjoyed working with Thomas. What did that mean? I was more confused than ever.

Chapter Twenty-seven

"Julieta?" Carlos's voice was coarse with emotion. "It is okay."

I rested the mug on the coffee table. It left a ring on an old skiing magazine. "It's not that. I like being able to help Thomas and the Professor, that's all."

Carlos pursed his lips, but didn't push the subject. "How is the tea?"

"Not bad, considering." I laughed, trying to keep my tone light. "It's slim pickings up here."

"It is tea bags, yes. I agree."

"So Whitney left the lodge, where do you think she went? She could have gone to the marina and shot Tony." I paused. "But then how would she have lifted him into the freezer? She must have had help. Maybe that's what the two glasses were for. Maybe she and her accomplice were plotting out their plan before you arrived."

Carlos dunked his tea. "Julieta, you must relax. This is not your problem."

I was in the zone. I couldn't stop. My mind was running so fast, I could barely keep up. "What did you do after Whitney left?"

"I came back here."

"But what about the wine?"

"I told you I did not see a wine bottle."

"No, I mean you went to the lodge to get a bottle of wine for us. What happened to that?"

"Oh, yes. That's true." Carlos scratched his head. "I went to the bar to find a bottle, but Mercury was there. She was going over some number calculations."

"Wait! You saw Mercury, too? Who else was at the lodge?"

"No one. Only Mercury and Whitney."

"Did you tell this to Thomas and the Professor?"

"About Mercury?"

I nodded emphatically. How had Carlos failed to mention that he'd bumped into two potential murder suspects last night?

"Yes, I did tell them."

"And what did they say?"

"I do not know. They asked a few questions. That's all."

"What kind of calculations was Mercury going over?"

"She was tallying the bar sales, I believe. She did not seem happy. She kept muttering and punching numbers on her calculator."

"Tony," I whispered. "It all has to be connected."

Carlos shrugged. "I do not know, but Mercury was upset about something. I asked her if she needed anything from me, but she did not. I decided to not worry about the wine. I did not want to disturb her in the middle of her work, so I left."

"And did you see anyone on the walk back to the cabin?"

"Julieta." Carlos laughed, but looked worried. "You sound like the police."

"I know. I'm just trying to piece it all together."

"But I think this is disturbing you, no? You discovered Tony's body. Do not distress yourself with this."

"I found his body. I was the only one up here who had any connection to the police. I feel responsible for figuring out what happened to him. It's not distressing me. I promise. It's something to focus on. Otherwise, I'll just focus on seeing his face over and over. At least this way I feeling like I'm doing something productive."

Carlos dropped it, but I could feel his body tense. Was it that he didn't want me involved in a murder investigation, or was it that he didn't want me spending time with Thomas?

We settled under the blankets and listened to the crackling fire in silence. I sipped my tea and let my mind wander. Carlos had given me two important clues. Mercury and Whitney were both at the lodge and had potential motives for killing Tony. What was Mercury upset about? I would have to try and find her first thing in the morning and see if she would confide in me.

I also needed Carlos to tell Thomas and the Professor about Whitney. What did we know about her? Not much. This was her first weekend on the job. I'd have to ask Lance where he found her, and if he'd checked her references when he hired her. He'd love nothing more than being looped in on the gossip.

The lemon tea warmed my hands and was making me sleepy. I drifted off again, only to wake up shivering a couple hours later. The fire had burned out. Carlos snored softly. He had managed to twist himself and the blankets in a tight knot against the back of the couch. I slid out from his arm.

Without the heat from the woodstove, the cabin felt colder than the walk-in freezer at Torte. I could see my breath in front of me. I didn't want to wake Carlos, but I didn't want him to turn into an ice cube as he slept, either. Carefully I cranked the door to the stove open and stuffed in newsprint and kindling. It lit with ease. As flames leaped from the paper, I added two logs.

Then I made my way down the chilly hallway to the back bedroom. We had been smart to sleep in the living room last night. A thin layer of frost had formed on the inside of the windows. Brrr.

I changed as quickly as I could, trying to stay in motion to keep my blood circulating. I would have to track Gavin down later, and thank him profusely for fixing the generator. Lake of the Woods was in a deep freeze without power.

My cheeks were red with cold. I splashed them with icy water in the bathroom. I brushed my hair into a high ponytail and coated my lips with Chapstick. The dry air was making them crack.

Coffee would have to wait until I got to the lodge. That was fine by me. Yesterday's less-than-Torte-worthy brew had left a bitter taste in my mouth. I bundled up, and tiptoed past Carlos.

Outside the snow had stopped. Even though it was still dim, I could see stars fading in the sky. The clouds had pushed north, a good sign that the brunt of the storm was past us. I wondered how long it would take for the team to arrive from Medford.

My boots crunched through a top coat of ice that had formed overnight. With each step, I sank to mid-calf. It must have dumped another eight or ten inches overnight. Debris from the storm littered the ground. Fallen pine needles and branches made the air smell like Christmas.

There was no sign of movement anywhere as I descended toward the lodge. I considered heading to the section of woods where I'd seen Dean shooting last night, but I had yeast to get rising and rolls to bake. Plus, it probably wasn't the wisest idea to go tromping through the deep snow alone with a murderer on the loose.

None of the outdoor lights were on when I made it to the lodge. Oh no! Had the generator stopped working again? I kicked snow from my boots, and unlocked the front door. Please let there be power, I prayed silently as I scrunched my face and reached for the light switch. In one motion the overhead lights hummed on.

Thank goodness.

The heat wasn't running. I turned that on next, and headed for the kitchen. If the last two days were any indication of how much more time everything needed to bake at this elevation, I had to get moving now. But first, I needed coffee.

Everything was prepped and ready to go, and waiting on the island for me. Sterling must have stayed late last night. Once Lance paid me, I was going to make sure to give Sterling a little bonus. He had been a godsend this weekend. I appreciated that he took charge, and didn't wait for me to direct him.

I ground fresh beans, opting for a medium-bodied breakfast blend. The scent of the caramel roast perked me up immediately. Next, I turned the oven onto high and started water boiling on the stove. I'd learned my lesson. We were going to end this weekend on a high note. Two meals left to go: breakfast and lunch. I wanted to dazzle Lance and his guests with our signature Torte pastries and have them leave happy and satiated.

I gathered yeast, butter, flour, and sugar. While the coffee brewed, I let the yeast rise and started making dough. I had originally planned to make puffed oven pancakes this morning, but since we had to swap things around yesterday, and after my almond bar rising disaster, I figured it was safer to stick with pastries. We could serve an assortment of pastries, hot oatmeal, and the previously missing sausages.

Soon the kitchen was alive with good smells—percolating coffee, yeast, and a slight scent of smoke that lingered in the pizza oven. I needed to light that, too, but it could wait. I planned to bake everything for breakfast in the main oven. We would use the pizza oven for our last meal, lunch. And I knew exactly what I wanted to make—pizza.

When Sterling arrived I would put him in charge of pizza toppings. In the meantime I filled a coffee mug with water and heated it in the microwave. I'm a creature of habit when it comes to my coffee ritual. My morning coffee always begins with a piping-hot mug. Mom and Carlos both tease me about it, but I swear a hot mug changes the flavor and the experience of drinking coffee.

I poured a cup of the aromatic brew and added a splash of cream. Taking three long sips, I stretched in a yoga pose. Now it was time to bake.

The yeast, not surprisingly, rose like a hot air balloon, I incorporated it into the flour and sugar and pounded the dough down. My thoughts wandered. I was eager to get home to Torte and Mom, but I couldn't shake how unsettled I felt about my future. Since I'd been back in Ashland everything felt simple and clear. I knew what I wanted. I wanted to run Torte and make it the best bakeshop in Southern Oregon. Having Carlos here complicated everything.

Would he really come to Ashland and live with me? As wonderful as that sounded, I couldn't quite imagine him in the idyllic village with its quirky theater troupe and revolving tourists. He was used to dealing with tourists on the ship of course, but it was different in Ashland. Tourists were our livelihood. They are like royalty. The whole town caters to the summer season. Would Carlos tire of Ashland? Of me? We'd always had a new destination to look forward to exploring together. I wondered what permanent life on solid ground would be like with Carlos.

Just bake, Jules, I scolded myself as I coated my hands in flour. The sweet bread dough had developed a nice elasticity, it stretched and sprang back to life when I pressed my fingers into it. I could stretch, too. I'd learned that being home.

"Good morning," a voice said from the doorway. It was Mercury. She wasn't wearing her pajama pants and snow boots. Her hair was twisted in a bun and the dark circles under her eyes looked less pronounced. I took that as a positive sign that things were returning to normal, or at least as normal as they could possibly be, given that Tony was dead.

"Come on in." I waved her in with pasty hands.

"I came down to make sure the generator was still running, and I smelled coffee. I had to come beg you for a cup."

"No need to beg," I replied. "Help yourself. It's fresh. I'd offer to pour a cup for you, but as you can see I'm sort of in the middle of this."

"That smells so good, too." Mercury walked to the cupboard and removed a mug. She was definitely familiar with the kitchen. "Are you always up this early?"

"Yep." I reached for a rolling pin. "It's sort of a job requirement for bakers."

Mercury poured herself a cup of coffee. "Yeah, I get that. We're usually up pretty early around here, too. It's one of the pros and cons related to running this place. We get to make all the decisions, but that means we get to make *all the decisions,* you know?"

"Tell me about it. My mom and I have talked about that at length with the bakeshop. It's great to be your own boss, but sometimes not so much."

"Especially when it comes to staff." Mercury sank onto a barstool.

"Have you had a problem with staff?"

"You mean other than Tony?" Her voice was laced with bitterness as she said his name. She sipped her coffee and sighed. "It hasn't been so bad. The usual kind of thing, especially in the summer when we're really busy. We have a bunch of teenagers who help Gavin run the marina. He gets irritated when they show up a few minutes late or spend their lunch breaks flirting with girls at the swimming area."

"Teenagers." I made a goofy face and laughed.

"Right. What can you do? I keep telling him they're good kids, but he's so protective of this place. I guess that's a good thing. Better than having staff who don't care, right?" She paused and drank her coffee. "This is amazing."

"Thanks, it's a new blend from a roaster in Ashland who roasts all of her beans by hand. I brought it up here to see what kind of feedback we would get on it. I'm thinking about adding it to the daily rotation at Torte."

"I give it a ten out of ten." Mercury flashed ten fingers at me. "Of course, I'd probably drink coffee out of the lake bottom today. It's been such a long weekend."

"How are you holding up?" I asked as I pressed the rolling pin onto the dough.

Mercury exhaled. "It's been rough. I wish I could speak to my husband. That's been the worst part. Why did something like this have to happen while he wasn't here?"

"It seems like that's always the way things go. They never quite turn out the way we planned them." I thought about Carlos.

"Can I tell you something in confidence?" Mercury looked to the doorway to make sure we were alone.

"Sure."

"It's about Tony."

I sprinkled more flour over the dough. "What about him?"

Mercury rested her elbows on the island. "I think he was stealing from us."

"Really? Why?"

"I was going over the books last night and they don't add up. I told my husband that I didn't trust Tony months ago. Things have been disappearing in the bar. Like Lance's order. We're barely scraping by, even this summer when every cabin in the resort was in use."

Last summer I had a similar fear about Torte. Our cash flow was in the red, and I was worried that one of Mom's employees had been skimming the profits. It turned out that Mom had been lending a helping hand to everyone in town. When the recession struck, she refused to let some of her loyal customers, who had lost their businesses, pay. It was a kind thing to do, but meant that we'd been saving every penny to get the bakeshop back in the black.

Mercury finished her coffee and poured herself a second cup. "I confronted him about it. Claiming that he lost Lance's order made me snap. I'd had enough. Did you hear what he tried to do?"

"No, what?"

"He tried to sell Whitney our stock for double the price." Mercury walked to the fridge, and took out the cream.

I had heard that, but I let her talk.

"That's when I finally figured out what he'd been doing. He was pocketing the difference, plus who knows what else. I think he's been scamming us for months."

"How did he react when you confronted him?"

"He flipped out. It didn't surprise me. I expected him

to. He got defensive, said it wasn't him. I asked him if it wasn't him, then who was doing it. He wouldn't say. I know he was lying. I planned to fire him yesterday. I just needed to talk to my husband first and make sure there wasn't anything that I needed to do from a legal perspective before I let him go." She swirled the cream in her coffee, turning it into a gorgeous beige color. My hands were still covered in flour, but as soon as I finished rolling the dough I could go for another cup.

"Now he's dead." Mercury rubbed her forehead. "Everything is a mess. News of a murder at the resort isn't going to be good for business, and with Tony dead there's no way we're going to get back any of the money he stole from us."

"Have you told Thomas and the Professor this?"

Mercury sipped the coffee. "Most of it. Not everything. I told them that I thought he was stealing from me. I didn't tell them I was planning to fire him. I probably should have, but I was worried that they would think I had something to do with his death."

They probably would, I thought to myself. Learning that an employee had been stealing from her was a potential motive for murder. Especially because it was evident that Mercury was desperate to make Lake of the Woods a success. I knew that feeling, and I respected her drive. At the same time I wondered if that drive could have led her to murder Tony.

Chapter Twenty-eight

"You should tell the Professor and Thomas everything. They're both intelligent and reasonable, and they'll understand, but if you don't tell them and it comes out later, it won't look good for you." I didn't tell her that at the moment I thought Thomas wasn't being reasonable about Carlos.

Mercury hung her head. "I know. I don't know why I didn't. I know it was wrong. It's been a stressful few days, what with the storm, losing power, Tony—the whole thing."

"Stress has a tendency to make us do crazy things sometimes."

"Thanks for listening. I appreciate it. You're right. I'll tell the police everything this morning." She finished her coffee and put her cup in the sink. "It looks like the storm has cleared. A crew should be here sometime today. I can't wait to have the phone lines up and running again. I have so much to tell my husband. He'll never believe it."

Pausing at the kitchen doors, she glanced around the room. "Is there anything else you need?"

"Nope. I'm all set." I waved as she walked away. Mercury seemed sincere, but I was more confused than ever. I wasn't going to take any chances. As soon as the Professor or Thomas showed up I was going to tell them what I'd learned.

I didn't have to wait long. The Professor came in as I slid the first batch of sweet rolls into the oven.

"Good morning, Juliet." He stared longingly at the coffeepot. "I see my nose did not deceive me. I thought I smelled a refreshing brew. Might I bother you for a cup?"

"No bother." I wiped my hands and reached for a mug. "It's been sitting for about a half hour. Would you like me to make you a fresh pot?"

The Professor scoffed. "You are so like your mother. She won't touch coffee that's been sitting for more than fifteen minutes. I say coffee is coffee."

"I promise you coffee is not coffee." I poured the remaining coffee into the mug and handed it to him. "Drink this. I'll brew another pot, and you tell me the difference."

"A challenge. I like it." The Professor savored the stale coffee. "Tastes good to me."

"Just wait." I ground beans and added cold water to the coffeepot. "Once you taste this, you won't be able to go back."

"That could be true, but I'm afraid we don't have the luxury of brewing fresh coffee in my line of work."

"Good point. Well, at least you can experience it here." I pressed start on the coffeepot and returned to the island. "It looks like the snow finally stopped."

"Indeed. I'm expecting the coroner to arrive anytime this morning."

"Any new leads in the case?" I wanted to see if the Professor said anything about Mercury first.

"It's a messy business, murder." The Professor ran his fingers along his beard.

"Did you talk to Mercury?"

"Not recently, why?"

I shared what I had learned from Mercury.

The Professor nursed his coffee and listened intently. Twice he stopped me and jotted something down in his notebook. "I think that money is at the root of this murder. You know what the Bard said?"

I shook my head.

"He said, 'How quickly nature falls into revolt when gold becomes her object.' "

"So does this mean Carlos is no longer a suspect?" The coffeepot beeped. I poured the Professor a new cup. "Here." I placed it in front of him. "See if you can taste the difference."

Before he answered my question, the Professor carefully drank from each cup. He swished the coffee in his mouth like he was tasting wine. Finally, he placed his mug on the island. "You are correct, this one is better." He pointed at the new cup of coffee. "However, this one is cold, so it might not be that we are comparing apples to apples here."

"I can warm it in the microwave for you."

"That won't be necessary. You've convinced me."

"Have I convinced you about Carlos?"

"Perhaps." The Professor studied my face. "You know what the Bard said about love?"

"He said a lot about love, didn't he? I mean isn't most of his work about love?"

"Indeed. He is one of the most prolific writers on love of all time. Regardless, a quote keeps running through my mind, but I can't remember if it's from the Bard. I think this particular quote often sums up love and angst so eloquently."

"What?"

" 'Expectation is the root of all heartache.' "

"Does that have something to do with Tony's murder?" I wasn't sure how we had moved from the subject of murder to love, or how the professor memorized so many quotes.

"Expectation always has something to do with murder." He drained his coffee cup, leaving the first stale cup half empty. Then he stood and gave me a little bow. "As always, thank you for the stimulating conversation and my morning stimulant."

"Happy to help."

"Juliet, I want to caution you to be careful. We are closing in on the killer. I've found that desperation often leads to danger. I know that people tend to open up to you. You get that from your mother too, but remember, whoever killed Tony might still be dangerous. If you hear any other news, please come find me or Thomas right away."

"Of course." The Professor didn't need to worry. There was no way I was going to try to take down a killer in the snowy woods. I was quite content to stay put in the lodge's cozy kitchen.

"Before you go, can I ask you one more question?" I asked as the Professor started toward the door.

"Ask away."

"It's about our conversation yesterday."

"You're wondering about my intentions with your mother," he answered before I could even form what I wanted to say.

"No, not exactly."

"I assure you, Juliet, I have nothing but your mother's best interest in mind."

"I believe that. Definitely. But I guess I'm confused about what you want from *me*? Are you wanting me to say something to her?"

"Juliet, I trust your excellent judgment. Proceed however you feel most comfortable." He gave me a half-smile and walked away.

What did he mean by that? Was he hinting that he

wanted me to scope out the situation with Mom? I wasn't sure I wanted to be in the middle. In fact, I knew I didn't, but I had to admit that I was more than a little curious to find out how Mom felt about marriage in general. We'd never talked about it. There wasn't a need. After Dad died Torte became Mom's life. I had a new appreciation for Mom's dedication to the bakeshop for all these years. The question was, was she ready to let go a little and focus on herself for a change? When I got home I was going to have to figure out a way to broach the subject.

For the next hour, I was a one-woman baking machine. I refused to let the altitude or the murder investigation rattle me. Sterling arrived a little after six. His dark hair, which he normally styled with gel to make it look intentionally messy, was tucked under a knit cap. His eyes were dull and his walk was sluggish.

"How late were you here last night?" He looked like he could use more sleep.

"Not too late. I don't know, maybe eleven or so. Carlos really put on a show. Everyone loved him, and the wine helped, I'm sure. I left right after Lance."

"You look like you're still tired."

"I didn't sleep at all. My cabin was freezing. Was yours?"

"It was okay until the fire went out, and then yeah—it was like a freezer."

"Exactly." Sterling tied on an apron and waited for instructions. "Mine went out twice last night. I gave up the last time. I think I had every single blanket over me and I was still cold. Makes you appreciate the small things like heat, doesn't it?"

"That's for sure." I grinned. "If it helps, I just made a fresh pot of coffee."

"Now you're speaking my language." Sterling helped himself to coffee. "What do you want me to do?"

I went over the menu. "I've pretty much got breakfast under control. The sausages can be grilled right before we serve everything, so maybe you can start lunch prep."

Sterling agreed. We brainstormed pizza flavor combinations over coffee. We decided to do a traditional red sauce with salami, black olives, and peppers, a white sauce with marinated chicken, sundried tomatoes, Kalamata olives, and artichoke hearts, and an olive oil base with pears, prosciutto, and gorgonzola.

He marinated chicken breasts in balsamic vinegar, olive oil, garlic, red onion, and a healthy dose of salt and pepper. I continued to rotate rolls in the oven. Once they cooled I frosted, and drizzled them with chocolate, marmalade, and jam.

Lance stopped in for coffee. "Did anyone else barely make it through the night?" He wore a new turtleneck sweater that covered his chin, a cashmere scarf, and tight black leather gloves. "I thought I might actually freeze to death."

"Stop being so dramatic." I handed him coffee.

"Darling, drama is what I do. I am drama."

"Touché." I raised my mug in a toast.

Lance blew me a kiss. "Did I miss out on any juicy details while I was trying to avoid hypothermia last night? I sent Thomas up to check on you, and Carlos was hot on your trail right after that. How does it feel to be pursued by two heavenly male specimens?"

"You sent Thomas to my cabin?"

"Darling, I was only trying to help you out. Plus, I can't resist a good love triangle."

I rolled my eyes.

"Don't be pouty. It's not a good look on you." Lance tapped the bottom of his chin. "Chin up. And do tell, how did it go with your dueling leading men?"

"First of all, I don't have dueling leading men."

Lance looked to Sterling for support. "Don't put me in the middle of this," Sterling replied. The coffee perked him up. His eyes were as bright as the sky outside. He massaged a juicy chicken breast and winked at Lance. "I'm working on my chicken."

"Or you are a chicken." Lance flapped his arms. "Come play along, Sterling. I'm just having a bit of fun with Juliet."

"She's not your boss. A little fun could get me fired."

"Ha! Like that would happen. Everyone in town knows that Torte's become a gathering spot for teenage girls since Juliet had the brilliant idea to hire you."

Sterling doused the chicken with olive oil. "Still, I'm not getting involved with this one."

"You're no fun." Lance tossed his scarf over his shoulder.

"Hey, speaking of firing staff members, what do you know about Whitney?" I asked, trying to change the subject. If there was anything Lance liked more than a love triangle, I knew it would be murder.

He bit. "What do I know about her?"

"Yeah. How long have you known her? Did she come recommended by someone, or did you hire her sight unseen?"

Lance put his hand to his heart. "Ouch. How could you even consider that I'd hire anyone for the company sight unseen? That's absurd. I happen to run one of the biggest and most famed festivals in the world, do you think I would really leave hiring a personal assistant up to fate? No, no, darling, Whitney was personally recommended and then vetted by the board."

"Who recommended her?"

"Dean Barnes, of course. He's her uncle."

"Dean Barnes is Whitney's uncle?"

"Didn't I just say that?"

"Why didn't you tell me this before?"

"What's to tell, darling? I was in need of a personal assistant. I happened to mention it at our last board meeting, and Dean recommended his niece Whitney. We flew her up to Ashland for a series of interviews. She passed with flying colors. She might be young but she's very mature for her age. Quite an eye for detail, too."

"She seems convinced that you're going to fire her."

Lance sipped his coffee. "Now why would she think something like that?"

"Because of the alcohol debacle."

"Well, that wasn't her fault, was it? Why would I fire her over something like that?"

"Oh, I don't know—high standards, perfectionism, being upset that there was no alcohol for your retreat. Those all sound like valid reasons to me."

"Darling, your imagination is too much sometimes. I assure you I have no intention of firing Whitney. I'm quite pleased with her work thus far. She has more to learn, of course. And she needs to ditch that silly tablet. I keep telling her this isn't L.A."

"You're sure?"

"Yes, I'm sure." Lance sounded incensed. "What are you trying to get at?"

"Nothing." I shrugged.

"Juliet, don't be coy with me. Does this have something to do with Tony's murder?"

"I'm not sure."

Lance scowled and ran his fingers along his goatee.

"Honestly, I'm not. Maybe. If Whitney was worried about you firing her, could she have killed Tony?"

Lance threw his head back and laughed. "Oh my, you have really been cooped up here for too long! Or perhaps the thin air is messing with your head. Whitney, a killer?

Impossible. Absolutely impossible. That girl couldn't kill Tony any more than I could. I don't think she could kill a spider even if it was about to bite her. You must be joking."

"You never know. Like Thomas said, 'people can do things you'd never expect when under pressure.'"

"Thomas said that?" Lance winked. "Did he say that over a glass of wine last night, or was he too busy trying to fight off your Latin lover?"

"Lance." I shot him a hard look.

"Truce. Truce." He threw his hands up.

"Maybe Whitney and Dean paired up. I found him shooting in the forest last night."

"Really?" Sterling looked up from his marinade.

"Yeah! He had a hunting rifle and claimed to be target shooting."

Lance twisted his scarf. "Whitney and Dean? You can't be serious. Dean is our most elder board member and I think Whitney would struggle to lift that." He pointed to the sack of open flour on the island. "You're slipping. This fresh mountain air must be getting to you."

"Not if they worked together," I insisted.

"You deal with her," Lance said to Sterling. "I have some work to do before the masses arrive and want to be fed, but let me part with these words—Whitney is not your killer. Nor is our creaky British gent. Better get back to your sleuthing." Lance turned on his heels and blew me kisses. "See you for breakfast, soon. Ta-ta."

I knew that Lance had a flair for the dramatic, but he seemed certain that neither Dean nor Whitney could have had anything to do with Tony's death. Was he right? What about their connection? She was his niece. Could that be who she'd been sharing the bottle of wine with the night that Tony was killed? I remembered that Dean said he had a hangover. Lance might be convinced, but I wasn't. It was certainly possible that working together, Whitney and Dean could have killed Tony.

Chapter Twenty-nine

Sterling trekked back into the cold and recovered the sausages from the cooler. We had finally figured out baking at this altitude, just in time to head home. Breakfast prep was a breeze. Within the hour everything was baked to perfection and ready to go.

We got a jump start on the pizza dough and desserts for lunch. I couldn't believe how quickly the past three days had sped by, and I couldn't stop reviewing the potential murder suspects in my head.

Whitney had a motive whether Lance believed it or not. She was genuinely concerned about getting fired. Dean was her uncle. Could he have killed Tony to protect her? Or had they teamed up and killed him together? Dean was an accomplished hunter. I still wondered what he was doing shooting in the woods last night.

Then there was Gavin Allen. He was a burly guy, who also knew how to operate a hunting rifle. He had the physical strength for murder. But what was his motive? I couldn't figure out a reason he would want Tony dead.

And Mercury. She seemed genuinely rattled about Tony's death, but maybe it was an act. She was desperate to make the resort a success. If Tony had really been stealing from her that was certainly a motive for murder.

But how would she have done it? She would have needed an accomplice.

Focus, Jules. I flicked my wrist. You are here to bake.

Sterling and I served breakfast to grateful guests. The board members devoured all the sweet rolls and sausages. Apparently, the morning after a wine-tasting tour called for sustenance. Carlos joined everyone for coffee. They all chatted amicably about how much fun they'd had with him as their vintner, and encouraged him to come to OSF.

The Professor and Mercury both nibbled on breakfast. Thomas was noticeably absent. I wondered when the coroner and a team of workers would arrive. I also wondered how hard it was going to be to drive back to Ashland in the deep snow.

I didn't have too much time to worry about it. As soon as we cleared the breakfast dishes, we turned our attention to lunch. Carlos wasn't needed in the bar, so he offered to teach Sterling how to throw pizza dough.

It was hilarious to watch them take turns flipping the dough into the air.

I wanted to wow Lance with a parting dessert. I decided on cherries jubilee. The classic flambé is an artful sweet dessert that would send the guests off in flames. It's an underutilized simple technique that would be sure to leave a lasting impression. Flambéing caramelizes the sugar and deepens the flavor. I would set it aflame at the table and serve it over vanilla bean ice cream.

Carlos tossed the dough, twirling it in a spiral first. "You see," he said to Sterling. "It is all in the wrist. Flick like this. It will give more air to the dough for a light and crispy crust."

Sterling watched as Carlos made it look easy. I knew it wasn't. When it was Sterling's turn, the dough hit the ceiling and stuck for a moment before landing on the stove.

"That is okay, you try again. Keep it spinning, yes?" Carlos was calm and encouraging. Some chefs run kitchens by force, berating and yelling at young sous chefs. Not Carlos. He had a different approach. He infused fun in everything he did. From blasting Latin music to playing practical jokes, his relaxed style put everyone at ease. That didn't mean he wasn't in control of his kitchen. Quite the opposite. Staff respected him, and worked twice as hard to please him.

Sterling tossed the dough again. This time it made a full rotation and landed on his outstretched hand. A smile spread across his face. "I did it!"

"Yes, yes." Carlos clapped him on the back. "Bravo. Try it again."

"Has anyone seen the rum?" I asked.

Sterling concentrated on the flying pizza dough. He shook his head, but didn't speak.

"There is a bottle of very good rum behind the bar," Carlos replied, keeping one eye on Sterling. "Do you want me to get it for you?"

"No, you guys keep working on the pizza. I'll go find it."

I left to the sound of them laughing as dough landed on Sterling's head.

"Do not worry. This happens all the time." Carlos grabbed the dough and plopped it on his own head. He posed with it for a second and then said, "We have a rule in the kitchen. If it lands on you—you eat it. This one becomes your pizza. What do you want on it?"

Lance was explaining his new fund-raising strategy to the board when I scooted past the table en route to the bar. The bar was dark and empty. Two long shelves were framed in the window. Bottles of gin, vodka, and vermouth glimmered backlit from the sun. "Sun, ah, sun," I said aloud. I hadn't been this happy to see the sun for years.

The resort looked picturesque. Icy crystals sparkled under the sun's warming rays. Last night's snow had covered most of the fallen debris. It looked as if a blanket of white had been cast on the ground. The dark evergreen branches stood in stark colorful contrast to the sea of blinding white.

I scanned the shelves of alcohol, looking for a bottle of rum. There was one bottle, but it only had a quarter inch of rum left. Not enough to flambé my cherries jubilee.

There had to be more rum somewhere. It was a staple in so many well drinks. I turned around and checked the cupboards under the bar. There were two cases of wine in the first cupboard, and boxes of clean glasses in the second. I opened the third cupboard where standalone bottles of hard alcohol sat in perfect rows.

I checked the labels, finally finding a full bottle of rum near the back.

Jackpot.

As I pulled the bottle from the cupboard my hand hit something. I scooted closer, and pushed the bottles to the side. In the far corner of the cupboard was an envelope. Without thinking, I pulled it out and opened it.

Inside the envelope was a giant stack of cash. At first I thought it must be tip money, but when I looked closer at the bills they were twenties and hundreds. There had to be a few thousand dollars in the envelope.

There was something else in the envelope. I shoved the cash back in and removed a piece of paper. It had the Lake of the Woods logo on the top and read: "Lake of the Woods Marina." Someone had written a ledger on the paper. It documented cash transactions in the bar and at the marina. I scanned the paper until I found OSF's order. It was for two cases of wine—one white and one red. The total order was for seven hundred dollars, but that number was crossed out and in the column next to it someone had written a price of fifteen hundred dollars.

I had found proof that Mercury was right. Tony had been skimming from her.

I read through each entry. Something didn't add up. Not only was Tony overcharging customers in the bar, but the same thing was happening at the marina. There were entries for fishing boat rentals that were more than double the listed price.

That didn't make sense. How was Tony skimming from the marina, too?

I dropped the paper on the floor. All of a sudden I realized how. Gavin. Gavin had to be in on the scheme. Gavin and Tony had been working together to steal from Mercury and guests at the lodge. The paper was tangible proof.

I had to get this to the Professor or Thomas, without anyone noticing.

Poor Mercury. She'd put her trust in Gavin and he had been stealing from her, too. I couldn't believe it.

I tucked the note back into the envelope, and stacked the bottles in place. Then I hid the envelope in my bra, and closed the cupboards.

I hurried back to the dining room with the bottle of rum. Maybe I could catch the Professor's eye and motion him into the kitchen.

When I walked past the dining table, the Professor wasn't there. Neither was Mercury. Where had they gone?

A new thought popped into my head as I returned to the kitchen where Carlos and Sterling were hurling pizza dough in the air. I hadn't been able to figure out what motive Gavin might have had for killing Tony. Now I had one resting against my chest. What if Gavin wanted all this cash for himself? With Tony out of the picture, and knowing that he had Mercury's unyielding trust, he stood to pocket all of this cash. Gavin had to be the killer.

Chapter Thirty

Why hadn't I figured it out before? Mercury had said that Tony claimed he wasn't the one stealing from her. Was that because he planned to put all the blame on Gavin?

I thought about the hunting rifles at the marina. Gavin had access to them and knew how to use them. Had he and Tony had a fight about their scheme? All Gavin would have had to do was grab a rifle from the rack and shoot him. He could have lifted Tony into the freezer. He had the strength.

"Jules, are you okay?" Sterling's voice startled me. I almost dropped the bottle of rum on the floor.

I caught it on my elbow. "Yeah, sorry." My hands shook as I set the bottle on the counter. "How's the pizza lesson going?"

"Good." Sterling smiled and ran his hands across a line of thin round circles waiting to be transformed into pizzas.

"Those look great," I replied. My hands wouldn't stop shaking.

"Julieta, what is wrong?" Carlos noticed.

"Nothing. It's nothing," I lied. "How are we doing for time?" I wanted to go find the Professor and Thomas right now. The envelope felt like it was burning my skin.

"We're good," Sterling said, pointing to the clock. He was right. There was plenty of time, and cherries jubilee didn't take long. If worse came to worse I could cook them while Lance and the board were noshing on their pizzas.

"Do you guys mind if I step outside for a sec?" I asked.

"Step outside into the snow?" Carlos said with a disapproving look.

"I won't be long, and you know the drill, right, Sterling?"

He pointed to each pizza. "Red sauce, white sauce, olive oil, right?"

"Exactly."

"No problem. We got this. Right, Carlos?"

Carlos nodded, but he didn't take his eyes off me.

"Okay, I'll be back as fast as I can." I turned and hurried away.

I checked the bar one more time, just in case the Professor or Thomas had come back while I was in the kitchen. It was still empty. They had to be outside. I zipped up my coat and placed my hand on top of my chest. I didn't want the envelope to slip out.

Maybe they were at their cabin. I would try that first. I ran up the hill.

The resort looked welcoming and picture-perfect under the winter sun. Smoke spiraled from cabin chimneys. If I wasn't on the trail of a murderer, I would have stopped and snapped a picture for Mom. She would love this.

You can admire the view later, Jules, I told myself as I raced toward Thomas and the Professor's cabin, kicking powder into the air.

My breath came in shallow gasps. The Professor and Thomas were sharing the cabin directly across from mine. It had the same layout, only theirs was larger and had a ramp leading to the porch. I grabbed the hand railing to steady myself as I flung my body up the ramp. With the storm gone and the roads being clear, Gavin could get away. This was his chance to escape.

Did he suspect that anyone was on to his scheme?

I banged on the screen door.

There was no movement inside.

I tried again. "Thomas, it's Jules! Are you awake?"

Still nothing.

He was either asleep or somewhere else. What about the Professor? I thought, scanning the grounds. Where had he gone? Had he gone to find Mercury?

I considered my options. I could go back to the kitchen and wait for Thomas or the Professor to show up, or I could go look for them. Daylight stretched across the brilliant white grounds. I was relatively safe, right? I knew I should probably just go wait for them, but the money in my bra felt like it was weighing me down. I had to find them—now.

I ran around the back of the cabin and tapped on the bedroom window. Maybe Thomas was snoozing. There was no answer. I peered in the cold windowpane. The bed was undisturbed.

Onward, Jules.

My best bet was the marina. Maybe they were reviewing evidence now that the storm had cleared, or waiting for the coroner to arrive. I felt a twinge of trepidation as I trekked down the hill. The marina was Gavin's headquarters. It might be morning, but I didn't want to run into him alone. If he'd killed Tony, he could do it again. I needed an excuse in case he was there. What could I tell him?

Think, Jules.

I could tell him I was looking for supplies. He didn't need to know that Sterling had stored our cooler on the lodge's deck. I would simply tell him that I needed to check the freezer for sausages.

Perfect, Jules. That's foolproof.

Twice I thought about turning around. Power lines and tree branches were strewn around the lake. The storm had packed a mighty punch. Mercury was going to have a big cleanup project on her hands, and if I was right she was going to have to do it without her right-hand man, Gavin.

Shadows seemed to jump from behind the evergreen trees. I knew that it was a simple trick of the light, but that didn't stop me from flinching anyway. Sun reflected on the frozen lake and filtered through the quiet forest.

When I made it to the marina, I stopped in mid-stride. The roped-off crime scene was fully visible in the morning light. I'd been so distracted by the blizzard yesterday that I didn't really have a chance to take it in. A wave of nausea swept over me as I relived opening the chest freezer and finding Tony's body. He was still in there. I couldn't see him, but just knowing that his body was resting on ice made the coffee in my stomach churn.

"Need something?" A gruff voice sounded behind me.

I jumped and whipped my head around at the sound of the voice.

Oh no. It was Gavin. He had a hunting rifle slung on his back and a fishing tackle box in one hand.

"Whew, you startled me." I smiled. Stay calm, Jules.

Gavin didn't return my smile. "What are you doing?"

"I'm in search of sausage this morning." My voice sounded shaky. I hoped that Gavin wouldn't pick up on it. Where were the Professor and Thomas? I was sure that they would be down here.

"Sausage?" Gavin didn't look convinced.

"Yeah, I think Sterling, my sous chef, stored some of our supplies down here. There wasn't space in the main freezer."

Gavin motioned toward the marina. "Go ahead. You can take a look in there, but I don't remember seeing any food."

I froze. I didn't want to go inside the marina with Gavin, especially since he had a gun slung over his shoulder. I also didn't want to give away that I suspected he killed Tony. Was the gun loaded? Would he use it against me? At least this way we were out in the open, and I could make a run for it if I needed to. He wouldn't shoot me in broad daylight? Would he?

"What's the problem?" Gavin stepped closer to me.

The veins in my neck pulsed. My throat felt like it was about to cave in. Think fast, Jules.

I gave Gavin a pained grin. "It's Tony." I pointed my thumb in the direction of the chest freezer. "I'm not sure that I can walk past him. It's kind of creepy, you know?"

Gavin frowned. "You're scared of a dead body? He's not going to jump out at you or anything."

"Right. I know. I'm just kind of creeped out by the whole scene."

Gavin considered my words, then he shrugged. "I'll go look for your sausages if you want to wait here."

"Thanks, that would be great."

Well played, Jules. I commended myself for my quick thinking as Gavin brushed past me and tromped into the marina. Now what? Should I wait for him to come back, or should I go try and find Thomas or the Professor?

I decided to wait. Gavin bought my story, which wasn't entirely untrue. I didn't want to go anywhere near the freezer. If I took off, it might make Gavin suspicious. My best bet was to stay put, stay calm, and get back to the lodge as soon as I could.

My eyes kept darting back to the chest freezer. Tony's body was only a few feet away from me, and his killer wasn't much farther away, either. How had I gotten myself into this position? And the even more important question was, how was I going to get myself out of it?

Despite the sunny skies, the air was still frigid. I rubbed my hands together for warmth and bounced back and forth on my toes. I hoped that Gavin would hurry up and return.

In the distance, I could hear the sound of Lance's board members outside. Good. They must be taking a mid-morning break. Surely Gavin wouldn't risk hurting me with people around, right? I considered shouting to the crowd to come help, but Gavin would hear me before they would. My nose began to drip with the cold. What was Gavin doing in there? It was taking him forever.

Every few minutes I caught sight of a flash of light from inside. Gavin must be searching everywhere for my sausage, I thought. But that didn't make sense. The only two places the sausages could have been were in the chest freezer with Tony's body, or in the pizza kitchen. Why was Gavin searching the entire marina? A new thought invaded my swirling head. Gavin had to be looking for something else. But what?

Chapter Thirty-one

Was Gavin looking for a piece of evidence linking him to Tony's murder? Was he packing getaway supplies? Or worse, was he trying to buy time and figure out a way to silence me?

I was just about to take off for the lodge, when he stepped onto the porch. "Where are you going?"

"You were gone so long, I figured you couldn't find them. I should probably get back to work." I nodded toward the main lodge.

Gavin scowled. "How did you know I couldn't find them?"

"What do you mean? I didn't know. Like I said, you were gone for a while, so I assumed you couldn't find them, that's all." I hoped I sounded convincing.

Gavin didn't have the fishing tackle box any longer. One hand firmly held the gun strapped to his chest.

I took a step backward. "Thanks for checking. I really appreciate it."

"Not a problem. Why are you backing away?" Gavin hardened his eyes.

"I'm not. I was just going to head back to the lodge and get baking again. I guess the guests will have to go without sausage."

Gavin shifted the gun.

I let out a little scream and jumped backward.

"What's your problem?" He stepped from the porch, swinging the rifle into his free hand.

I really needed to calm down. I knew I was acting jumpy and suspicious. What if the gun was loaded? People do crazy things when they're under pressure, and if Gavin realized that I knew he killed Tony there was nothing to stop him from killing me, too.

"Sorry," I said, through chattering teeth. "Being down here again has me totally on edge. I found his body, you know."

"Tony? You found Tony?"

"Yeah. I came down here to look for the sausage yesterday and found him like that." I scrunched my eyes shut and nodded to the cooler.

Gavin clutched the rifle tighter. "You already looked for the sausage?"

"No." I shook my head. What was wrong with me? "I mean, yes, I did start to look, but when I found Tony, I stopped and ran to get help."

"Why are you acting so jumpy all of a sudden?"

"Honestly, I'm just freaked out to be back here. That's all."

"What do you know?" Gavin didn't exactly aim the rifle at me, but he moved it into a position to make it clear that he could.

"What do you mean?" My hand went to my chest.

"You know what I mean." His gaze turned severe. "Did you find my money?"

"What money?" I stepped back again.

"Stop moving. I'm not going to hurt you, but we are going inside to have a talk—right now." He motioned with the barrel of the gun. "Get moving."

I dug my boots into the snow. I had to stall. I knew

that going inside with Gavin was a bad idea. "Gavin, let's talk this through."

"There's nothing to talk through. I want my money."

"I don't have your money," I lied. "I don't know what you're talking about."

"Get inside." Gavin flicked his head toward the marina. He kept the gun aimed in my direction.

"All I want to do is go bake, that's why I'm here."

"Look, I know what you town folks think of me. You think I'm some kind of backwoods idiot. I've worked at this marina for most of my life and I've learned a thing or two about people. They may not notice me, but I notice them. No one is this jumpy over sausage."

His expression shifted. I felt a flash of empathy for him. "What do you mean, people don't notice you?"

"No one notices the help. Rich kids and their families come up here and tool around the lake, leaving their garbage behind for me to clean up. I've had enough. I'm done."

"Is that why you killed Tony?" I asked quietly.

Gavin snapped to attention. "Who said I killed Tony?"

"No one." I shook my head. "Just a guess."

"Get inside," he said, waving the rifle. This time I could tell he meant it.

I stepped forward slowly.

"Move it."

I was out of options. Where were the Professor and Thomas? The Professor said that the coroner was on his way. How long ago had that been? How long would it take him to get through the roads? Carlos and Sterling would have started to wonder why I wasn't back by now, right?

With a longing glance at the lodge, I continued inside.

Right away I knew what Gavin had been doing in the marina. The rental counter was a disaster. Receipts, supplies, and fishing supplies were strewn across it. The cash register drawer was open and emptied. Gavin had been looking for something—frantically looking for some-thing. I was pretty sure that something was tucked into my bra.

"Gavin, what's going on? You're a good guy. You don't want to do this."

He clicked on a flashlight.

I shielded my eyes.

"You're right. I want my money. Give me my money and I'll be on my way."

For a moment I thought maybe I should just hand over the cash, but it was my only bargaining power. If I gave him the cash and he really was crazy there would be no reason for him to keep me alive. I decided to try another tactic. "I think I know where the money is. Let me take you to it."

"Do you think I was born yesterday? You'll take me to my money, or to your police friends?"

I looked at my feet.

"That's what I thought." Gavin's voice was laced with bitterness. "You're no better than the rich kids who come up here to play with daddy's money."

Gavin had a huge chip on his shoulder. Mercury had been wrong about his gruff exterior hiding a softer side.

"I don't get it. If you didn't like it here why didn't you leave?"

"That's what I was trying to do until Tony ruined it."

This was good. He was talking. I just had to keep ask-ing him questions.

"How did Tony ruin things?"

Gavin scratched his head. "He stole my money."

"Then why not go to the police? They can help you get it back."

"Not this money."

I pushed him. I knew that he'd been involved in Tony's

scheme, but he didn't know that. "But if it's your money then the police will help."

"It wasn't exactly my money."

A bird chirped outside. Gavin whipped the flashlight in the direction of the sound. He sighed. "I'm done catering to rich kids. These frat boys come up here for party weekends in their daddys' SUVs. They don't care about this place. They just want to get drunk and go crazy. It's not like it used to be."

"So why didn't you quit?"

"I couldn't. This is the only place I've ever worked. It started by accident a few summers ago. A group of boys took out one of the party boats and trashed it. I had to spend a week cleaning out their vomit and putting in a new motor. When I confronted them about it, they didn't care. They gave me daddy's credit card and a couple hundred bucks. It was easy to pocket the extra cash. I didn't feel bad about the resort, it was a way to make the rich kids pay. They didn't care. It wasn't their money they were spending."

"How did Tony get involved?"

"He found out this summer. Damn. I'd almost saved up enough. I found a property out near Burns. Land is dirt cheap out there. I don't need much. A small shack away from people is fine with me. I'm going to pay cash for it. I'll fish and hunt. No more cleaning up after rich kids."

Rich kids was a recurring theme for Gavin.

"He threatened to tell Mercury if I didn't cut him in. When Mercury and her husband bought this place I knew it was time for me to hit the road. The old owner didn't care about this place. Let it go to shambles, didn't care if the kids were drunk when they were out driving on the boats. Not Mercury. She wants to return the resort to the fishing getaway it used to be. Tony took it too far.

He couldn't keep his mouth shut and he was too obvious. He ruined everything I had worked for."

I wanted to point out that technically he hadn't *worked* for anything. He'd stolen from guests and the resort.

"When he was jacking the price up on that young assistant, I had enough. I told him the deal was off. Then he stole all the cash that I'd saved."

"So you killed him?"

I noticed Gavin's hand shook slightly on the gun. "It was an accident. I caught him drinking an expensive bottle of Mercury's wine and telling that theater girl that she would have to come up with another thousand dollars. I dragged him out of there and down here to make him show me where my money was. We got in a fight. He punched me. I reached for my rifle. I didn't mean to shoot him. It all happened so fast."

I felt sorry for Gavin, and equally terrified. He had just confessed to murder.

At that moment footsteps sounded on the porch outside. Gavin leaped past me and made a break for the pizza shop.

Chapter Thirty-two

"Jules, what are you doing here?" Thomas walked into the room.

"It's Gavin," I whispered as loud as I could and pointed to the pizza shop. "He's getting away."

Thomas reached to his holster and pulled out his gun. In two quick moves he was in the pizza shop and out the side door. I heard him yell, "Stop!"

I held my breath, nervous for Thomas. Who knew how Gavin might react.

"Please don't let Thomas get hurt," I said aloud.

Gavin must have surrendered. The next thing I knew, Thomas was directing him with his hands cuffed behind his back through the marina.

"Jules, can you run up to the lodge and get the Professor for me?"

I sprinted to the lodge. The Professor and Mercury were sitting in the bar drinking coffee. "Thomas needs you down at the marina," I said, panting.

"Juliet, sit." The Professor stood and gave me a look of concern.

"It's okay." I tried to slow my breathing. "It's Gavin. He killed Tony. Thomas has him, but he wants you to come down there right away."

The Professor walked to me and placed his hand on my shoulder. "Thank you, but please relax and breathe for a moment. I'm sure that Thomas has everything under control."

Mercury wrinkled her brow. "Gavin? Did you say Gavin killed Tony? That can't be right, Gavin wouldn't hurt a fly."

"I'm afraid he did. He confessed." I unzipped my coat and reached into my shirt. The envelope was damp with sweat. I handed it to the Professor. "Gavin's been stealing from you," I said to Mercury.

She walked over and looked through the envelope with the Professor while I explained what Gavin had told me.

"I can't believe it." Mercury looked stunned. "Out of everyone here, I trusted Gavin the most."

"If it's any consolation, he said that he was done. That's why he and Tony fought. I don't think he planned to kill Tony. He was trying to do the right thing." Well, sort of. He was going to tell you all about it. I paused and turned to the Professor. "What will happen to him?"

"It's too soon to tell." The Professor placed the envelope in his tweed jacket. "I'll see that this gets returned to you," he said to Mercury. "But I'll need to catalog it as evidence."

Mercury nodded.

Bright blue, red, and yellow lights flashed out the bay window. The coroner and the power company had arrived. Mercury and the Professor left together. I needed to check on breakfast.

Lance and a few board members sipped coffee in the dining room. He waved me over. "What's all the commotion about, darling? I heard raised voices in the bar."

"They've arrested Tony's killer."

"Do tell, darling. Don't leave me hanging like that."

"It's Gavin."

"Gavin? The burly mountain man? Well, that is a twist, isn't it?"

"Listen, we can talk later, I've got to make sure that Sterling has everything under control in the kitchen." I shook myself free from Lance's grasp.

"Fair enough, but we are not finished. I need to hear all the gory details. All of them."

The smell from the kitchen made my stomach growl. Pizza sauce was simmering on the stove. Garlic, onion, basil, and tomatoes lingered in the air.

Sterling stirred the sauce. "Hey, what happened to you? Carlos and I were about to send out a search party."

"You don't want to know." I walked straight to the sink and ran my hands under hot water. The tips of my fingers had turned bright red.

Carlos was arranging an artful tray of fresh fruits. It reminded me of the extravagant food displays he used to create on the ship. "Julieta, your lips are blue and you are shivering."

I kept the water running on my hands. My body quaked, but I had a feeling it was due to the adrenaline pulsing through me. Gavin had said he wouldn't hurt me. I didn't think he would, but now that I was safely back in the kitchen fear assaulted my body.

"Julieta, sit." Carlos swept me onto a barstool and shut off the water. He wrapped his arm around me and rubbed as fast as he could. "Sterling, can you bring some coffee, yes?"

Sterling left the sauce simmering and headed for the coffeepot.

"It was Gavin," I said. My voice sounded distant and foggy. Sterling placed a coffee in front of me. I nodded thanks and explained how I found the money stashed under the bar and how Gavin was the one skimming from Lake of the Woods. The words spilled from me. I told them about looking for Thomas and the Professor, but finding Gavin instead.

Carlos didn't loosen his grip on me. "Julieta, this is very dangerous. I am glad you are safe, but I do not think you should have done this. This is what the police are for. You should have stayed here and waited for the police to come."

He was right. I knew that Thomas and the Professor would say the same thing. I couldn't tell any of them that the real reason I went in search of Thomas myself was because I didn't want to foster the love triangle I seemed to somehow be in the middle of.

"You should eat," Carlos said, studying my face. "You don't look so blue anymore. This is good."

"I've got it," Sterling said. He walked to the stove and removed a plate with sausages and rolls. "We saved you some."

No wonder that Lance was impressed with breakfast. The delicate and fluffy pastries would rival any French pâtisserie. Paired with the citrusy fruit and spicy sausage it was comfort on a plate. I cut into the sausage. The center was firm, there was no pink, and the juices ran clear. "Nice cooking on these," I said to Sterling.

"Carlos kept an eye on me." Sterling winked at Carlos.

"No, no." Carlos shook his head. "He has it, you know. He cooks from here." He pointed to his heart. "He cooks with love."

"He does," I agreed.

Sterling looked embarrassed.

"He asked me for my recipe for the pizza sauces." Carlos massaged my back as he spoke. "I told him I could give him the recipe, but every great chef knows the most important ingredient is love. Without it everything tastes flat."

Everything had tasted flat while Carlos and I were apart.

"Do you want to taste this?" Sterling ladled pizza sauce onto a spoon and brought it to me.

I blew on the spoon, letting my nose take in the flavors. It smelled like a summer garden. The tomatoes had been puréed and blended with herbs. This was going to be *divine,* as Lance would say, on a wood-fired crust.

"Very nice," I said.

Carlos nodded happily. "*Sí,* I told you, he is good, no?"

"He's good."

"Should I start making the pizzas?" Sterling asked.

I moved to get up. Carlos held my shoulder firmly. "No, you sit. You eat. Sterling and I will make the pizzas."

My core temperature rose and my anxiety faded as I watched Carlos and Sterling spread sauce on the pizza crust. Carlos flicked his wrist in a rhythmic and sexy motion. It looked like he was flirting with the dough as he layered on red sauce. I couldn't believe we were about to serve our last meal at Lake of the Woods, and that Gavin had been arrested. I wondered what happened next. Would Thomas and the Professor take him to Ashland, or would they wait for the authorities to arrive from Medford?

"This pizza, it will become a bridge to pass your emotions to someone else," Carlos explained to Sterling as he lovingly massaged olive oil on the dough with his hands. "You nurture your food. You nurture your guests."

Sterling followed Carlos's lead.

"*Sí!* That is it."

I smiled. Was this how Carlos interacted with Ramiro? It warmed my heart to see him take Sterling under his wing, but unanswered questions still sounded in my head.

Like why didn't Whitney tell Thomas and the Professor that she had seen Tony before he was killed, and that he'd been trying to get more money out of her? Why hide the bottle of wine? And why was Dean shooting in the woods? My mind wouldn't rest until I'd talked to both of them.

For the moment I had a singular mission—finish lunch service and then go home. I had never been more excited to return to Ashland.

Chapter Thirty-three

I polished off my breakfast. Who knew that being alone with a murderer would give me such a ravenous appetite? Then I tied on my apron and started rinsing cherries. This is where I was supposed to be.

Sterling and Carlos sliced steaming hot pizzas and delivered them to the guests. I heard cheers and applause, as I reduced cherries, sugar, and water on the stove. If they were that excited about pizza, just wait until they saw my flaming cherries jubilee.

Every once in a while I caught a glimpse of the activity down at the marina through the kitchen window. A team of police in blue uniforms traipsed the perimeter, snapping photos and collecting evidence. Another crew of power workers had scaled an electrical pole, as high as the evergreen trees, and were working on restoring power.

"They're ready for you," Sterling said, bringing in pizza trays without a single crumb.

"Showtime." I mimicked Lance's tone.

Sterling laughed. "What do you need me to do?"

"Bring out bowls and the ice cream. You can go around the table and scoop ice cream into everyone's bowl, while I set the cherries on fire."

"You seem pretty excited about this. I never knew you were a pyro."

Carlos held up the bottle of rum. "Julieta has a fierce and fiery side, you know."

I snatched the bottle from his hand. "Don't give away all my secrets. I've worked hard to display a professional attitude with my team, right, Sterling?"

"Ha!" Sterling laughed.

"You two are trouble together." I pulled the cherries off the heat and doused them with rum. "Let's do this."

I carried the pan to the table. Sterling followed with a tub of vanilla bean ice cream. "Who's ready for dessert?" I struck a long match. The rum ignited, and the room erupted in cheers. I swirled the wild flames until they died out.

"Darling, now *that* was a show." Lance clapped. "Talk about sending us out on fire. I love it. I absolutely love it."

"You haven't tasted it yet."

"I don't need to. I know it will be divine." Lance addressed the board. "A final round of applause for our lovely chefs."

My cheeks warmed as I ladled the hot cherries over ice cream. It was a striking color combination.

The guests applauded and lavished us with praise. I felt like I was on stage. I couldn't wait to escape back to the kitchen.

When the last of the cherries had been dished up, I made my exit, but not before Lance stopped me. He pressed something into my hand and whispered, "Kidding aside, darling, you did a brilliant job this weekend. Many thanks." He kissed the top of my hand. "Absolutely brilliant."

His sincerity gave me pause. Then he quickly returned

to his normal role as theater director, commanding that everyone dive into dessert. I snuck away.

Inside the kitchen, I realized the paper Lance had given me was actually an envelope with a stack of tidy one-hundred-dollar bills and a note written in Lance's beautiful scrawl. "Another smashing success. We do make a stunning team, don't we? Treat yourself to something special. Well done, darling. XOXO."

Lance's tip was generous to say the least. I removed a few bills and walked over to Sterling who was cleaning up at the sink.

"I have something for you."

He turned around and dried his hands on a gingham dishtowel.

I placed the cash in his hands.

"What's this?"

"A tip." I smiled.

"What?" He stared at the money, then tried to give it back to me. "It's too much. I can't take this."

I stepped away. "It's all yours. I'm not taking it back."

"But, Jules?"

"Nope." I held up my hand. "It's a tip from Lance, and that's how we work at Torte. We share tips."

"Yeah, but not tips like this."

"Sterling, you've been invaluable to me this weekend. Take it as a token of my appreciation for a job well done. I couldn't have done this without you." I checked to see if Carlos was with us. He wasn't. "I couldn't have done *any of it* without you."

"Thanks." Sterling's voice was thick with emotion. "It means a lot to have you trust me."

I patted him on the shoulder. "Like Carlos said, you cook with your heart. It comes through."

Sterling folded the cash and stuck it into the front

pocket of his hoodie. "What's the plan now? I'll finish cleaning and then pack up?"

Carlos stepped into the kitchen. "Are you making plans to leave?"

I nodded.

"I was hoping you would drive with me."

I looked to Sterling. "Is that okay with you?"

He shrugged. "As long as it's okay that I drive your mom's car."

"She'll be fine with that."

"It is settled then," Carlos said. "I will pack our things at the cabin and come back for you."

Sterling and I finished clearing the breakfast dishes and cleaning the kitchen. There wasn't much to pack. Lance and his guests had polished off most of the food. We boxed up the remaining supplies and the kitchen tools we'd brought. Sterling gave the kitchen one last walk-through after he loaded the car with all our stuff.

"You're sure you're good?" he asked.

"I'm good." I gave him a thumbs-up. "Drive safe. Take your time, okay?"

"You got it." He paused at the doorway. "Thanks again for the tip, Jules."

"*Thank you* for all your help, Sterling." I waved. "See you back at Torte soon."

As he left, I smiled. I couldn't wait to tell Mom how far he had come this weekend. Having Carlos here made a major impact on Sterling's ability and confidence level in a short amount of time. When we got back to Torte I was going to talk to Mom about continuing Sterling's cooking lessons. We had the perfect team—Andy manning the espresso bar, Stephanie training on pastries, and now Sterling working as a sous chef. Torte was in great shape for the new OSF season. And Lance's tip was going into our fund for new ovens. My wish list now also included a wood-fired oven.

Despite the storm and Tony's murder the weekend had been a success. I flipped off the lights and bid good-bye to the cozy kitchen.

It was time to go home.

Chapter Thirty-four

Most of the board members had dispersed. A couple sat by the fireplace, but otherwise the dining room was empty.

When I walked past the bar, I noticed Mercury and Whitney going over an invoice. I ducked my head in. "Just wanted to say thanks and good-bye."

Mercury motioned for me to come in. "We were just talking about you. Your ears must be burning."

"Me?" I walked to the bar.

"Yeah, I was telling Whitney that we have you to thank for catching Gavin."

"Oh, I don't know about that." I shook my head. "Thomas and the Professor were already on to him."

"Yes, but they told me he might have already been on the road if you hadn't stalled him."

"I doubt he would have gotten far." I pointed behind them to the snowy scene outside.

"True." Mercury glanced out the window. "But he knew the back roads around here better than anyone. There's a lot of forest to disappear into."

"Good point."

Whitney held up a paper invoice. "I have you to thank, too."

"What for?"

"This." She pointed to the invoice. "It's the exact price we first discussed. Hopefully, that means I'll get to keep my job."

"Lance would never have fired you," I said.

"He might have when he saw how much Tony was going to charge us."

"But that wasn't your fault."

She gulped. "It kind of was. I was telling Mercury that I lied. I did lose the order. I tried to blame Tony. When he found out, he jacked the price up. I should have told Lance right away."

"Losing an order isn't grounds for having Tony charge you double."

"More than double," Mercury said, shaking her head. "I can't believe that he and Gavin were stealing from us and our customers this whole time."

"What are you going to do now?" I asked.

She sighed. "Start over, I guess. My husband isn't going to believe everything that happened, but if there's a silver lining, it's that the resort is probably in much better shape financially than we thought."

I paused for a moment and then looked at Whitney. "Before I go, I have a question that's been bothering me."

"What?"

"Why didn't you tell Thomas and the Professor about Tony? You were the one drinking wine with him the night that he was killed, right?"

She turned as red as the pizza sauce. "Yeah. I apologized to Mercury for that. I told her I would pay for the wine."

Mercury placed her hand over Whitney's and said gently, "And I told you not to worry about it. The fault was all Tony's, not yours."

Whitney smiled up at her. "I don't know why I didn't

tell the police. I was so scared. Tony threatened to tell Lance. He said Lance would fire me for sure. I needed this job. My uncle worked hard to get it for me and I didn't want to let him down."

"But the police would have understood."

"I know." She hung her head. "I guess I just caved to the pressure. Tony told me to meet him in the kitchen after everyone left. He was already half drunk when I arrived. I thought maybe I could convince him that I didn't have that kind of money and that I was too new to OSF to know how to expense extra fees. He wouldn't listen. He just kept drinking more wine, and laughing about drinking the expensive stuff. He said not to worry, that he would fake an invoice and Lance would never know."

"So that's how he did it," I said. "He created fake invoices."

Mercury nodded. "Yep. I found a stack of them in the back of the cash register. I can't believe how much money he stashed. The Professor is going to work with me to make sure we return the money to our customers. At least the ones we can. It will be hard to track down people he overcharged in cash, but the customers that he invoiced will get their money back."

I spotted Carlos putting our bags in the back of his rental car. "I'm glad that the Professor is going to help you," I said. "I see my ride out there. I better go."

"Thanks again for everything," Mercury said. "You're welcome here anytime. Come back this summer and stay as my guest."

"I'd love to." I gave them both a hug and headed for the car.

Before I got to the front door, I ran smack into Dean Barnes. He had two suitcases in his hands.

"Sorry," I said, taking a step back.

"The fault is mine." He set the suitcases on the floor. "I've come to find Whitney. I'm her ride home."

"She's in the bar." I pointed to my left.

"Excellent." He smiled and extended his hand. "It's been a pleasure. I'll be frequenting Torte. You have a fan in me for sure."

"Thanks." I returned his handshake. "We're open every day. Come by anytime." I started to walk past him, but stopped in mid-stride. I had to know why he'd been shooting in the woods. "Can I ask you one thing, before I go?"

"Of course."

"Why were you shooting in the woods?"

"For practice. I told you this."

"I know, but it's kind of weird, don't you think, to shoot at night?"

He shook his head and chuckled. "Oh, it's becoming clear to me. Did you think I had something to do with the murder? Is that why you were so skittish when I saw you?"

I nodded.

"I assure you, the only thing I enjoy shooting is fowl, and an occasional fox."

"At night?"

"Shooting is my way of letting off steam. I don't do well when I'm cooped up for long stretches of time. I needed the fresh air and the sound of my gun."

"Got it."

"A murderer, me?" He laughed. "I thank you for considering me a suspect. It makes me feel quite young, actually." He gave me a half salute and walked to the bar.

I continued toward the car. All of my questions seemed silly. I should have trusted my initial instinct that there was no way Whitney or the elderly Dean could have killed Tony. I guess murder messed with my head, too.

Speaking of messing with my head. Carlos stood with his legs crossed and his back against the car. He looked like an ad for a skiing magazine with his posture and his puffy jacket. I had a feeling he was going to mess with my head.

Thomas and the Professor were busy with the investigation as Carlos and I drove past. Thomas held up his hand in a wave. His face looked wistful. I thought about asking Carlos to stop, but I didn't. I caught Thomas's eye in the side mirror. He smiled, gave me a final wave, and returned to the crime scene. I knew that we had more to say to each other, but for now it would have to wait.

Carlos and I took the opposite route home—through Medford. Gavin had been right about the storm. Work crews and snowplows lined the two-lane highway. The sound of chain saws and heavy construction equipment made it hard to speak. I gazed out the window at the massive piles of snow.

"Julieta, you are a million miles away," Carlos said as he steered the car around a giant log.

"Sorry." I smiled. "I just need some time to think. My head is kind of swimming in this murder and everything that happened this weekend." What I didn't tell him was that my head was running on a constant loop about him. Our conversation about Ramiro hadn't left me feeling any clearer on why he had lied to me. If anything, it made me even more confused. He clearly loved his son, yet had chosen to shut me out of that part of his life. What else could he have lied about?

Carlos took one hand from the wheel and placed it over mine. "It is okay. It is good for you to think, *querida.*"

Trees blurred out the window as Carlos returned his hands to the wheel and sped around a curve. It wasn't only the trust issue that was bothering me. There was no denying the chemistry between us, but was it enough? Everything about our relationship felt like the surface of the sea. We worked great on smooth water, but did we have enough depth to weather this rough patch?

A police car zoomed past us on the opposite side of the road. I wondered if it was heading to Lake of the Woods. "I can't believe it was Gavin," I said, watching its blue and red flashing lights. "The lodge was so important to him. It was his life. It was all he had. Why would he ruin that?"

Carlos was quiet for a moment. When he finally spoke, his voice held a trace of sadness. "He made a mistake." I knew he wasn't talking about Gavin.

We drove on in silence. The storm had left its mark on the forest. Snow was heaped as far as I could see. Debris was scattered on the ground and roadway. Uprooted ancient trees had caved to the power of the wind and the weight of the snow. I felt sad for them, and for Gavin. If only he had gone to Mercury. She would have been upset, but she trusted him so much, I'm sure she would have found a way to forgive him. There was no chance of that now. I wondered what would happen to him, and his forest retreat.

Before I knew it, we passed a sign saying it was ten miles to Ashland. Ten more miles and I would be home again. Home! I couldn't wait to see the staff at Torte and Mom. Mom and I had so much to discuss, like Tony's murder and Sterling's first successful outing as a sous chef. Not to mention trying to figure out where she stood with the Professor, and then Carlos.

Carlos was coming home with me. Things were not the same between us, but I owed him a chance. I thought back to the quote that Sterling had shared on the drive to

Lake of the Woods. I couldn't step twice into the same river. Was I doing that with Carlos? Or was there a way we could find a new river together? I didn't know if there was space for him in the new life that I'd carved out in Ashland, but I was about to find out.

Recipes

Orange Cardamom Rolls

Ingredients:

DOUGH:

  1 package quick rise yeast
  ¼ cup warm water
  1 teaspoon sugar
  ½ cup melted butter
  ½ cup sour cream
  ½ cup sugar
  ½ teaspoon salt
  1 egg
  2¼ cups flour

FILLING:

  ¼ cup butter
  ½ cup brown sugar
  ½ orange—juice and grated rind
  1 teaspoon cardamom

GLAZE:
  ½ orange—juice and grated rind
  1 cup powdered sugar

Dough:

Preheat oven to 350 degrees. Dissolve yeast in warm water with the teaspoon of sugar. Let stand 5 minutes.

Combine melted butter, sour cream, sugar, salt, and the egg in a mixing bowl. Gradually stir yeast mixture into butter mixture. After the yeast has been incorporated slowly stir in flour, one cup at a time, until it forms into a soft dough.

Lightly flour a cutting board and knead dough until it is smooth. Add a couple tablespoons of flour as needed if dough is sticking to hands.

Place dough in the mixing bowl, cover with a towel and let rise for one hour or until doubled in size.

Filling:

Combine butter, brown sugar, orange rind, cardamom, and half the juice of the orange with a fork.

Form dough into two equal balls. Roll the first ball into a rectangle about an inch thick. Sprinkle with half of the filling. Roll into a log, beginning with the long side. Repeat with remaining dough. Cut each roll into 12 (1-inch) slices. Place slices in a buttered 13 × 9-inch baking pan. Cover and let rise 30 minutes or until doubled in size.

Bake for 20 minutes.

Glaze:

Whisk powdered sugar, juice from remaining half of orange and grated rind. Drizzle over warm rolls. Sprinkle with cardamom.

Roasted Chicken

Ingredients:
  Whole chicken (Jules prefers to use organic free-
    range chicken)
  1 yellow onion
  6 cloves garlic
  4 carrots
  4 celery stalks
  1 lemon
  1 clementine
  6 sprigs of fresh rosemary
  6 sprigs of fresh thyme
  6 sprigs of fresh pineapple sage
  Olive oil
  Sea salt
  Pepper

Directions:
Preheat oven at 400 degrees. Drizzle olive oil in the bottom of a roasting pan. Rinse and clean chicken. Be sure to remove everything from the bird's cavity. Chop onion, carrots, celery and place in the bottom of the pan. Peel garlic and place whole cloves in the bottom of the pan. Poke small holes in the lemon and clementine and stuff in bird's cavity along with the fresh herbs. Place on top of the vegtables. Massage bird with olive oil, salt and pepper. Roast at 400 degrees for 1 to 1½ hours, or until juices run clear. Remove from the oven, cover with foil, and allow to rest for fifteen minutes before carving.

Braised Green Beans

Ingredients:
  1 pound fresh string beans
  4 pieces of center-cut bacon
  3 cloves garlic
  2 to 3 cups chicken stock
  Salt
  Pepper

Directions:
Rinse and drain beans. Chop bacon and fry in a sauté pan.
Add chopped garlic and beans to bacon and fat. Sprinkle
with salt and pepper. Add enough chicken stock to cover
beans. Bring to a boil. Cover. Reduce heat to low and
simmer for 40 to 45 minutes. Serve hot.

Double Chocolate Cookies with Chocolate Cream Cheese Frosting

Ingredients:
  1 cup butter
  1 cup sugar
  1 cup light brown sugar
  2 eggs
  1 teaspoon vanilla
  1 teaspoon baking soda
  ½ teaspoon salt
  ⅔ cup unsweetened cocoa
    powder
  3 cups flour
  1 cup milk chocolate chips
  1 cup semisweet chocolate chips

Directions:

Preheat oven to 400 degrees. Cream butter and sugar together in an electric mixer. Add vanilla and eggs, beat at medium speed. Sift dry ingredients, blend at low speed until combined. Stir in chocolate chips by hand.

Form dough into one-inch balls and place on cookie sheets, two inches apart. Bake at 400 degrees for ten minutes. Cool and frost with chocolate cream cheese frosting below.

FROSTING:

½ cup butter
8 ounces cream cheese
1 teaspoon vanilla
½ cup unsweetened cocoa powder
2½ to 3 cups powdered sugar

Directions:

Bring butter and cream cheese to room temperature and whip together in an electric mixer until light and fluffy. Add vanilla. Slowly sift in unsweetened cocoa powder and powdered sugar, mixing on low until blended. Spread on cooled cookies.

Beef Stew

Ingredients:
   1 pound stew meat
   1 large yellow onion
   2 stalks celery
   4 carrots
   4 cloves garlic
   2 large russet potatoes
   4 cups beef broth
   14.5 ounce can of diced tomatoes
   2 tablespoons flour
   1 teaspoon salt
   1 teaspoon pepper
   1 teaspoon brown sugar
   Fresh thyme
   3 dried bay leaves
   Olive oil

Directions:
Add two glugs of olive oil to frying pan and heat on medium high. Dredge stew meat in flour. Brown meat on both sides. Remove from heat and set aside. Peel and rough chop all vegetables. Add another few glugs of olive oil to a hearty stew pot. Sauté vegetables on medium low until translucent. Add beef broth, tomatoes, salt, pepper, brown sugar, thyme, and bay leaves.

Bring to a boil. Reduce heat add browned meat. Cover and simmer on low for four to six hours.

Cherries Jubilee

Ingredients:

  1 pound of fresh Oregon Bing cherries (pitted and
     halved) or frozen if not in season
  ½ cup sugar
  1 teaspoon freshly grated orange rind
  1 tablespoon orange juice
  ½ cup rum
  1 pint vanilla ice cream

Directions:

Rinse and drain whole cherries. Cut them in half and discard pits. Add pitted cherries, orange juice, orange rind, and sugar in a sauté pan. Sauté on low heat for five minutes or until the sugar dissolves. Bring heat to medium and cook cherries in their juices for an additional five minutes.

To flambé using a gas stove, remove cherries from the heat and add rum. Light the rum with a long match, being sure to swirl the pan until the flames subside.

To flambé using an electric stove, add rum to a saucepan and warm it on low for 3 minutes. Remove pan from heat, light rum with a long match, and carefully pour ignited rum over the cherries, swirling the pan until the flames subside.

Serve warm cherries over ice cream.

*Jules likes to flambé the cherries tableside for a showstopping presentation.

Snowflake Latte

Andy's prayer for snow in the form of a snowflake latte worked. Try his delicious creation at home in front of a roaring fire.

Ingredients:
  Good quality espresso (Jules and Mom serve Stumptown at Torte, but are always open to trying new blends)
  2 % milk
  2 tablespoons white chocolate sauce
  1 teaspoon almond extract
  Whipping cream
  White chocolate shavings

DIRECTIONS:
Prepare espresso and steam milk. Mix white chocolate sauce and almond extract in the bottom of your favorite coffee mug. Add steamed milk and stir. Pour over espresso. Top with whipping cream and white chocolate shavings.

Read on for an excerpt from the next installment
in the Bakeshop Mystery Series

Caught Bread Handed

Available in July from St. Martin's Paperbacks!

They say that home is where the heart is. That could be true. But what if my heart was lost? What if my heart couldn't find its way home?

Technically I'd been *home* for six months. Home for me was my childhood town of Ashland, Oregon. It's a magical place with its Elizabethan architecture, charming Shakespearean-themed shops and restaurants, inviting outdoor parks and public spaces, and mild Mediterranean climate. Not to mention the warm and welcoming locals who can make a stranger feel like they've lived in Ashland for decades upon meeting for the first time.

Our family bakeshop, Torte, sits in the center of my hometown. Ashland has something for everyone from its world-famous stage productions, to its funky artistic community, and wide open spaces perfect for adventure lovers. The only thing it didn't have at the moment was snow. Usually in January, Mt. Ashland's slopes were coated in deep layers of snow. But not this January.

I looked out Torte's front windows. The sun hung low in the late afternoon sky. A group of musicians with banjos and an accordion was busking in the center of the plaza. It looked like spring outside. Bistro tables had been set up in front of restaurants and shop doors were propped open. It was hard to believe that people were meandering through downtown without coats in January, especially since winter had begun with an epic storm.

A week ago I had been at Lake of the Woods Resort, a remote alpine lodge, for a catering job and had ended up snowed in. Thick white flakes dumped from the sky for three days. Snow fell in record levels causing power outages and making travel impossible. Ashland had been hit by the blizzard too. Customers had to strap on cross-country skis for their morning coffee fix. After the storm blew over the sun emerged from the clouds. It melted the snow and ushered in a stretch of unseasonably warm weather.

I had to admit that I was a little disappointed. I hadn't experienced a winter in over a decade and I had been looking forward to a change of seasons. My work as a pastry chef for a renowned cruise line had taken me to every corner of the globe. It had been an adventurous ten years. I'd seen nearly every tropical port of call, but the ship always sailed under sunny skies. Winter meant island hopping in the Caribbean and swimming in the Mediterranean Sea. Snow was unheard of in the warm blue waters where tourists took refuge from winter's harsh winds and swirling storms.

In anticipation of the cold weather months in Southern Oregon, I had purchased a new wardrobe of sweaters, jeans, and thick wool socks. From the looks of the busy plaza outside, I wasn't going to need them anytime soon. People milled around the fountains and information kiosk wearing shorts and thin sweatshirts. Definitely not winter attire. They looked like they belonged on the upper deck of the cruise ship, not Ashland in January. Since I'd returned from Lake of the Woods the temperature in Ashland had been holding in the mid-sixties. At this rate, I was going to have to break out my summer clothes again.

The sound of mixers churning in the background and the smell of sweet rolls rising in the oven made the lack of snow more manageable. Breathing in the comforting scents brought an instant calm to my body. Being home again had been better than I had ever expected. When I returned to Ashland six months ago with a broken heart, I thought it would be a temporary stop until I found my land legs and figured out what was next for me. That quickly changed. The community had welcomed me in, and working at Torte with Mom and our incredible young staff had given me a new sense of purpose and direction. There was just one lingering problem (literally and figuratively)—my estranged husband, Carlos.

I glanced across the plaza and shook my head. Carlos was at the Merry Windsor chatting with a bell boy in a green and gold striped uniform. Of course. I couldn't escape him. I wasn't sure I wanted to.

I watched them talk. Carlos's dark hair fell in a soft wave over one eye. The sleeves of his casual white shirt had been rolled up to the elbows, revealing his bronzed forearms. He'd been telling everyone in town that he brought the Spanish sun with him. "You see, this is how we winter in Spain. We drink in the sun along with some lovely Spanish wine."

Everyone was charmed by Carlos, myself included. It was impossible not to fall under his spell. His sultry dark eyes and Spanish accent were practically irresistible as was his naturally relaxed personality. He'd been in Ashland a little over a week and had managed to bewitch everyone in town.

Almost everyone. Richard Lord, the owner of the Merry Windsor, where Carlos was staying, didn't look

pleased that Carlos was distracting the bell boy from his
work. I shook my head again as I watched his animated
speech with large hand motions. The bell boy chatted
happily as if he and Carlos had been friends for years.
Carlos had that effect on people.

My mom, Helen, had the same gift. She used it differ-
ently. Her approach was to offer up a hot cup of coffee, a
fresh pastry, and a listening ear. Carlos tended to lure
people in with his witty banter and whimsical pranks.
Both approaches achieved the same result. Mom and
Carlos had a way of putting people at ease.

Carlos turned in my direction and caught my eye. He
blew me a kiss and then waved with both hands in an
attempt to get me outside. I shook my head and pointed to
the kitchen. Heat rose in my cheeks as I left the window
and walked back to my work station. My husband had
caught me staring at him. Normally that wouldn't be a
bad thing, but right now it was for me. Having Carlos in
Ashland for the last week had been equally wonderful
and confusing. He was leaving for the ship in three days.
I couldn't get distracted now. I had too much to do. Like
getting our wholesale orders out the door, I said to myself focusing on the stack of orders resting on the kitchen
island.

I leafed through them, making sure everything was
ready for tomorrow morning's shift. Thanks to some
new restaurant accounts, Mom and I would finally be
able to get the new ovens that Torte so desperately
needed. We'd been barely getting by with one functional
oven. New kitchen equipment came with a hefty price
tag. We had been saving every extra penny for the last
six months, and taking on extra wholesale accounts. It
had paid off. We were so close that I could almost taste
the fresh bread baking in shiny new stainless steel commercial ovens. I'd even gone so far as sketching out how

we might make some minor tweaks to the kitchen floor plan and modernize our ordering system.

Having the new wholesale accounts had been great for our bottom line, but it meant that things were very tight in Torte's already small kitchen. I had been coming in earlier than usual in order to bake and deliver bread to our wholesale clients before the morning coffee rush. The long hours were taking a toll on my body. I shifted my weight as I restacked the order forms and surveyed the kitchen. Everything was running smoothly, as usual.

Stephanie, the college student who had been helping with pastry orders in the back, rolled sugar cookie dough on the butcher block. "Is this thin enough, Mrs. Capshaw?"

Mom tucked a strand of her brown bobbed hair behind her ear and nodded in approval. "Perfect."

"I'm going to grab a coffee. Need anything?" I asked.

Mom dusted a pan of brownies with powdered sugar. "No thanks." Her brown eyes narrowed. She caught my apron as I passed. "Hold up there, young lady."

"What?"

"How many cups is that for you today?"

"Uh. I don't know. Not that many. Maybe a couple. I haven't been keeping count." I looked at my feet. If I made eye contact with her I knew that she'd catch me in a lie.

Mom threw her head back and laughed. "Ha!" She turned to Stephanie. "Did you hear that? Not many. By my count you've had at least a gallon."

"A gallon?" I over-enunciated my words and played along. "Hardly." Then I folded my arms in front of my chest. "Plus it's my duty to carefully sample our coffee offerings. You wouldn't want us serving bitter coffee to customers, would you?"

Mom flicked my apron and shook her head. "Stephanie, you and I may need to stage a coffee intervention."

Stephanie looked up from the cookie dough and offered us both a rare grin. "I'm in."

I left them brainstorming ways to keep me from the espresso bar and headed for the front of the bakeshop. As I was about to ask Andy, our barista, for a double Americano, a woman's voice called my name.

"Juliet! You are just the person I wanted to see. Can I bother you for a moment, dear?" An elderly woman with silver hair stood near the pastry case holding an almond croissant in one hand and clutching the counter with the other.

It was Rosalind Gates, the president of the Ashland Downtown Association. She wore a black t-shirt with the words "SOS—Save Our Shakespeare" written on the front.

"Sure." I scanned the dining room and pointed to an empty booth near the front windows.

Rosalind looked a bit unsteady on her feet. "Let me help." I offered her my hand and guided her to the booth.

"Thanks, my dear," she said as she carefully lowered herself into the booth. "My hip has been creaky lately."

Before I could ask her what she needed she pointed a bony finger across the street. "Look at that monstrosity. We have to put a stop to this right now. That woman has gone too far this time. Way too far."

My eyes followed Rosalind's quivering finger. She was pointing to ShakesBurgers. The chain restaurant had opened last week. Many local business owners weren't thrilled about it. Downtown Ashland is known for its eclectic shops and restaurants. The plaza is a hub for small, family-owned businesses. ShakesBurgers was the first chain to take ownership of a building downtown and most people weren't happy about it. Not only was the neon fast-food burger joint out of place in the historic Shakespearean village, but they had also taken over one of Ashland's beloved restaurants, The Jester.

Alan Matterson had opened The Jester last February. He was an old family friend who had run an extremely successful food booth at the farmer's market since I was a kid. His hand-dipped corndogs were legendary around town, as was Alan's entertaining personality. In any place other than Ashland, Alan might have struggled to find his niche. Here, though, he blended right in. No one gave his black and white checked jester jumpsuits or his zany hats a second look.

Locals flocked to The Jester for Alan's home-style cooking. The restaurant was themed after a medieval court. Tourists loved the restaurant's brocade façade and funky collection of jester hats and scepters that hung from the walls and ceiling. Alan greeted each customer who walked through the door with a goofy joke and a little jig. Kids' meals came with a gag gift—like waxed candy lips or a fake camera that squirted water. The Jester's food was equally irreverent. Alan served his signature corndogs along with pink and blue swirled cotton candy and banana splits piled high with Umpqua Valley ice cream and topped with sprinkles and maraschino cherries.

It seemed like The Jester was a success, but in early December right before the holiday season a "Closed" sign was posted on the front door. A week later the building was listed for sale. Before anyone could blink, a construction crew began ripping down the Shakespearean façade and removed the cotton candy machine.

One of the issues with running a seasonal business in Ashland is calculating for the slow season. Sadly, many shops and restaurants open in February when OSF kicks off their new season, only to close in November and December when the tourists return home. Watching it happen to a friend like Alan had been devastating. What made it even worse was having a chain like ShakesBurgers move in.

Mindy Nolan, a wealthy real estate developer who owned a number of chain restaurants, swooped in, purchased the building, and gave it an overnight makeover. She opened ShakesBurgers two weeks later. The two restaurants could not have been more different. ShakesBurgers had over thirty stores in eight western states. They specialized in fast food—burgers, fries, anything coated in grease. Unlike the other shops in the plaza, ShakesBurgers had painted the exterior of the building in a shocking lime green and installed neon flashing signage that included an animated dancing milkshake and hamburger and a dialog bubble pulsing their tagline: "Our burgers make your buns shake."

It all happened so fast. One day The Jester was there and thriving. The next day it was gone. Some of my fellow business owners had expressed concern about Mindy and how she had handled the takeover. The word "hostile" had been tossed around. Rumors tend to spread quickly in a small town. I've learned that it's best not to make assumptions. I hadn't had a chance to talk to Alan. He'd gone in hiding since ShakesBurgers had opened.

While Mindy was in the middle of renovations, she caught me in the plaza one day and asked if we'd be willing to source all of the bread and buns for ShakesBurgers.

"You're Juliet, right?" She hoisted a box of pre-cut frozen potatoes in one arm and extended her hand. "I'm Mindy Nolan. Word is you bake the best bread in town. I want to source all of our buns from you. We try to partner with local businesses, you know, throw the small guy a bone, when we launch a new store. I don't take no for an answer. You might as well say yes."

Mindy's condescending attitude was off-putting. "I'm not sure," I replied. "We're pretty busy right now."

"A small business owner turning down thousands of dollars per month in new revenue before you've even had a chance to hear my pitch, are you crazy?" She set the box of frozen potatoes on the sidewalk and folded her arms across her chest. Her lime green shirt with a cartoon logo of a burger oozing with melting cheese blended in with the garish color of the building.

I didn't appreciate Mindy's approach. "I'll have to talk it over with my mom," I said, trying to end the conversation.

Mindy continued to press. "I'll make it worth your while. This could be a very lucrative deal for you. Shakes-Burgers is one of the fastest growing chains on the West Coast. You're going to want to be in on what we have to offer."

I disagreed. Working with the chain would anger my fellow downtown business owners. I couldn't betray Alan, and I didn't want Torte's products associated with a giant corporation. "Like I said we'll talk about it, but I don't know that it's going to be a match," I said to Mindy.

My instincts were right. When I told Mom about Mindy's proposition she held up her hand to stop me before I'd even finished speaking. "Juliet, no. No amount of money is worth it. We can't do that to our friends."

"It would be more money, though," I said. My voice didn't sound convincing. "It would get us even closer to new ovens."

Mom was adamant. She stood firm. "No, it's not worth it. She can get her buns from Richard Lord. They seem like a match made in heaven, don't you think?"

I agreed. "Absolutely. I'm glad you think so too. She accosted me with a box of frozen potatoes in her hand. That was my first red flag."

"And Alan." Mom put her hand to her heart. "We couldn't do that to him. He's still upset about losing The Jester. I saw him the other day and he wasn't even wearing one of his funny hats."

*   *   *

"Juliet, you're not working with the enemy, are you?" Rosalind's voice brought me back into the present moment.

I tore my gaze away from ShakesBurgers. "The enemy?"

She ripped off a bite of flaky croissant. "There's a rumor going around that Torte is supplying ShakesBurgers with buns." Her hands trembled slightly as she spoke.

"That rumor is false. I promise. Mindy approached us about using our products, but Mom and I both declined."

"Thank goodness." Rosalind let out a long sigh. "I told everyone that there was no way that Torte would agree to such a thing." She paused and took another bite. "The rumor mill is working overtime. The latest is that Mindy has hired two OSF actors to dress up in hideous hamburger and milkshake costumes to hand out fliers around town. It's absolutely sacrilegious. The woman is single-handedly destroying Ashland and I intend to put a stop to her."

"How?"

"The city has design standards and unfortunately they've become too lax. Mindy might meet the letter of standards on paper, but not intent."

"I'm not sure I understand."

"Juliet, that thing is an eyesore." Rosalind pointed again. "Look at it. It belongs in a strip mall, not downtown Ashland. ShakesBurgers? What kind of a name is that? Mindy has a blatant disregard for the caliber of development downtown. Neon and, God forbid," she made a cross in front of her chest and continued, "hamburger mascots prancing around town! Nothing about ShakesBurgers is compliant with the vision of this community."

I had to agree with Rosalind. Everyone was irritated that Mindy had torn down the old façade. Part of down-

town's charm is the nod that businesses give to the Bard.
Like the flower shop, A Rose By Any Other Name, Puck's
Pub, and even the Merry Windsor, the hotel across the
street, owned by Richard Lord, my least favorite person
in town.

"I'm still not clear what you need from me," I asked.

"I need the support of all business owners. I've called
an emergency meeting tonight. We are going straight to
the city council and demanding that the design standards
be tightened. I've already worked up a rough draft. The
new standards will specify materials, quality of finishes,
that sort of thing, and trust me, neon green paint is not on
the list." She glared in the direction of ShakesBurgers
again.

"Tonight?"

"Yes. At the Black Swan. At 5:00." Rosalind stuffed
half of her croissant into a paper to-go bag and checked
the silver watch dangling from her thin wrist. "Oh dear!
It's almost time. You'll be there, won't you, Juliet? We
have to put a stop to this."

Before I could reply she was already limping toward
the door to catch up with the owner of Puck's Pub. I had
a feeling he was going to get an earful about Shakes-
Burgers too.

Mom came up behind me with a tray of petit fours as
Rosalind left. "What was that about?" she asked.

"Rosalind has called a town meeting tonight to talk
about ShakesBurgers."

The smile lines on Mom's cheeks deepened. "Talk,
huh?"

I shrugged and helped her arrange the petit fours in
the pastry case. They were hand-dipped in pastel-colored
white chocolate. Each one looked like a dainty present.
"That's what she said."

Mom handed me a pink petit four with a white

chocolate heart in the center. "Let me go. You look exhausted, honey."

"No." I took the petit four and bit into it. Layers of vanilla sponge cake, buttercream, and blackberry preserves melted together in my mouth. "You have a date with the Professor. It's fine. I'll make a quick appearance and call it a night."

We walked to the kitchen with the empty tray. "Those are so good," I said. "Are there more?"

Mom pointed to the island where Stephanie was drizzling white chocolate over a tray of petit fours. "Plenty."

Carlos and Sterling had their heads bent over a notebook at the counter. I hadn't noticed them come in while I was talking to Rosalind. Sterling could almost pass for Carlos's younger brother. His black hair matched Carlos's, although he wore his in an intentionally rough cut. When I had first met Sterling I judged him based on his skateboarder style and tattoos. What a mistake. He's a wise soul with a kind heart and the most piercing blue eyes.

"It looks like you two are plotting something," I said, interrupting their concentration.

They both looked up.

"Julieta, I have decided tonight I will teach Sterling how to cure meat and make an antipasto. We will serve this as the starter for the Sunday Supper, is this good?"

"Great."

"And it is okay that we can have the kitchen tonight?" He sounded surprised.

I picked up another petit four. The chocolate hadn't hardened. It melted onto my fingers. "It's all yours. I have to go to a town meeting."

Mom scowled. "We're not done discussing that."

Carlos clapped Sterling on the back. "Okay. It is decided. We must go to the market."

We'd been hosting specialty dinners affectionately known as "Sunday Suppers" each week. Customers paid a flat rate for a three course meal served family style. They'd become so popular around town that we had to start taking reservations. This weekend's supper was already sold out. I had a feeling that it had to do with the fact that rumors had spread that Carlos would be preparing the meal.

Sunday's supper would be his last meal before he had to return to the ship, and everyone wanted a taste of his cuisine. I couldn't blame them. Carlos was the best chef I'd ever met, and not just because I'm biased. His food is simple and elegant. It's an experience. You don't eat a meal prepared by Carlos, you linger over it, savoring each morsel. He says the secret is infusing his food with love. I'm a believer. In addition to his culinary talents, Carlos is an excellent teacher. That's a rarity in the world of chefs. While he was in Ashland I had asked him to take Sterling under his wing.

They had worked together at the catering event at Lake of the Woods. Carlos had been impressed with Sterling's instincts and eagerness to learn. He was a natural in the kitchen. They hit it off immediately. Carlos loved having a young protégé to nurture. I loved not having to worry about the menu for Sunday and that every seat in the house was taken.

I yawned and stretched. The clock on the wall ticked in a steady rhythm in the empty room. It was almost five. The long hours had finally been getting to me. I'm usually an early riser. I tend to thrive on little sleep.

Mom noticed. "You're exactly like your father, Juliet," she complained. "He used to work himself sick. He was always the first person here in the morning and the last person to leave at the end of the day."

"I'm fine, Mom," I said. I grabbed a cup of coffee and held it up. "This is all I need."

She frowned. "Juliet, your eyes are bloodshot and you keep staring at that whiteboard in a daze. We need to adjust this schedule."

"No," I protested. "It's okay. I promise. I just need to get through this weekend."

The truth was that having in Carlos in town wasn't helping. We'd been going out each night. In part because Carlos wanted to try every restaurant, and because we had a lot to discuss. Ramiro, Carlos's son who I had only recently learned about, had been our main topic of conversation. He had failed to mention that he had a son when we got married. I'd been struggling with coming to term about why he hadn't told me, and Carlos had been doing everything he could to try and regain my trust.

The clock dinged, signaling that it was five. Usually at five, I'd be on my way home, but I'd made a promise to Rosalind. I would have preferred to call it an early night with a glass of wine and the latest issue of *Bake and Spice* magazine, but duty called. It was off to a town meeting for me.

Little did I know what would be in store for me that night . . . .

34